I Adopted My Mom at the Bus Station

Savannah Hendricks

Grand Bayou Press

First published by Grand Bayou Press 2020

ISBN PRINT 978-17344553-8-0 ** ISBN EBOOK 978-1-7344553-7-3 ** ISBN HARDCOVER 978-1-7344553-1-1

Cover design by The Red Leaf Book Design / www.redleafbookdesign.com

Library of Congress Control Number 2020901223

Foreword

Please note, prior to publication, this novel was professionally edited and copyedited. However, it has come to our attention that this was not a quality job and has since been re-edited. If you have a Kindle copy, please check for an update to the file.

We apologize greatly for the grammar errors, and while we're well aware that even big-name authors have errors in their books, it's often the "little guys" that get called out on it.

> "I am careful not to confuse excellence with perfection. Excellence, I can reach for; perfection is God's business." — **Michael J. Fox**

Dedicated to the motherless children, may you find your "adoptive" mom.

Author Tidbit

In 1994, a movie based on John Grisham's book, *The Client,* was released. I was fourteen and became instantly obsessed with all things John Grisham and Joel Schumacher's films (in 1996; he directed John Grisham's *A Time to Kill*). So when my dad asked me what I wanted to do for my sixteenth birthday, I begged to go to Memphis. To say my dad regretted asking me would be an understatement. But we went anyway.

He planned a loop-road trip from Memphis to Nashville and back around to Memphis. While we visited Elvis's house, grabbed some ice cream at Gladys' Diner, we only visited the Peabody Hotel to see the ducks and didn't spend the night. We grabbed lunch at BB King's Restaurant; I had cottage cheese and peaches. And my dad was nice enough to drive us around downtown Memphis, so I could see the pyramid and bridge that was in *The Client*.

Even though I'm older now, I remain fascinated with where movies and TV shows are filmed. And my dad admits the trip wasn't half bad.

*Chapter 11 - Since 2007, the scale ratings are under EF – Enhanced Fujita scale

Contents

Chapter 1 - How it all started

Summer was the best time to run away from home. To be exact, July 24, 1993, ended up being perfect.

The screen door slammed shut before I'd reached the over-grown grass at the edge of the yard. The door didn't creak back open, and Nana didn't holler "Sandy, you come back right this instant and close this door properly!" Nana always hollered loud enough to require an exclamation mark.

I didn't say goodbye to Nana or Gramps. As I rushed past Heidi and Hazel grazing on hay, I waved, but they didn't look up. I kept on going past Little Pete, Medium Pete, and Grand Pete, but with their faces deep in their trough, they didn't see me leave either. Running away meant I even left my favorite books and my few photos of Mama behind.

I ran away on that exact day because in 1984, on July 24, Mama became an angel. Sometimes the thought made my heart suffocate.

I sure kicked up a lot of dust on the two-mile run to the bus station. My legs throbbed, and my feet hurt, as a layer of sweat glued my flip-flops to my soles. The sun beat down on my bare legs, as my shorts only covered my thighs. My arms were protected since I always wore a long sleeve shirt regardless of the weather.

I pulled my sleeve over my hand and yanked the heavy bus station door open. Cool air smacked my face, sending goosebumps through my whole body. Reaching up, I touched my hair, forgetting the wind couldn't have possibly messed it up. In my haste of running away, I'd forgotten my cap to cover the wild frizz of curls that resembled a tumbleweed.

The bus station sat between Diamond City and Clayton. Being a one-horse—or about a ten-horse town, to be exact—it was possible to see someone I knew. Maybe even two people I knew.

And why it was called Diamond City in a place that had nothing shiny made no sense to me. This place didn't have jewels of any kind unless horse poop sparkled.

Dang, how I wish I hadn't forgotten my cap. I flopped on the wood bench, my sweaty back sticking to it through my shirt. Except for a teller behind the counter reading a book with a dinosaur skeleton on the cover, the station was empty. I shoved my hands into my pockets, realizing they were as empty as the pigs' trough after supper. When you run away, it's best to bring money.

I scanned the departure board. The names of cities I'd learned about in social studies were up there in bold white letters. Some letters were missing. DAL AS, meant Dallas. W CH T meant Wichita. ME PH S meant Memphis. OK OMA TY meant Oklahoma City.

Tallahassee or T ALLA was not up there. That's where my father is, at the Tallahassee prison. I still don't know what to think about my father. Thoughts of him always made me feel mixed up inside the way the stomach flu does.

Also, not on the board, MOBILE or M B LE, but I wished it were. Mobile, Alabama, the birthplace of Mama. A city with a beach. I was always thinking about Mama. She filled even my simple thoughts like what clothes to wear for the day.

My eyes started to water, and I wiped the tears away even though there wasn't a soul to see them. Why had I run away to the bus station? I knew it would be impossible to get on a bus without an adult accompanying me. I guess when your heart controls your feet, they leave your brain out of it.

A lady swung through the station doors as though the wind had decided where she belonged. Her wavy hair was the same color as maple syrup, and long enough it reached her waist. She wore a pretty floral dress; the kind mamas wear as they hold their baby on their hip and chat with the neighbors about someone's casserole dish.

The lady dug through her purse and slapped some money on the counter for the teller. She had a soft voice so I couldn't make out where she bought a ticket to. The lady glanced at me, strolled over, and took a seat on the bench. She crossed her legs at her tan cowboy boots.

"Hi, sweetheart," she said.

"Hi," I replied.

The lady pushed her hair off her face, and I noticed a bruise around her left eye. She glanced at me and moved the hair back over her eye like it was something I shouldn't have seen.

She set aside her black backpack, opened her pink purse, and removed her round Cover Girl compact.

"My name is Belinda," she said without looking at me or offering a handshake.

She held her compact in one hand, applying the coral pink lipstick with the other. Had Mama worn coral pink lipstick too? I thought about my mini Avon sample lipstick Nana gave me for special occasions. The name of the color in a circle on the bottom. I wore it to my best friend Molly's birthday party last spring. But it felt as though everyone was staring at me with it on, so I took a lavender party napkin and rubbed it off. At the rate I wore it, I should still have some left for high school graduation.

"I'm Sandy," I said.

The station door swung open with a swish. When I turned to see if it might be Nana and Gramps, Belinda's amber eyes had frozen with fear. A man in gray cowboy boots and a fire truck red shirt made his way to the counter. Belinda made a heavy sigh.

"Where are you going?" I asked Belinda.

"Little Rock."

The white letters on the board read: LIT LE RO K.

"Where are you going?" Belinda asked.

When I took off running, my mind had had too much. All I knew was my feet and heart joined forces and took control. Maybe I ran to meet my father finally. Maybe to finally see the beach Mama loved so much. All I knew was that I wanted the exact opposite of Diamond City.

"Somewhere," I said, focusing on my flip-flops, "and nowhere."

"I'm sure your family and friends would miss you if you left."

"No one will miss me. Molly, she might miss me, but she's still at camp, so she won't miss me until she gets home and realizes I'm gone. Is anyone going to miss you?"

"Sometimes you need to..." Belinda said, peeking back at the door. "Sometimes, you need a start fresh, even if people might miss you. Like the difference between a fresh loaf of bread and one that's been sitting in the breadbox for a week."

"Fresh bread is the best," I said.

"Exactly."

When Belinda said my favorite word, I knew it must be a sign from Mama. She must have known how desperately I wanted to experience having a mom. But Little Rock?

"What's in Little Rock?" I asked.

"Nothing, it's just the first stop along the way."

"The way to where?"

"I'm sure you learned about the Gulf of Mexico in school," Belinda said, returning her compact and lipstick to her purse.

"Lots of beaches there," I said, a smile breaking free on my face. Oh, how I wanted to visit the beach. "Are you going to the beach?"

"I'm from the beach, or darn near it."

I must get on the bus with Belinda, even if it might be the wrong thing to do. Belinda didn't appear as a stranger might. She looked like someone familiar, someone safe. How I imagined Mama might look now. I don't know how my brain worked up the courage to spill out the words, but it did.

"We could go to Little Rock together," I whispered.

Belinda stood up, dug through her purse once more, and slapped some money into my hand. I would have moved my hands away if I knew she was going to put the dirty money in them.

"Oh, you're breaking my heart," Belinda said. "But we can't go together. Buy yourself a pop and some chips. Rest until you're ready to go back home."

I let the money sit on my hands like an injured bird, not sure what to do with it, but I didn't want to drop it. Belinda went right back through those bus station doors as though the wind came back for her. It even took the man with the fire truck red shirt. My body felt cold and hot at the same time, my mouth dry, and my brain a box of puzzle pieces needing to find order.

I counted the money Belinda had given me. Three dollars. Yet, when I studied the bills, I noticed towards the bottom it

4

said SERIES 1984. Then, the number 7 around the sides of the same bill. I examined the other two dollars and saw 12 around the sides. The seventh month, July, twelve plus twelve equaled twenty-four. July 24, 1984. I slid the money into my pocket and bolted to the restroom.

I pumped the soap holder four times, scrubbing until foam covered the backs and palms of my hand before rinsing it off under the steaming water. Ripping the paper towel from the holder, I used it to swing open the door and bolted for the bus station's main doors. I tossed the used paper towel into the trash and yanked my sleeve over my clean hand before throwing the door open.

The bus leaving the parking lot was heading onto the main road. I got as close to it as possible, waving my arms like a rooster in distress.

The bus jolted to a stop, and the door flew open with a pop.

"What are you doing, child? Trying to get run over?" the driver, who looked like Santa on vacation, scolded.

Think of something quick, my mind screamed.

"My mom, she's on the bus," I stammered.

"Your Mama left you behind?" the driver asked.

"She gets caught up in her thoughts sometimes," I said, placing a foot on the first bus step.

My legs, weak and tired, took all I had to climb onto the step with both feet.

"Well, hurry up, go sit down."

I walked down the aisle as though walking on a tiny pier over a lake—a lake, which I couldn't see the other side of, only to the sides. I had exactly no idea why my heart controlled my feet that day. All I knew was they were looking for what my heart wanted.

"Sandy?" Belinda asked.

I sank into the empty seat next to her. She might be a stranger, but she was my stranger.

"Sandy, I have to tell the driver to turn the bus around. You can't be here alone."

"I'm not alone. I'm with you," I said.

I breathed deep. My thoughts were waves at the beach I needed to see.

Chapter 2 - Present Day - 2009

It takes me all of three seconds to realize my father is standing in front of me on the other side of the front door. His deep brown hair is unbrushed and greasy—grays streak through it like veins of lightning. My mouth hangs open enough for a wayward fly to come swooping in if it weren't for the screen door stopping it.

"What are you doing here?" I place my left hand on my hip as though I have authority over him.

The sun pushes through the limbs of the trees as the hot and humid evening air eases through the screen. Regardless, goosebumps crawl up my arms.

"I finished my time," my father, Robert says.

His words stab my chest like a knife, not that I know what it feels like to be stabbed by a knife. Sixteen years, of course. Not that I'd forgotten.

"And you decided to come here?" My left hand falls from my hip.

Robert glances behind him as though the sunset might be able to help him come up with an answer. "I had to." He turns back around.

Even through the worn screen door, I spot what the years in prison have done to him, aged him like a president at the end of a term.

"Could I at least have some water?" Robert wipes his brow like he just hopped off a horse after a long ride.

"Sure." I step back a few before turning and heading to the fridge. I can't very well allow him to pass out from dehydration. It's July in Oklahoma, and the humidity attacks you a like a cockroach on a crumb. An extremely hot, slightly aggressive, cockroach.

The house I'm living in, once gorgeous, is currently in disrepair. From the front door, one can see back into the kitchen. The pine floors hold marks of dropped cans and scratches from the chairs. If I close my eyes, my bare feet can tell you every room I'm in just by the gouges.

Chester, my seven-year-old Australian cattle dog, lifts his head as I pop open the freezer door. He was nearly deaf when I rescued him, so he can't hear worth a darn at this point, but his nose still works.

I lower myself to pat him on the head. Even though he can't hear me, I say, "Maybe your nose is taking after your hearing."

To Chester's defense, the wind usually blows south, carrying the scent of my father away from the house.

I remove a tray of ice, drop a few into a glass, and fill it with water. From where I stand, my father can't see me from the front door. But I know I can see him if I peek around the corner by the wall phone. Growing up in this house benefited me after my grandparents suddenly passed away. I understand every ache and moan of the tired wood. Of course, it doesn't keep me from sleeping with a bat underneath my bed.

With Robert's glass of ice water in hand, I stand by the phone, taking in his form outlined by the glow of the setting sun. The last thing I need is for him to look like an angel back from heaven, but there it is, right in front of my screen door. Chester steps past me and heads down the hall. Don't walk towards the light, Chester. It's not what either of us thinks.

The ice taps against the glass as my feet, covered in today's dirt, patter down the hall to the door. I open the screen. It creaks, and my father glances at it.

He takes the glass from me, avoiding our fingers from touching. There's no telling where his hands have been. "I can fix the screen door if you like?"

"I like it squeaking. It alerts me when someone is trying to break in." I watch as Chester sneaks past me and sniffs Robert's jeans.

My father swigs some of the water, and I watch his Adam's apple move under what must be a week or so of unshaved facial hair. He doesn't have an odor to him, although looking at his disheveled clothes, it's probably the breeze keeping it from me. Not that I'm one to pass judgment. When I woke this morning, I dressed in jeans and a white tank-top I'd worn two days in a row before spending the better part of my day drinking thick black coffee and reading three-hundred-some pages of a novel. Once I'd willed myself off the couch, I spent the afternoon on the riding lawnmower, trying to tackle the overgrown grass. Being a teacher allows for a lazy summer, but also reminds me I'm a huge procrastinator.

"You're here alone?" Robert wipes the droplets of water resting on his mustache with the back of his hand. "Where are your grandparents?"

"They passed a few years back. Car accident, I kept the house." I shove my hands into my jean pockets and stare at the freckles dotting the length of my arms.

"I'd assumed if you didn't leave Oklahoma you'd stay in the house, with or without your grandparents. Your Mama loved this home." He returns the glass to his lips and finishes off the water. "I'm sorry to hear about your Nana and Gramps."

His apology for their passing means nothing to me. My grandparents were not a part of his life during prison, and from what I understand, not much at all before prison. And I won't fault him for not knowing "sorry" is the most useless word in all of the English language. So, I nod.

"I'm glad you stayed. Your mama being raised here and all." Robert eyes the weathered molding around the windows and the peeling baby blue paint.

"What are you here for? I assume it was a daunting task to make it from Florida."

The edge of the sun's sphere has melted into the landscape in the distance, and nothing but tangerine and hot pink filter the sky around the fields.

The long lost cries of the pumpjacks that once filled the countryside haunting and soothing me as a child are gone. Gramps and I used to take walks near them, calling them oil birds and watching their rhythmic motions as they thumped.

"I needed to come to ..." His eyes drift beyond the porch as though the words are hidden in the branches of the dogwood trees. "I can't rightfully say. But I needed to see you. To try and find a way to fix what I did."

"There's nothing you can do to take away the horrible thing you did." I don't have the strength to shove him off the porch, or I would. Frankly, since my grandparents passed, life has been rougher than steel wool—something I never expected. Countless failed relationships have left marks on my heart and weakness in my soul, and the last thing I need in my life is him.

"If ya don't mind, could I at least help you out around here?" My father bends over and scratches Chester under the chin. "All I'd require is food and shelter."

"Why do you think I'd even want you here to help?" I run my tongue over the front of my teeth.

"Sandy." Robert leans away from me as though my rudeness leaves him off-balance. "Regardless of what happened all those years ago, I'm still your father."

"Do you think that matters to me after what you did?" I spin around and fling open the screen door, causing the weakened hinge at the top to completely give out. The bottom of the frame scrapes on the wood deck planks below.

Chester follows me inside as I slam the door shut, leaving Robert alone on the porch with the broken screen door and an empty glass of water. With a deep sigh, I lower myself to Chester and pull him in for a hug. He flops to the floor and insists on a belly rub instead. As I scratch at his mix of black and white fur between my fingers, I listen for the sound of my father walking down the porch steps, but don't hear it.

Standing, I go to the living room and peek out the side of the window onto the porch. Robert's hand is wrapped around a column, his other around a backpack. I watch as his shoulders raise and lower, and then he steps off the porch, only to sit on the step. Why won't he leave? Doesn't he see I want nothing to do with him?

Darkness washes over the house with the setting sun's color long gone. It has to be about nine as I make my way into the kitchen. I open the cupboard, pour myself a bowl of Powdered Sugar Squares, and tossed an uncoated one to Chester, who catches it like a pro. After pouring too much milk into the bowl, I lean against the countertop and face the front door.

"The nerve of him for showing up," I whispered to Chester, even though he can't hear me, my father might be able to. "Why would he think I'd want him here, let alone allow him to live with me?"

A fan oscillates in the corner of the kitchen, causing a much-needed breeze. My dishwater blonde hair hangs like a horse's mane down my back, sticking to my neck with sweat. I place the empty cereal bowl in the sink, give it a quick splash of water, and tip-toe down the hall.

Out of the corner window by the front door, my father's shadow remains. His back is toward the house, hunched over, and resting against the column. Clearly, he's not about to give up without a fight. It isn't like he has other plans, another life to go to. I watch as he lifts his hand in a sweeping motion, probably to wipe the dirt and perspiration off his forehead. It's far from relaxing porch weather out there.

I scrunch up my face. It's not my job to care about him. He deserves to sit out there in the heat and wilt away. While he owes me everything, I owe him nothing. I back away from the front door, tiptoe to the steps, and turn off the lights with Chester at my heels.

After changing out of my jeans and into jammie-shorts, I rinse the dirt of the field from my face and brush my teeth. As I climb into bed, the house settles for the night with a few pops. From upstairs, I can't see if my father is still on the porch.

The wind drifts through the open window and lifts my white curtains in a slow dance. I pick up the dog-eared paperback from the nightstand and click on my bedside light, staring at the words as they blur. Trying to focus on reading is impossible with my father outside.

On my nightstand rests a photo of my birth mama, and my adopted mom and her family. After my grandparents passed, I put a framed photo of them in my room. Our relationship had always been strained, but I didn't realize how much they meant to me until they were gone. It wasn't their fault our bond was weak. They were dealt with an unforeseen change in their lives when they had to suddenly raise me. With a sigh, I pick up the phone and dial my best friend of so-many-years–I've-lost-count.

"Hi, Molly," my voice is low as though my father can hear.

"Hi, I'm busy right now. Mark is over. We're about to watch a movie." Molly whispers into the phone.

Ever since Mark, her boyfriend, came into the picture mid-way through her pregnancy, our friendship has been non-existent. I hate that he took my best friend away from me, not to mention he rubbed me the wrong way. Of course, I could never tell Molly because she's in love. I do, however, worry about her newborn baby girl, Dixie Lynn. Mark has made it clear he doesn't want children of his own, so I don't understand why he is in a relationship with her.

When Molly announced she'd became pregnant from a random one-night stand, neither I nor the entire town of Diamond City was shocked. Molly kept the corner stop n' rob in business with her seemingly endless purchases of pregnancy tests. If she'd bothered to buy some of the other items in the same section, she would've been a lot better off.

"Never mind then." I prop the book open on my knees.

"Okay, bye, Sandy. We'll chat later."

The line drops, and I set the phone back on the receiver. I know very well that Molly and I won't be chatting anytime soon. My heart aches thinking of Dixie Lynn, probably lying in her crib, all alone while her mom makes another bad decision.

Chester jumps onto the bed and sprawls out on what has become his side since I adopted him a few years back.

I take the book and re-read the same paragraph at least three times before deciding to grab some water from the kitchen.

Descending the stairs, I pause at the landing. The view through the side window lines up perfectly with the left side of the porch. And sure enough, laying down, his feet hanging off the wooden swing my Gramps built, is my father.

The porch light, although nearly burnt out, is on nightly and allows me to see Robert. He pulled a trucker cap over his eyes and rested his feet on the arm of the porch swing, using his backpack as a pillow. Honestly, he looks too comfy. Maybe I should call the sheriff, have him arrested for trespassing. But I know better. The sheriff is on vacation, and his back-up, green-behind-the-ears, is making out with my so-called best friend at this exact moment.

I fill up a cup of water, dump half a tray of ice in it, and head back upstairs. My feet pause on the steps at the top of the landing. If I'm thirsty, Robert must be too. Too bad. He made it all this way from Florida; he can survive. I'm not taking care of or caring for him regardless of who he is. What he did was inexcusable. Yet, why is it so hard to remember that right now?

Returning to bed, I open the book back up and say a little wish to whoever might be listening. When I wake up, I don't want to find my father on my front porch.

Chapter 3 - My name

I gazed out the window as the red brick buildings of Diamond City faded, my stomach tightening. It felt like double-knotted shoelaces. I was running away. I didn't bring a jacket or even a pair of socks. The first time I ran away, I hid behind the hemlock tree in the front yard. The last time I ran away, I made it to the bus station. But spent all my money on pop and candy from the vending machine before Gramps found me. I think if Molly had not been away at camp, she would've come with me. This time, no tree, no food, no Gramps, no Molly.

Belinda opened her purse and pulled out a floral printed notebook and matching pen. She turned to where a purple ribbon held her spot.

"What are you writing about?" I asked.

"This and that. I've been writing in a journal since before I was your age."

She took a sigh the size of the Oklahoma panhandle. Her eyes filled with tears.

"Are you writing about something sad?" I asked.

"Oh no, sweetheart, I'm sad because ... well, it's not important."

Belinda's pen and journal rested in her lap as she pushed her head against the seatback. I'm sure if it caused Belinda to get teary-eyed, then it was important, but I knew enough to take a hint. I knew if I wrote about Mama, I would be sad too.

"I like your name," I said, trying to snap her out of her thoughts. "Belinda, Be Linda."

Belinda's face warmed with a smile.

"No one has ever broken my name up like that," she said. "Be Linda. I love it, Sandy, thank you."

"You're lucky to have such a name. My name ... it, doesn't fit me."

"Why is that?" Belinda asked.

"It reminds me of the beach."

"What's so wrong about the beach?"

"First, Mama was born by the beach. Second, Nana said Mama loved the beach and that she would take me someday, but someday hasn't come, and I'm already eleven."

"So the sandy beach is a good and bad thing at the same time," Belinda said.

I thought about what she said, how it might be something smart a mom would say.

"What do you want me to call you?" Belinda asked.

For the first time, someone asked me what name I wanted. I'd thought about it often and written it in cursive a hundred times on my schoolbook covers.

"Felicia," I said.

"That's beautiful," Belinda said. "How'd you come up with it?"

"It was my mama's middle name."

"Then Felicia it is," she said and winked.

It hit me right then, like when you get the wind knocked out of you from going down the slide backward and slamming onto the bark below. Belinda was not just Be Linda. She was Mrs. Williams, my first-grade teacher. I didn't recognize her until the wink. Her hair used to be a pixie cut and blonde. Mrs. Williams seemed to have disappeared over the summer after that year, never to return. And I guess with all my heart-over-mind-like thinking, I didn't notice who she was at first.

I guess she didn't recognize me either, with my blonde tumbleweed mistake of hair. In first grade, I had hair long enough that I usually sat on it. Until Nana had the hairdresser cut and perm it to match Rebecca on the channel seven news, who was at least fifty years old.

This meant I was not running away with a stranger after all, but a safe teacher. They had to be background checked out somehow to teach a room of kids. She probably even has her fingerprints on file with the FBI. Talk about luck. Mama was making everything perfect for getting me where I needed to be.

"I bet you're starving," Belinda said.

I shook my head. If I opened my mouth, all my thoughts might come flying out. Was she keeping it a secret that she knew me too?

"We'll get you a big milkshake with a cheeseburger and a pile of fries in Little Rock," Belinda added.

Milkshakes, another reason to love summer. Ice cream tasted far more delicious in the summer than in the winter. My stomach rumbled at the thought of the food, even though I'd eaten breakfast. Nana had whipped up some cheesy scrambled eggs and an English muffin with red raspberry jam. When she turned her back, I snuck a long sip of her hot black coffee.

I started drinking coffee a year ago. Nana didn't know this, but Gramps did. He came in from the field and caught me with both hands wrapped around Nana's steaming ceramic mug. We locked eyes as he paused in the doorway for what must've been forever, and then he pulled out a chair and sat down. Nana brought him his breakfast plate, and he said, "Sandy sure is growing up." That was that. Gramps never said anything about the coffee.

I shifted from my thoughts and set my sights out the window as the bus drove over a bridge. A sign read: LEE CREEK. It appeared awful muddy, a real thick mess. Like when the tractor broke or when Mrs. Haung wore her homemade hat with crocheted bunnies and plastic flowers on them. Lee Creek was a real thick mess.

The rhythm of the bus rocked my thoughts and me. I let my head relax on the headrest. I would need to wash my hair as soon as possible and remember not to touch it until I did.

❧❧❧❧❧ ❧❧❧❧❧

"Sweetheart?" Belinda rubbed my arm to wake me. "We're in Little Rock. Let's go find us some food."

Belinda and I made our way through crowds of people milling about, in and out of stores. I squeezed my arms to my sides like suction cups with every brush of a stranger's shoulders. My neck muscles tightened, and I had to remind my shoulders to relax. I couldn't catch germs from shoulders, could I?

We walked under a sign that read: RIVER MARKET DISTRICT in white and blue.

"Look, Felicia," Belinda said, pointing at a sign in the distance.

"River Grill, I bet they'll have our burgers and milkshakes."

Hearing my new name made the knots in my stomach loosen some. As we headed towards the River Grill, my hands were still suctioned to my legs.

Chapter 4 –
Present Day –
2009

"Here." I hand Robert a mug of coffee and an apple, aggravated yet amused to find my father right where I left him last night. Steam wafts up from the dark liquid. "I don't have creamer. I don't use any in my coffee."

Robert takes the floral mug, one Nana often used, and sits upon the swing. "Thanks, I appreciate it." He holds it to his nose and takes a sip. "I don't take creamer in mine either. I was lucky if I got coffee that didn't burn a hole through my stomach in prison, let alone French vanilla flavor."

The broken screen door rests up against the house. I'm already dressed for the day in jeans, boots, and a blue tank top, and take a long sip from Gramps's potbelly mug. Since he passed, I've been drinking from it religiously. The coffee over the years has left stains in a ring around the inside, and no matter how hard I scrub, it never comes completely clean. This, of course, takes a lot of mental strength to continuously remind myself that the mug is clean, even if it doesn't look that way.

The sun continues to rise behind the house, keeping the front porch cool and shaded. Chester trots up the steps and finds us after taking his morning bathroom break. I'd let him out the back slider while the coffee brewed. His tail wags as my father reaches out to pet him. If you'd asked me sixteen years ago, if this moment would ever take place, I would've said not a chance in hell. And probably not even if this was hell.

"Your hair is just like your mama's, dishwater blonde." Robert sips his coffee.

"I never thought my horrible perm would ever grow out. Honestly, I was ready to go GI Jane on it at one point."

"I use to watch your mama stare off at the sun rising and setting from this very porch all those years ago. Back when we first started courting. She loved the view from here." Robert stands, stiff, and shakes out his legs. "I'd appreciate it if I could help you out around here."

I'd spent most of my night tossing and turning. My thoughts were consumed by the fact he had the nerve to show up in the first place—but also because I could use the help.

"It doesn't change anything between us if you stay." I switch my mug from my right to my left hand.

He nods in response. A breeze whispers through the leaves of the tree as I cross my arm over my stomach.

"I figured you'd have a husband, or at least—"

"There are a lot of things that happen differently than I would've wanted." I go to the screen door. "Honestly, let's not rehash the past. Bringing anything up now is pointless."

"I don't think it's pointless." He scratches his brow. "I'd appreciate it if we could work on it now, too."

"Focus on chores around here; I'm not looking to mend anything other than the screen door."

Chester enters the house, and I follow behind. If I stay outside with my father, my words will turn to daggers, stabbing him where it hurts the most. I might hate him, but I'm not that evil. When it comes down to blood, I can't completely remove him from my life. There was a reason Mama had married him. And I at least need to respect that, especially since he made an effort to come all this way.

"The saying is: I've done my time. If the system can forgive me, I'd hoped you could too," Robert states.

"I've never liked the system," I holler back over my shoulder as I head into the kitchen, leaving the front door wide open. "Finish your coffee; we have a lot to do today."

A spark ignites in me when those words fill my mouth. I'm telling my father what to do, and it's about time too. Maybe having his help will resolve some of the feelings of what he owed me.

I remove a notepad from the drawer, along with a purple pen, and start on the list for Robert. If prison didn't kill him, these chores might. Glancing around the kitchen, I write down: paint, refinish cabinets, install new windows.

Nana and Gramps had left me a substantial bit of money with their passing. While I knew I wanted to spend it on fixing things up around the home, I continued to put it off because I didn't have the motivation. Gramps was great at working on automobiles, and I could easily rebuild a carburetor or replace a starter, thanks to all he taught me. But anything involving a hammer and a nail, I needed help.

Taking the notepad with me, I move down the hall and into the living room, adding: paint halls.

Making my way upstairs, I add: re-stain steps, fix missing spindles, wallpaper removal, and downstairs bathroom (all).

Once on the upstairs landing, I note: remodel the upstairs bathroom, paint all rooms.

Chester waits for me at the bottom of the steps as I return to the open door. Eyeing the screen door I broke yesterday. I write outside at the top of the list: screen door, scrape and paint exteriors, and trim trees.

In the distance, at the end of the driveway, the sound of a truck's engine draws close. Dust floats up, and I don't have to look to see who it is. I know. Justin Witherspoon. He's driven the same truck for as long as I can remember, a 1976 Chevy, burnt orange with white stripes.

The sunshine reaches the roofline as it continues to rise in the sky, casting a spotlight as though Justin is entering from heaven in a spaceship. And everyone who knows Justin knows it just might be true.

"Expecting company?" Robert steps forward on the porch, Chester at his side.

I lean inside, snatch my worn crimson Sooners cap off the hook by the door and pull it on.

"It's Justin." As I step off the porch, my father follows.

"Who's Justin? I thought you weren't with anyone?"

"I'm not."

Justin parks the truck in the drive behind my 1997 Toyota pickup.

"Good morning, beautiful," he says, climbing out of his Chevy.

"Why good morning, fine sir." I curtsy as I approach him.

"Are you ever serious?" Justin raises an eyebrow at me.

I shake my head no.

"Mama sent me with breakfast for you." He leans forward, peering around me. "Who's that?" Justin's smile melts like butter in the sun the second he spots Robert.

I watch as Justin takes a step forward as though he's going to confront the stranger.

"It's my father, Robert." I cross my arms and widen my stance.

Justin runs his hand through his chestnut hair. I remember the pleasure I had of running my hands through it once. The memory of the silkiness between my fingers sends goose-bumps through my body. If he told me he owned stock in baby shampoo to keep it as soft as a feather, I'd believe him.

"Your dad?" he whispers.

My father approaches me and reaches his hand out. "I'm Robert Evans, Sandy's dad."

Justin takes my father's hand, gripping it and giving it a stern shake. I can see the muscles in Justin's neck as though he's grinding his teeth.

"Justin." He drops my father's hand. "Must admit, I never expected to see you here. Did Sandy invite you?"

I move my hand and touch Justin's muscular arm. Another reminder of why I keep my hands to myself. "It's okay. He's staying to help me around the house."

"I can help you." Justin shoots me a glance, his forehead wrinkles with concern. "I've offered more times than I can recall."

Robert shoves his hands in his dirty jean pockets. "Sandy never mentioned you."

I turn to my father. "Because you and I've been chatting for weeks, right? So you know all the current people in my life?" My lips press together in anger.

"Sandy and I have been friends since the childhood you missed. I've always been there for her." Justin crosses his arms. His muscles flex in the movement, and I see them peek out at the edge of his T-shirt.

"You've been watching out for my daughter then, I presume." Robert scratches at his hairline, pushing the trucker's cap up a bit.

"Always." Justin tilts his head.

Robert turns. "Good to hear." He starts to walk back toward the house.

Justin throws his hands out as though a silent scream of what the hell is going on right now. I lean toward him, and my hands drape over his arms. The only time I'm not freaking out about germs is when I'm around Justin. At school, my students know proper hand washing and like to remind me about my germ phobia, so I don't have to even mention it much after the first week of school starts. Strangers are a whole other story. It's not to say Justin doesn't have germs, but I'm more concerned about catching cooties from him. One wrong move and I'll surely make-out with him as though I've been dared on the playground.

"It's okay. I can handle this," I say.

"Are you sure, because I can't."

"Thank you for your concern. I didn't plan this, but I can't send him away. He has no one."

"Good." In all my years, I've never heard anger in Justin's voice before. Sexy, yet firm. "He doesn't deserve to be here. He doesn't deserve any kind of hospitality."

I push Justin to spin around and open his truck door for him. "I'm twenty-seven years old. I can handle my father."

Justin huffs as he climbs into his truck and slams the door. His arm leans over the edge of the doorframe, and it takes all my strength not to touch it. His vision is fixed on my father, now on the porch. "You call me if you need anything."

"I'll be fine." I reach both hands out. "Now, give me what your mama sent." I love Justin's mama, although technically she's his step-mom. His biological mom moved to Wisconsin to chase after some cheese-loving man she met when Justin was only five years old. He's repulsed by dairy as much as I am with germs.

Without taking his eyes off Robert, Justin hands me a Tupperware container. I take it and peek under the cream-colored lid. "Oh, raspberry muffins." I lick my lips in anticipation of eating them. "Tell her, thank you."

Justin starts up the truck. "I will, and I'll be driving by here often. I don't like this one bit, Sandy."

Our eyes meet, and we stare without words for a few seconds longer than needed.

"I know you don't, and I don't either, but I'm a big girl. I can handle myself." As I step back from the truck, I glance at the porch and then back at Justin. His chivalrous nature is warm and welcoming. "See you around." I give him a half-smile and head toward the house.

"You'll see me around," Justin hollers as he backs his truck up and drives toward the main road.

I step onto the porch holding a raspberry muffin with crumble topping already out of the container and a bite missing.

"I thought you said you didn't have a boyfriend?" Robert eyes me, and then the truck disappearing down the road, dust swirling around it.

"I don't," I say between bites.

"You might want to let Justin know. I might've been locked up for a long time, but I still remember what love looks like, and it just drove off in a Chevy."

Chapter 5 - Milkshakes & laughter

I took a long time reviewing the menu, my hands covered by my sleeves. Summer and milkshakes, the perfect pair of perfection. The menu had at least thirty different milkshake choices. Strawberry sounded good, but so did mint, caramel, cookies and cream, banana, chocolate, and black cherry. I searched for my favorite.

"May I please have a raspberry milkshake?" I asked the waitress.

"I'll have a peppermint shake, and we'll have cheeseburgers and fries," Belinda said.

Belinda tucked her wavy hair behind her ears. I could see the bruise better in the restaurant's harsh lighting.

"What happened to your eye?" I asked.

"Oh, don't you worry about that," Belinda said. "The next big city stop is Jackson, Mississippi. M-i-s-s-i—"

"—s-s-i-p-p-i," I finished, and we fell back in the booth laughing.

Belinda smiled widely, like in the commercials where they want you to buy toothpaste. I noticed she had a side tooth missing. I didn't remember if that was missing in first grade. Plus, I didn't want to ask about the missing tooth because maybe she was a klutz like me. I've opened cupboard doors into my face. I've tripped over my own feet when nothing was in their way. I've even run into the patio slider—all embarrassing things I wanted to forget. And I didn't want to embarrass Belinda. Nana always said you couldn't unembarrass someone, so you had better not start to embarrass them in the first place. Mrs. Morgan, my teacher before summer started, said "unembarrass" is not a word. But, I knew telling Nana her word wasn't a word might embarrass her, so I left it alone.

"What's in Jackson?" I asked.

"I don't know right now, but it'll be fun to find out," Belinda said. She opened her backpack and pulled out a map.

"After Jackson is Mobile, right?" I asked.

"Indeed."

The map took up most of the table. The fold lines held small rips, as though some of the places would forever be lost without the help of tape.

Maps had always fascinated me. If a city were listed in a book, I would search the map for it. When I didn't have a map for the place, I'd arrive early to class and have Mrs. Morgan pull down the big one rolled up over the chalkboard.

"Do you have a highlighter?" I asked. "We can use it to mark our journey."

Our shakes arrived as Belinda searched her bag for a highlighter. I took a long sip and felt the ice cream travel down my throat, cooling me off. When you haven't drunk anything in a few hours, and you're hot, you can feel it slide down towards your stomach. Almost as if you can feel all the organs it soaks into. I hoped the food would help the funny pain in my stomach go away.

"I found a pink one," Belinda said, holding up the highlighter.

Of course, she would have a highlighter. Don't all teachers? But why had she not mentioned she was my first-grade teacher yet?

The burgers and fries arrived, and I focused on the map between bites.

"Does Jackson have a zoo? I've always wanted to go to a zoo," I said.

"You haven't been to a zoo?" Belinda said, scooping the last of her fries into her mouth. "There are two zoos just outside of Diamond City."

24

"The truck is always needing fixing," I said. "Gramps said we could go once he got the part in, but then something else would break. After a while, I stopped asking."

"Sweetheart, I think we need to get on our way to Jackson and find us a zoo. But first, I need to make a quick call. I saw a payphone outside. Finish your shake, and I'll be right back."

Belinda returned a few minutes later, paid for our meal, and then we headed back out into the sticky July air.

"How about we visit the river's edge before we get on the bus to Jackson?" Belinda asked.

"Okay." It wasn't the beach, but it would have to do for now.

Belinda found an open path through the crowd, and I followed. The crowd grew with each step. I focused on not bumping into anyone. When I looked up, Belinda's wavy maple syrup brown hair wasn't in front of me. My heart thumped loudly as blood rushed to my face, turning my cheeks flush.

"Belinda?" I called.

I stopped walking. The crowd went around me as though I were a statue. What do you do when you get lost? It's hard to think when your mind is in panic mode. Stay where you are so they can find you? Go to where you were supposed to go? Signs, look for signs.

My steps forward felt like I was going in slow motion. I'd lost Mrs. Williams, I mean Belinda. She was a teacher, so shouldn't she know how to find kids? That must be a requirement for a teacher.

There were too many people to see around and spot a sign. But I'd moved from my spot, which meant I had to find my way to the river now. Every step was more difficult than the last with the growing pain in my stomach.

The smell of sweet, sugary candy caught my attention and directed my feet into the open door of the shop.

"Hi, there little Missy," a lady with cotton candy white hair piled high on her head said from behind the counter.

"Hi, can you tell me how to get to the river?" I asked.

"Oh dear, where is your Mama? You're not lost, are ya?" Ms. White Cotton Candy Hair asked.

I didn't want her to call the police. I had to get to Belinda. I had to get to Mobile.

"Lost?" I asked, looking around me as though she was talking to someone other than me.

"Yes, why don't you have a piece of chocolate while we find your mama."

"Oh, no, my mom, she's just outside," I lied. "Her sweet tooth is strong, so strong she can't even set foot in here. She wanted me to come in and ask for directions to the river."

"Walk out the door, go left. Then when you get to From Bark to Book, the bookstore, go right, and then you'll see the river ahead."

"Thanks," I said. My mind repeating the directions so I didn't forget. "Is From Bark to Book a bookstore for dogs?"

She chuckled. "I guess I never thought of it that way before. But, rightfully so, the owners mean it as the bark from a tree, where paper comes from—"

"Oh," I said. "From paper to a book. I get it." I smiled.

"Take this with you, but finish it before your Mama steals it." She handed me a piece of chocolate the size of a half-dollar in a paper cupcake holder. Because she had on clear plastic gloves, I took it without hesitation.

I beamed. "Thank you."

Ms. White Cotton Candy Hair lifted her hand in a wave as I turned and made my way out of the store. I went left as directed, then looked for the bookstore. With each step, I avoided the bumps of strangers. How far could Belinda have gone? Did she not stop and look behind her to see that I wasn't there anymore?

When I reached From Bark to Book, a hand grabbed my hand.

"There you are, Felicia!" Belinda said. Her face flushed as though she had finished running in a marathon.

"Belinda!" I exclaimed, not even trying to wiggle my bare hand from hers.

"You scared me half to death." She gave me a quick hug.

The hug happened before I could react. Belinda pulled away, my hands suctioned back to my legs. I couldn't hear what Belinda said because my thoughts focused on washing my hands as soon as possible.

"Felicia?" Belinda asked. "Are you okay?"

"I'm good. I found a candy shop, and the lady gave me chocolate and directions to the river."

"Let's never have that happen again," Belinda said as a question, but a rhetorical one.

I answered anyway, "Never."

26

Chapter 6 –
Present Day –
2009

"What happened to the lady who brought you to see me in prison?" Robert asks as he works the drill, re-hanging the screen door.

"Mom, a.k.a Belinda. We're still close, but she and her husband, Paul, moved to Springfield. So they're a bit further away than I'd like. I don't get to see Jessica and Miles, Paul's kids, as much as I'd like anymore either, but we're all grown up now. Before they moved I spent a lot of time watching the daughter they had together, Pamela. Mom and Paul received a competitive offer from Missouri State University. They both used to work at OU, but Springfield offered them a better deal, so they moved."

"You call her mom?" My father glances at me.

"Yes, she's been there for me no matter where she's lived for the last sixteen years. As I mentioned before, things don't always work out the way we want them to."

I work the scraper as it peels off another strip of weathered paint from the exterior siding, the rhythm already familiar and soothing to me. While I put all these chores on the list for my father, I dove into some of them, trying to get my thoughts in order. With Robert here, the last thing I can do is focus on a book. Even Chester wants to spend time with him.

"What's the deal with Justin?" Robert stands back and eyes the screen.

"If there were a deal, which there's not, I'm not discussing it with you." I continue to scrape in a linear motion as my hand begins to cramp.

"Hmmm," he hums.

I spin around, my brow furrows. "Fine, I'm not relationship material, and I'm not going to be in a relationship with him."

"Because?"

I return to scraping. "This is not a father-daughter therapy session."

"Alright, I'll hush up."

The wind picks up, and the trees' branches bend with the gusts. Blue skies give way to clouds and hide the sunshine. Being mid-July, it's not tornado season, but it's happened before. My vision moves toward the skyline at the front of the house. Mammatus clouds dip down like bubble wrap, and I walk to the edge of the porch railing and gaze at them. I can spend hours staring at clouds developing across the prairies.

"Tornadoes usually don't happen in July," Robert states because he knows. His history is here, his life before prison.

When I look at him, I notice dust has settled into the creases of the crows-feet near his eyes. His skin is freckled by the sun, his smoke gray T-shirt sleeves are hitched up and expose his lack of muscles.

"Usually not." I turn back to the sky and rest my elbows on the railing. The thought of how many germs are on my father makes me shiver. "When was the last time you cleaned up?"

"Don't ask. If you have some soap, I can bathe in the garden hose." He pets Chester, and I can't help but flinch.

I've been petting Chester too, and he sleeps in my bed. Somehow, I overlooked this, and my vision darts to the steps inside. I must wash my bedsheets and bathe Chester.

"Use the shower. I'm not a warden. Do you have any extra clothes?"

"Yes, I went to Macy's on the way here and picked up a bunch of stuff, but I left them in my limo." My father grins.

I shake my head. "I'll grab you some of Gramps's clothes. They'll fit."

As I open the front door, I trip over the lip of the floor, but catch myself. Out of the corner of my eye I see my father's hand reach for me. I pause and glance at it just as he pulls it away. We don't say a word as our eyes met.

After setting out Gramps's clothes, a fresh towel, and a bar of soap, I grab a glass of raspberry iced tea and my cell phone from the kitchen. My father's outline stands at the front door.

"Thank you. I appreciate it." He starts up the steps, his germy hand on the railing. I'll clean it as soon as he's in the shower. I remind myself to scrub down the bathroom's light switch, door handles, shower knobs, and toilet once he's done.

"Don't thank me. The showerhead sprays every which way, and the water is ice cold. You might've preferred the garden hose." I watch him continue up the stairs and listen for the bathroom door to close.

In the hall closet, I pull out disinfecting wipes and rub the banister and door handles. Then I let Chester out the kitchen slider with a bottle of dog shampoo. He's rather pleased by the bath until I scrub the top of his head. Then I become the worst dog owner ever.

Once inside, I point at the raised bed in the kitchen.

While Chester flops into place, I take the steps two at a time and enter my room. I yank the sheets from my bed and toss them into the washing machine downstairs in the laundry room. I stand where Chester can see me and pat my leg for him to come to me. We make our way to the porch and watch the sky continue to shift and change.

The light on my cell phone blinks, and I flip it open. I'm alerted to two voice mails and one text message. I don't like people being able to reach me no matter where I am or what I'm doing. Yet, Mom didn't like that excuse, so I gave up arguing with her and have a flip phone, even though the rest of the world has smartphones. I have a laptop with internet, so I can't fathom why I need it on my cell phone. I'm hopeful the fad will end sooner rather than later. Although, my students tell me I'm crazy not to have one. Even in this tiny town, most kids carry cell phones with them and can use them as though they came out of the womb with one.

Molly has texted me: `I'm sorry`

Perplexed by the message, because she knows how much I hate the word "sorry," I listen to the first voicemail.

"Sandy, I can't do this. I thought I could. But I can't. Please call me."

Can't do what? I wait for the second voicemail to play.

"Sandy, I'm a horrible mother. I can't do this anymore. Please meet me at the bus station."

I check the time of the call, about an hour ago. Leaving my iced tea on the porch, I reach inside the front door, snatch up my keys and bolt down the steps.

I pat the side of my leg multiple times, the universal sign for Chester to come here quickly. He springs up, hurries down the steps, and trots to the truck's passenger side.

He's been my co-pilot since the first day he came home with me. I fling open the door, and he jumps onto the floorboard first and then from there to the seat. I think the distance from the ground to the truck is a bit too high, and again, I'm reminded he probably needs a ramp.

I jog around the front of my truck and climb into the driver's seat. Without a clue as to what I'm racing towards, I throw the truck into reverse and then whip the wheel around as I speed down the driveway toward the bus station.

Chapter 7 - Candy & girl stuff

"The bus driver mentioned the Jackson Zoo is right around the corner," Belinda said as we turned the corner from the bus station.

We'd slept on the bus all night, and it took a minute to get my legs used to walking on land again.

The Jackson bus station had a small gift shop, and I was happy to use a bathroom that wasn't bumping down the highway.

"Thanks again for my cap," I said, pulling the Ole Miss cap down so the sides were snug to my ears. I'd been so focused on hiding my tumbleweed that I didn't notice the cemetery until we were upon it. The iron entry gates cast dark shadows even in the middle of the afternoon sunshine. Shivers traveled up and down my body. I didn't like being anywhere near a cemetery, other than to visit Mama.

"Felicia?" Belinda said. "Are you okay? Don't pay any mind to that. We're going to have fun at the zoo. Come on."

Belinda bought us both a jumbo cup of lemonade with curly straws and a bag of popcorn. And we enjoyed it as we viewed animal exhibit after exhibit. She bought a disposable camera and took pictures of us making ridiculous and funny faces. If I stuck my tongue out, Belinda would cross her eyes. If I put my thumb on my nose and wiggled my fingers, she would stick her tongue sideways as though she was trying to reach her ear.

My favorites were the indoor animal ones. Their air-conditioned exhibits were a nice break from the hot and sticky heat. When Belinda wasn't looking, I raised my arm a bit and smelled my armpit, *phewww*. I could knock a skunk over with that stink. My Teen Spirit from the other morning didn't last long enough.

"Let's rest our tootsies," Belinda said.

I'd never heard the word "tootsies" used in such a manner before. I assumed she meant our feet, but it made me think of candy.

"What's your favorite candy?" I asked Belinda as we sat on the bench under a magnolia tree. It's probably important for an adopted daughter to know about their adopted mom's favorite candy.

"I love Now and Later."

She took off her boots and rubbed her feet.

"Oh, those are hard as concrete," I said. "Molly lost a tooth on one. It ripped it right out of the socket. A baby tooth, not an adult one. Plus, she already had a missing tooth from falling on the railroad tracks, another baby one. She's adventurous."

I took a long sip of my now warm lemonade, watching as the last of it sent bubbles through the straw's loops.

"Do you want to call your family back home?" Belinda asked.

"I don't know." I shrugged my shoulders.

"I've got some quarters. We can call them and tell them you're okay."

"I don't think Nana and Gramps care that I'm gone."

I stood up, my shorts stuck to my butt from the humidity. A headache started to form. My stomach still felt odd too, and it hurt, but not stomach flu hurt.

"Sweetheart, are you okay?" Belinda stood up next to me.

"My stomach, it has a sharp pain."

"Let's take you to the restroom and splash some water on your face. It'll make you feel a whole lot better."

Maybe I was homesick. Maybe I was just plain sick. I washed my hands and then splashed water on my face, but I didn't feel any better. And, I found out why.

"Oh, no!" I cried from the bathroom stall.

That sharp feeling in my stomach. My period had started.

"Are you okay?" Belinda asked.

Of all places! Of all times! THIS had to happen. Tears welled up in my eyes.

"Did you start your period?" Belinda whispered.

I cried, wrapping my hands around my stomach. I wanted to be home with Gramps and Nana. In my clean bathroom, not at some stupid zoo. No, I wanted to be with Mama. Mama in the ground. Covered with dirt, in a box. Death didn't seem so bad right now.

"I'm sorry, sweetheart."

Sorry—my least favorite word of all the words in the world, other than lima. Lima went with beans. Lima beans were almost as bad as sorry. Together they made the worst sentence possible: "Sorry, but we're having lima beans for supper." Sorry doesn't change anything, and that's why it's my least favorite word. Plus, I still had to eat those lima beans. And I still had to have my period.

I heard a machine clicking out by the sinks.

"Here," Belinda said. "Put this in your undies."

I looked down through my tears and saw Belinda handing me a pad under the bottom of the stall door. I took it in my sweaty and shaky hands.

"It'll be okay," she said.

I imagined a mom would say such a thing in this type of situation. But it didn't change anything—the stall walls were covered with words in markers. Gum stuck in a corner. I closed my eyes. Germs were everywhere around me. What a mistake I'd made running away. I opened the wrapper, not able to see much through my tears.

"Felicia," Belinda whispered, "it will be alright."

Even my new name didn't make it better.

Chapter 8 – Present Day – 2009

The parking lot of the bus station is vacant, except for two cars. The red one is held together with duct tape, and the rusted car belongs to the teller who hands out the tickets. She's been there for all of eternity.

It's been some time since I stepped foot into the bus station, but the most life-changing instance was sixteen years ago, give or take. I went back off and on during my teenage years, but the one I remember the most was on July 24, 1993.

Chester sticks to my side as I open the bus station door with my pinky, trying to touch as little as possible since I don't have on a long sleeve shirt.

A section of wooden benches welcomes us. The station's empty, and I hurry to the counter. Memories flood back, and my heartbeat speeds up. I have to wash my hands or at least wash my pinky, but I'll handle that in a minute. Even all these years later, my OCD with germs remains the same.

"Excuse me. Have you seen Molly in here? Molly Dwyer?" I lean toward the counter but don't make contact.

"What does she look like, honey?" The teller mutes the small television on her desk and sits up in her chair. "Is she a child?"

I want to say she acts like one, but I refrain. "Tall as me, in her late twenties, stick thin, poorly bleached blonde hair."

"Come to think of it, I recall seeing someone like that about an hour ago. She came in with a baby in a carrier, but I don't remember seeing her leave."

My heartbeat continues to race, and my breathing sharpens. I nearly gasp as a thought enters my mind. I push it out of the way as quickly as I can. She wouldn't. I turn around and search behind all the benches and every spot a baby carrier might fit. Then I hear it, a cry. No, a muffled scream.

The teller stands up from her chair. "Did you hear that?"

I squeeze my eyes shut so hard I see stars as my heart tries to escape my chest. Chester whimpers and paws at me, sensing my anxiety. Moving toward the sound, I push open the restroom door as the crying erupts. In the corner, under the hand dryer is a baby in a carrier, swathed in pink.

"Dixie Lynn," I gasp.

Hurrying to her, I halt, thinking of the door germs I touched with my palm and pinky. As the baby continues to cry, I scrub my hands at the sink. Once they're clean, I lift Dixie Lynn from her carrier and press her to my chest. The teller remains holding the restroom door open with her mouth gaping, as Chester's tail wags.

"That Molly girl left her baby?" the teller squawks.

I rock Dixie Lynn, holding her tight until her cries turn into tiny gasps that sound like little hiccups.

As I pick up the carrier to head out of the restroom, I spot a folded up scrap of paper in it. Sitting on a nearby bench, I place the carrier on the ground and remove the note. The teller is still standing at the bathroom door even though Chester and I are far from it.

Sandy,

Why I ever thought I could be a mama is beyond me. Every time I look at Dixie Lynn, I see regret and sadness. I can't give her the life she deserves or needs. I've made so many mistakes. Please don't tell her she was one of them. You must be her mama. I hate to say this, I know it'll only make it worse, but I'm sorry. I'm sorry.

Molly

The paper falls from my hand and drifts to the floor like a leaf. Dixie Lynn's eyes are closed, and her tears have soaked through my tank top.

"Should we call the sheriff?" the teller asks, picking up the note from the floor.

"It won't do any good. I have a feeling the sheriff's office is suddenly short-staffed."

Holding tight to Dixie Lynn, I lean back on the bench and cross my ankles at my boots. Memories of meeting Belinda flood into my mind, and tears well up at the edges of my eyelids. My chin quivers as though I'm eleven again, terrified but needing to run away from my life. Can I blame Molly for doing the same thing?

"Looks like this baby might've adopted a mama in a bus station," the teller states, crossing her arms.

"You don't know the half of it." I press my cheek against Dixie Lynn's head.

Her licorice black baby hair is wavy and soft against my face. As I take in the scent of baby powder, fear and joy engulf me. Molly left me with her baby. Embracing an innocent child in my arms comes surprisingly natural, but the fear of holding this child's future in my hands overwhelms me. I've worried about her daily since her birth only a month and a half ago; after all, I'm her godmother.

As Dixie Lynn's breath goes in and out, her heartbeats match the rhythm of mine. With my eyes closed, the bus station disappears.

"Are you sure you're alright?" the teller asks.

The few seconds of peace disappear, and I state, "We're okay." But I don't believe my own words.

I uncross my legs, stand, and pick up the carrier. Chester sticks to my side as we exit the bus station and load into the truck. The extended cab barely fits the carrier; thankfully, the base is attached to the bottom. After buckling it up with Dixie Lynn, I drive us home.

Once I park in the driveway, I remove my cell phone from the dashboard and place a call to Molly's cell phone. Immediately it goes to a message I feared would come, "This number is out of service. Please hang up and try again."

Taking a deep breath, I climb from the truck and slide my cell phone into my back jean pocket. Chester hops down, and I unload Dixie Lynn in her carrier. As I make my way to the porch, I realize I have absolutely nothing for a baby, not even food.

"Thanks, Molly, you're right. You couldn't handle being a mother," I mumble.

My father is rocking on the porch swing as I go up the steps. "You have a baby?"

"I have a baby. Robert, meet Dixie Lynn." I lift the carrier as my father takes a peek at the infant, her eyes wide open.

"Why do you have a baby?" My father asks, continuing to stare at her.

I look at Dixie Lynn, her eyes sparkle and glance around. "Because I just adopted a baby at a bus station."

Chapter 9 – Motel 2

The sign outside didn't read Motel 2, but it should have; this place was it. Belinda unlocked the door and pushed it open. Instantly, I saw cockroaches scrambling, and I jumped back, remembering the Reba McEntire song that Molly and I always sang along to.

"You got to stomp it real hard," Belinda said, moving me aside. She took her cowboy boot and slammed down on a cockroach hard enough the floor rattled.

"I'm not staying here, unless they're staying over there," I said, pointing out into the hall.

"It's just for one night. We'll keep the lights on."

The room had black wallpaper with jumbo green palm leaves on them. A small television sat on the dresser opposite the two twin beds with bright orange comforters. The olive green carpet appeared like grass.

Belinda flipped on the bathroom light, and two more cockroaches met the underside of her boot. The bathroom had a tan toilet and brown linoleum. I decided I would be showering with my flip-flops on.

I found the television clicker bolted to the nightstand. I took a tissue from the holder and used it as a glove to swivel it towards the TV.

"Yes, let's see if anything good is on," Belinda said.

I searched the channels, but it seemed everyone had a commercial on. Belinda flipped through the TV Guide she found on the dresser. I needed to sit down. My stomach pain felt like it might rip my body in half. Sitting on the comforter, I took a few deep breaths.

"At eight, *Girls Just Wanna Have Fun* is on," Belinda said, almost like a song.

"What is *Girls Just Wanna Have Fun* about?" I asked.

"Well, sweetheart, just what it says, girls ... just ... wanna ... have ... fun. How about we walk over to the grocery store and see what they have for supper?"

"I don't know if I can walk," I said, clutching my stomach.

My stomach hadn't felt any better since the zoo. Molly got her period last year, right in the middle of gym class. The zoo didn't seem like the worst place now that I remembered that happening.

"Walking will be good for the pain. We can go slow," Belinda said. "Let's get some food, and we can come back and treat this like a slumber party."

Clouds formed above us as we headed to the store. Being the end of July, the tornadoes were not as big a threat as they were two months ago. As an Oklahoman, I learned what to look for in the sky. These clouds were nothing to bother with as we made our way through the parking lot of Beatty Street Grocery.

"Let's find your period stuff first," Belinda said.

She said it loud enough for my cheeks to turn pink when two boys looked our way. I didn't think moms were supposed to embarrass you about your period in public.

Belinda gave me an overview of each item and told me to pick what I felt would work best for me. How about none of them?

My cheeks were still pink as I kept peeking to make sure no one saw me trying to decide. I picked a box with flowers on it and placed it in the blue shopping basket Belinda held. I felt a million-trillion times better after that because now it looked like they were for Belinda since she had the basket.

"Let's get you a heating pad of some kind. It'll help," Belinda said, heading down another aisle.

She found a small rice-filled fabric pouch and placed it in our basket.

"We can put it in the microwave to heat it up. Now let's pick out some nail polish!" Belinda cheered. "Oh, and we'll get an avocado and make a mask for our faces."

I smiled. We each picked out a polish color. Belinda knew what color she wanted right away. Yet, I couldn't decide between purple and pink.

"Get both," Belinda said.

"Thank you!" I beamed.

She winked. Why had she not said anything about school yet?

We headed down another aisle, and Belinda picked the last two nearly black avocados from the small vegetable section.

"We can make sandwiches or microwave something for supper. Which do you want?" she asked.

"Can we microwave pizza?"

"How about we order a pizza? Have it delivered to our hotel room?" Belinda said.

"Yes!" I smiled.

Next, we headed to the candy aisle. By the time Belinda placed the basket on the counter for the cashier, all the junk food hid my embarrassing flower-covered box.

Outside, the sky had grown dark, and we were guided back by the few streetlights to the cockroach-filled Motel 2. Belinda called the pizza in and then went to the lobby for ice. She seemed to be gone a rather long time for just ice. With the heated rice pad on my stomach, I opened the licorice, eating four before she returned.

The pizza soon arrived, and we devoured three slices each while the avocado mush stuck to our faces. Thanks to the rice pad, I felt good enough to dance to the music in *Girls Just Wanna Have Fun*.

"Okay, I'm going to shower and get this off," Belinda said, pointing to the green mush, which had hardened.

I finished the last two bites of pizza crust as the movie credits rolled up the TV screen.

"We can do our nails next," Belinda yelled from behind the closed bathroom door.

I scooted off the bed and looked at my face in the mirror over the dresser. I heard singing coming from the bathroom. Belinda's soft voice sounded how I imagined a mom's might. Did Mama sing? Studying my face with the goop on it, I could easily ignore my nose that I never liked. And I didn't see any of the freckles across my cheeks.

"Ughhh!" I moaned. How I hated my freckles.

My hair curled everywhere, a tangled mess, but at least it appeared to be growing out a bit. The movie credits ended, and the news came on. I wondered if Nana and Gramps had reported me missing. Would I make the Jackson evening news or just the Oklahoma news? Was Nana making my favorite raspberry cake with marshmallows just in case I came back? She hadn't made it since my ninth birthday.

"Felicia!" Belinda yelled through the bathroom door.

"Yes, I'm here." My thoughts of cake disappeared.

"Please grab my pajamas out of my backpack, would you? They should be on the top. They're pink."

I snatched a tissue from the box and used it to lift Belinda's backpack onto the bed, and unzipped it. I didn't see anything pink. There were a few pairs of shorts and shirts. Then my hand brushed up against an envelope of some kind. I pulled it out and tossed it onto the bed to get it out of the way. It was plump and not sealed, just tucked in. Curious, I snuck a peek. Inside was money, but not five-dollar bills. They were all hundred-dollar bills. I'd never seen a hundred before, let alone this many. There must have been two hundred of those one hundred-dollar bills. Where did all the money come from? Had Belinda robbed a bank?

"Find them?" Belinda said, cracking the bathroom door open.

I fumbled with the envelope, shoving it back into the bottom of her backpack. Getting ready to throw the clothing back over it, I spotted something pink on the side.

"Found them," I declared, my voice a bit shaky.

"Everything okay, sweetheart?" she asked.

My stomach twisted in double shoelace knots again. Finding the money reminded me I'd run away from everyone I knew. And how much I didn't know about Belinda, aka Mrs. Williams. I stared at the television. My face wasn't there. I wasn't missing. I was anxious.

"They don't care that I ran away," I said, tears forming in my eyes.

"Of course they do, Felicia." Belinda emerged from the bathroom. "Do you want to go back home?"

"No," I mumbled.

I'd made it this far, and the beach was closer than ever. This was not the time to be frightened and have second thoughts.

Belinda crawled into her bed as I made my way to the bathroom to take a shower. I needed to wash the bus seat off my hair before I could place my head on the pillow.

With the water running, Belinda couldn't hear me crying. Beyond the tears, I thought about the envelope of money. Had Belinda quit her job as a teacher to rob banks? It would be a horrible mistake if I adopted a bank robber as a mom.

When I finished my shower, I realized I only had dirty clothes to put back on. I was the worst runaway-er ever. Three dollars in my pocket, flip-flops, shorts, and a long sleeve shirt, and starting my period at a zoo.

The shadows from the television danced on the wallpaper palm leaves as I crawled into bed. I wrapped my fingers around my wet curls. The moonlight snuck around the sides of the curtains as I closed my eyes. Who was Belinda? And why did she have all that money?

Chapter 10 –
Present Day –
2009

"How exactly do you adopt a baby at a bus station?" My father holds the screen door open, and I follow in behind him with Chester and Dixie Lynn.

Hopping awkwardly with my hands full, I kick off my boots by the door. "Long story, just like the summer of 1993." I set the carrier on the kitchen floor, next to the island, and unbuckle Dixie Lynn.

Taking the infant, I laid her in the crook of my arm and run my hand over the top of her peach fuzzy black hair. My father keeps his distance as though the baby might reach out and attack him. Remembering the unclean floor the carrier was sitting on, I make a mental note to scrub the bottom of it and the floor.

When I tilt my head in my father's direction, I spot the clothes, Gramps's clothes, on him. The jeans hang baggy around his thighs, and the striped long sleeve shirt lost its starchy stiffness years ago. If Gramps could see this now, he'd demand Robert remove his clothes and kick him to the road in his underwear. Then I notice his bare feet.

"Thanks for not wearing shoes inside." I point with my free hand.

"From what I've noticed, you're like me. You have a thing about germs." He wiggles his toes.

I squint. "Thank you."

"Whose baby is this?" Robert places his hands behind his back.

"Technically, Dixie Lynn is Molly's daughter. I'm the god-mother, but for now, she's mine." The aroma of chicken fried steak fills the air. I pivot on the balls of my feet. "Are you cooking?"

"I hope you don't mind me going through your kitchen. You had everything I needed for chicken fried steak. Since I was born and raised here, it's a requirement to learn how to make iconic Oklahoma meals." Robert steps over to the oven and pulls open the door as it squeals in protest. He winces at the sound and removes a steaming bowl of mashed potatoes. "Remind me to add that to the list. And yes, I figured you might be hungry. I know I am. But the potatoes were done quicker than I planned."

He sets the dish on the stove and continues to whisk the gravy. "Don't worry, I washed everything, including my hands. One thing I learned in prison was that it's not the place for those who are OCD about germs."

"It's nice having a break from cooking." I sway Dixie Lynn in my arms, as she continues to stare at me like I have all the answers in the world. "I didn't know you could cook."

"In my final years they allowed me to help out in the kitchen a few times a week. Plus, I used to cook for your mama."

Exhaustion from everything which transpired in the last twenty-four hours hits me, and my knees bow. I reach for the counter, supporting myself.

"Have a seat. I can serve you up." Robert points to the kitchen table.

Without hesitation, I shuffle my feet across the floor and slump into the worn wooden chair.

"What the heck am I going to do with Dixie Lynn? She needs her mother, not me. Sure, I'd spent my teenage years babysitting every little tyke in town, but this is a newborn."

Then it hits me, and I nearly gasp. Molly left Dixie Lynn at the bus station for me because of my past. She could've left her here at my house, but didn't because she wanted to trap my heart. The most important time in my life, the most fun, challenging, and life-changing experience, had started at that very bus station. She did it on purpose and to send me a big message.

"She's not coming back for her," I whisper.

My father places the olive green plate in front of me. Steam wafts from the gravy-covered chicken fried steak and potatoes, smacking me in the nose with buttery spices.

"Give her time. She'll realize her mistake and come back for the baby," Robert reassures me as he joins me at the table in Nana's chair.

"Molly left me with nothing. No diapers, formula, or even a change of clothes." I lift my fork and glance at Dixie Lynn, wide awake in my arms.

Robert nods as though I'm talking about a bag of flour someone left behind and focuses on the plate of food in front of him. A lump forms in my throat and all the swallowing in the world won't make it go away. I can't cry in front of my father.

Leaning my head back, I stare at the ceiling, but it puts too much pressure on the lump, and I lower my head back down, allowing the inevitable to happen. Tears spill from my eyes, dripping down onto the top of Dixie Lynn's only set of jammies.

I shake my head as the tears flood down my cheeks. "I can't do this. You show up. Molly leaves me with her baby. A baby! Why did she think I could ever do this is beyond me. She had such a loving mama. How can she not be the same with Dixie Lynn?"

I squeeze my fork. "While I was here with Nana, who didn't like me much. She never said it, but I knew she did. I ruined her life. And Gramps, he was always so depressed and angry. I'm the one who should've gotten knocked up and left my baby with my best friend."

My father's hand slithers across the tabletop toward me, and I drop my fork in response. It clatters as it hits the side of the plate and falls onto the floor. Chester hurries to lick the food off it.

"Because you're stronger than Molly."

"I'm not." I bounce Dixie Lynn in my arms. She's fussing thanks to my commotion. "I've gotten good at making it appear that way all these years."

I sit there at the kitchen table, holding my best friend's baby, eating supper my father cooked, and wanting nothing more than to run as far away as possible, yet again.

45

Chapter 11 – The storm

We boarded our bus for Mobile, Alabama, as the sun rose, turning the sky baby blue. I looked down at my horribly splotchy purple nails. Belinda's ruby red nails were perfect. I hadn't painted nails before. Thank goodness, with some extra hard scrubbing, I was able to get the polish off my skin around the nails.

"You'll get better with time," she said. "Practice, practice."

Belinda handed me a bottle of water, a banana, and the mini powdered donuts I'd picked out for breakfast. She had an apple, a cup of hot black coffee, and mini glazed donuts.

"There won't be much to see until we drive through Hattiesburg," Belinda said as the bus pulled onto the highway.

"May I please see the map?" I asked. Powdered sugar stuck to my lips and sprinkled onto my shirt.

"I think the first town is a tiny place called Star. It's as small a town as Diamond City," Belinda said, taking time to sip her coffee.

"Exactly how long until we're actually in Mobile?" I asked.

"About three hours."

"Where on the map are you from?" I asked, shoving another donut into my mouth.

Belinda took half of the map and held it with her free hand.

"Right there, Bayou La Batre," Belinda said, pointing to the spot on the map near Mobile.

"Can we visit there?" I asked.

"We'll see," Belinda said, crunching into her apple.

As the bus traveled through Star, I wished I'd planned better. I would've loved to have an R. L. Stine's *Goosebumps* or *Fear Street* book to read right now. Heck, I'd settle for reading *The Boxcar Children* all over again.

I thought about the envelope of money I found yesterday. I didn't think Belinda suspected that I saw it, since she didn't ask me about it. I wanted to ask her, but I didn't know how. After all, I'd been snooping around, and snooping was for raccoons in trashcans.

The bus rolled down the highway, the land to the sides flat and green. The further along we went, the more the sky transformed from all blue to streaks of white clouds, their tops beginning to puffy up.

As the clouds grew taller, they changed into shades of gray. My books taught me to look for a grayish-green shade of clouds. That meant a tornado might develop. I had my own way of telling when there might be a tornado. The air had a feeling and a smell. Yet, being on a bus, I couldn't smell or feel anything happening outside.

"Belinda," I said. "Can you maybe get me a new shirt and shorts?"

I looked at my sleeves; a layer of dirt had formed from all the stuff I touched, trying to prevent my hands from touching surfaces.

"Yes, it's at the top of our list as soon as we get to Mobile," Belinda said. "How are you doing with your period?"

My eyes widened. Could she have said it any louder? I don't think the bus driver heard her.

"It's fine," I said, attempting to disappear into my seat.

The tires continued to hum on the highway, with the open map across my lap, I waited for the bus to speed past the next road sign. According to the map, Mendenhall should be next.

A huge shake and squealing noise, followed by the bus braking hard, shoved everyone and everything forward.

"I think the bus has a flat tire," Belinda said, checking her shirt for coffee spills. "Let's get out and stretch our legs. Who knows how long until we're moving again."

We stepped off the bus, and I felt it. The breeze was a mix of cold and warm. We were too far from any town to hear the lengthy whine of the tornado warning sirens. But I could smell sulfur. It smelled like rotten eggs. There were a few times I thought I smelled a tornado inside the house. It turned out I'd only forgotten to take out the stinky trash.

The bus might've had a flat tire, but something else made the bus driver pull off the road. In the field beyond, the wind whipped the corn in a slow dance. Over the cornstalks, the grayish-green clouds were darkening.

"Crap-o-crap-o-shhh..," Belinda said, her coffee cup slipping from her hands, splashing onto the pavement below.

"Think it'll be a big one?" I asked.

But Belinda didn't answer.

The dark clouds stirred before us as a wall cloud started to rotate over the cornfield. The hail came quick and painful. It felt as though frozen peas were being thrown at us, bouncing off our heads and shoulders. This swirling cloud mass was about to drop a tail right in the middle of the highway!

"Belinda, are you okay?" I hollered over the hail and wind.

She turned to me, her face pale and eyes as wide as Nana's supper plates.

"I hate tornadoes!" Belinda shrieked.

"I love tornadoes!" I hollered.

In the distance, a tail formed, dipping down from within the cloud.

"Everyone in the ditch now!" the bus driver screamed, waving his hands in a come-here motion.

"Come on, it's the safest place out here," I said, not caring about germs and pulling on her hand.

Belinda had frozen in her spot, like a nail in a fence post. The pure white tail turned chestnut as it picked up debris from the fields.

"Belinda! Come on!"

My flip-flops dug deep into the edge of the ditch, trying to pull her my way. I put my other hand over her hand and yanked as hard as possible. With one final tug, Belinda's feet moved, and we made it into the ditch. However, in the struggle, I'd lost my flip-flops in the deep mud of the embankment.

"It'll be okay!" the driver yelled over the cries of the terrified passengers huddled together.

Belinda held her legs to her chest as the howl of the violent wind hurt my ears. They popped from the pressure as the tornado swirled closer. The worst part of a tornado was the things it threw. If the tornado went through a barn, then it would throw barn pieces at you. If it went through a herd of cattle, well, it would throw some super gross stuff at you.

I shifted my body to take a peek at the tornado. It looked to be an F1, but boy-o-boy, it kicked up a lot of dirt and made a horrid sound. I ducked back into the ditch next to Belinda.

The largest tornado I had seen so far had been an F3. F stands for the Fujita[1] scale, which goes to F5. The bigger the number, the more damage the tornado will leave. In school, we learned how to protect our bodies.

Remembering those instructions, I took my left arm and reached it over my head to my right ear. This covered both my ears. Then I took my right arm, placing my elbow on the back of my head and the palm of my hand between my shoulder blades on my neck. I lay as flat as I could on my stomach in the dirt. The tornado continued to hiss and whistle, and we waited for it to pass as quickly as possible.

Chapter 12 –
Present Day –
2009

After supper, I bring Dixie Lynn with me into the living room and click on the television. I need to wrap my mind around everything she'll need. Her diaper is full, and she must be starving at this point.

Thinking back to my babysitting days, I scribble out a list: bottles, formula, diapers, diaper cream, clothes, pacifier, blanket, crib, toys, books, bottle brush, baby shampoo, and a teething toy.

I run my hand through my hair, convinced I forgot to write down a million other things she needs.

With Dixie Lynn, yet again asleep on my chest, I lean back into the sofa and close my eyes for a brief moment.

Chester startles me, licking my hand. "What's up buddy? Do you need to potty?" Even though he can't hear me, I find I still talk to him. After all, even if he can hear me, he can't answer.

I stand up from the couch, taking Dixie Lynn with me, unsure how long I slept.

Everything is a blur, like someone wiped a film of mayonnaise over my vision. The house, outside of the television playing a re-run episode of *M*A*S*H*, is silent.

"Robert?"

The kitchen is empty, and the dishes are stacked in the strainer, clean. I head down the hall, past the empty bathroom, and up the stairs. The lights are off, and the rooms are all empty.

"Robert?"

With Chester at my side, we head back downstairs to the front door. I swing it open and push past the screen door. Instantly, I notice what's missing. My truck is gone.

"You've got to be kidding me! Way to kick me when I'm down." I clench my fist and punch it into the air. "People never change. I never should've let him back into my life and believed he had good intentions. Stupid."

I fling back to open the screen door; Chester is spinning in circles, not sure if he is to go inside or stay outside. I pick up the phone and call the sheriff's office.

"It's Sandy Evans. I need to report a stolen Toyota truck. *My* stolen truck."

"I'll let the sheriff know so he can keep his eye out for it." Gail, the receptionist, says. "Anyone you think mighta stolen it?"

"Yes, my father."

Gail chokes a cough into the phone. "Sorry, did you say your father? I thought he was in prison?"

Everyone in Diamond City knew my past, especially with Molly dating half the men in town and her inability to keep her mouth shut.

"He finished his time," I say. "Free man now." Without a goodbye, I hang up the phone.

At least I don't have to deal with my father anymore, a blessing in disguise, I guess.

I'm thinking of how I'll buy a new truck, something with more room for a baby, when the sound of a Chevy engine roars up the driveway.

A horn honks as I hurry onto the porch, and Dixie Lynn's fussing turns to crying.

"I know you must be hungry and need a diaper change." Stepping off the porch, I rock Dixie Lynn because it seems to be the only thing I can think to do most of the time. I'm hoping to quiet her, even a little, but her cries turn into squeals.

Justin climbs from his truck and slams the door shut. "I saw your truck at Crest Foods and assumed you left your father here alone."

He heads toward me in one swift motion. "So, I headed over to keep an eye on him. Now explain to me why you're here, and your truck is there?" He freezes in front of me. "And you have a baby."

"I do." My eyebrows raise.

"Why do you have—"

"Dixie Lynn."

"How nice of you to babysit for Molly with everything going on. Why's your truck at Crest Foods?" Justin observes the property around us, and he bites the side of his lip.

The sun set about ten minutes ago, and the sky has faded from sapphire to royal blue.

"Molly left Dixie Lynn for me at the bus stop and disappeared, and my father stole my truck." I switch Dixie Lynn from my left arm to my right.

As the words sink in, my shoulders slump, and inside my head spins. Justin's arms reach out for me as my legs wobble. "I can't do this," I gasp.

"You can and will." Justin directs me toward the porch swing, his arm gently around my back, supporting me.

I squeeze tight to Dixie Lynn, fearing I'll drop her. Chester whines from inside the house. Justin opens the screen door and sets him free.

My feet are bare. I ran out of the house without my flip-flops. My mind races to how many steps my feet have taken over the top of where my father's dirty shoes have been, and now Justin's.

He guides me by the side of my arm, lowering me onto the porch swing. "Sit, I'm going to get you some water."

When Justin returns, he takes Dixie Lynn from me and replaces her with a mason jar of ice water. The glass is already perspiring in my hand as I lean back. Justin is the oldest of five siblings and has more experience with kids and babies than I do.

"Pheww!" Justin holds the baby at arm's length. "This girl needs a new diaper."

My head sways. "She doesn't have any. Molly left her with nothing. I wrote a list of things to get Dixie Lynn, and I fell asleep for a minute or two, at least I thought. Must've been longer than that." I fling my hand in the direction of the driveway. "My truck." Tears pour from me along with an indistinguishable noise.

"I knew your father being here was bad news." Justin stomps his tanned cowboy boot on the porch. "I should've never left you alone with him."

Before I can agree with him, lights in the distance make their way towards the house, bouncing up the drive. My lights. My truck.

I lean forward, weak, but able to stand as I wrap my hand around the swing's chain. Setting the glass on the porch's banister, I stumble down the steps.

I charge at my truck so fast it almost runs me over.

"Where have you been?" An angry mama-bear voice I've never heard before erupts from me. "Who told you you could take my truck? I have Dixie Lynn, and she needs things."

"How dare you steal Sandy's truck!" Justin hollers from behind me, coming down the porch steps. He has one hand over Dixie Lynn's ear, closest to his mouth. "If I wasn't holding a baby right now!" he warns.

My father pops open the driver's side door and steps out. "Calm down. I took your list and went shopping for Dixie Lynn."

"With what money?" I throw my hands up in the air.

Robert reaches over to the passenger seat and loads up several paper bags into his arms. "The money from your wallet. You shouldn't have that much cash on you. It's not safe." He glances over his shoulder.

"Are you kidding me right now?" I can feel the blood rushing to the tips of my ears and my heartbeat speeding up.

With my father's hands full, he shoves the driver's side door closed with his shoe and heads toward the house. "I was only trying to help you out. Allow you to sleep. You've had a long day." He pauses, his hands at his side with grocery bags. "I'm your dad. Contrary to what you think, I wouldn't steal from you."

I glance at Justin, who glances at me and then back at my father. My eyes widen as if to scream, help me out here. But Justin shrugs his shoulders as though he doesn't know how to help.

"It's hard to know what you would do. You've been in prison for years."

"Not to mention some juvenile troubles you got into as a kid," Justin adds.

Robert stands on the porch, bags with the red Crest Foods logo weighing him down. "Have you been researching me?" His eyes squint together.

"I'm a lawyer," Justin says, patting Dixie Lynn's back. "And my father was the lawyer who defended you."

I watch as the news hits my father and his Adam's apple moves as he swallows. "You're Eric Witherspoon's kid?"

Chapter 13 – Mobile, Alabama

We didn't die. No one did. However, the tornado stabbed a cornstalk right through the side of the bus. It must've happened after the tornado knocked the bus on its side and spun it down the road a bit.

"Your bag!" I shrieked, remembering the money.

Without money, we couldn't buy food or my clothes, and thanks to the tornado, my clothes were covered in mud.

"It's right here," Belinda said, holding the bag as we boarded the new bus. "You were really brave back there."

"They don't scare me one single bit. My bookshelf at home has an entire section of earth science books. I've read them so many times the pages are falling out. You were really scared," I said.

"Indeed." Belinda looked right through me and out the window of the bus as the rest of the passengers took their seats.

"Where are your flip-flops?" Belinda pointed at my mud-covered bare feet.

In all the excitement, I'd forgotten the mud ate them right off my feet. I would never find them in that mess out there. Great, not only are my clothes dirty and muddy, but my feet have nothing to protect them from the dirty ground. The thought of all I've walked on just to get onto the bus made me shiver. I sat as far back in the seat as I could, my feet lifting off the bus floor until they dangled in the air.

We'd left the map on the bus that sat on its side, so I had nothing to keep my mind busy. I gazed out the window, keeping an eye out for the road signs. I'm not sure how much time passed before I saw the sign welcoming us to Mobile, Alabama, the birthplace of Mama.

I wondered how many times she saw that very sign. My heart ached for her. At least I assumed it did. It might have been the period cramps moving up through my chest.

Mobile looked nothing like Diamond City. Shiny buildings lined the streets, small shops ushered people in, plus it sat on the coast. Ocean water, not creek, river, or lake water. Ocean water like what I'd seen in photos of California's rolling, foam-white waves or Florida's Windex blue water.

As we made our way down the street, I focused on every step my feet made. Thankfully, the pavement wasn't too hot. But I'd need a bottle of bleach and Gramps's boot brush to clean off all the germs.

"Do you think we're walking down the same streets your Mama might have?" Belinda asked as we strolled along, looking for the first shoe store available.

"I hope so. I hope she had on shoes, though."

She laughed. "We will find a store any second now."

"Where is the ocean? I can smell the salt in the air."

"Oh, just beyond the buildings."

Forget flip-flops! Let's play where is the ocean!

"I should be able to find a job here," Belinda said.

Why did she need a job if she had all that money? How much longer could we keep pretending we didn't remember each other too?

"Felicia, look," Belinda said, pointing at the girl's baby-doll dresses and flip-flops displayed in the store window.

We rushed inside the store. Flamingo pink stripes covered the walls as Madonna played through the speakers. Skorts of all colors and patterns were on display, along with hats like the ones on the TV show *Blossom*. Overalls hung in the back next to a display of black army-like boots.

"You have ..." I started to say, thinking about the hundred-dollar bills.

Belinda had enough money to buy half the clothes in the store.

"Something on your mind?" Belinda asked.

"No, it's nothing."

We shopped until we dropped, or rather until we were super hungry.

My shopping bags were stacked next to me in the restaurant's booth. One bag contained two jean shorts and two long-sleeve shirts. The other bag had a pair of overalls I begged Belinda for and a pair of purple jammies. On my feet were flip-flops. I couldn't wait to shower and put on my clean clothes.

"We need to eat better," Belinda said, all mom-like as she read the menu. "Starting tonight with supper."

I rolled my eyes high enough in their sockets I thought they might not come back down. We were on an adventure. There shouldn't be rules.

"Order milk to drink, no pop," Belinda instructed.

"Milk?" I whined.

Belinda lowered her menu, her mouth in a stern line.

"Chocolate milk," I suggested.

"Okay, chocolate milk."

The waiter came and took our orders. He returned promptly with chocolate milk and a water.

"Why don't you tell me what's bugging you?" Belinda asked.

I took a jumbo sip of chocolate milk and held it in my mouth. Lots of things were bugging me, starting with Belinda, a.k.a Mrs. Williams, and the fact that I didn't have any books to read. We had yet to see the ocean or walk on the beach. My period cramps. The bruise that was still visible by her eye.

Belinda leaned back in the booth and crossed her arms.

"At the hotel, when you were showering, and you asked me to find your jammies. I found the envelope." I gazed down, playing with the wrapper from my straw.

"Oh." Belinda pressed her lips so tight together an ant couldn't squeeze through. "And you want to know where it came from?"

I nodded while twisting the white wrapper around my index finger.

"I stole it, kind of. It's all the money my husband and I had in savings. I emptied our bank account. I didn't ask him. That's the stolen part, I guess. The morning I showed up at the bus station, I'd just come from the bank. Technically speaking, it's just as much my money as his.

"What'll he do when he finds out it's gone?" I asked.

"I'm not sure. Hopefully, he won't come looking for me."

"Can he find you?" I asked.

My thought flashed to my father for the first time since I thought of Tallahassee at the bus station. I wondered if he wasn't in prison if he would look for me when I ran away from home. Gramps and Nana were probably not even worried about what happened to me.

"I've been paying in cash. He would be hard-pressed to find me. Especially once I cut and dye my hair tonight."

"Can I help?" I asked. "Can we do something with my hair too?"

I removed my Ole Miss cap, my tumbleweed curls stacked against themselves atop my head.

"Yes, you can help, but don't worry about your hair, it'll grow out. Besides, boys always like a girl in a baseball hat," Belinda said with a wink.

"No, boys or not, my hair is a bird's nest paradise."

Belinda laughed so hard I thought she might fall out of the booth. Even the waitress gave us the eye at all of Belinda's snorting commotion.

"Do you want to call your family?" Belinda said once she got her breath back from laughing.

"No, I still need to see the ocean."

Through the window, I noticed the streetlights had come on outside as the sky held the last bit of the sunset.

"You can see the ocean and call them."

"I'm not good at keeping secrets. They'll find out where I am and have the police bring me home before I ever see the beach."

"Just remember, when you want to go back to Oklahoma, to your Nana and Gramps, you can." Belinda took a drink of her water.

"I don't," I said. "I want to stay here with you."

"Fine, but we'll discuss this again tomorrow." Belinda smiled. "Tomorrow, we'll look for someplace to rent."

"I hope no Motel 2 tonight."

This time we laughed together just like a mom and daughter would about a secret only they knew about.

Chapter 14 –
Present Day –
2009

Not every time, but an awful lot of the time when I look at Justin, I'm reminded of what his father did. Or maybe what his father didn't do. Maybe something in between all that.

My father places the grocery bags on the floor, somehow knowing I would lose it if he puts them directly on the countertop. He washes his hands at the sink and then unloads the items.

"Here." Robert hoists a package of diapers at me. "It smells like you need these." I take them and the bin of wipes from him.

When I turn around, I bump into Justin. "I'd help, but please don't make me." He winces as though the smell was rubbed on his nose. "This one's a blowout."

"Can you at least carry her into the living room so I can set everything up?" I make my way to the downstairs bathroom and remove a towel from the under sink cabinet.

After I cleaned up Dixie Lynn and put on a new diaper, I carry her back into the kitchen.

My father has unloaded the bags and placed all the items on the island. Justin glares at my father, watching him as though he's on the side of the road and my father's picking up litter while wearing an orange jumpsuit.

"How'd you know what to get, I mean, the size of diapers?" I pick up the container of formula. "And the right bottles and formula?"

Robert leans over the sink, washing the bottles as steam rises from the water coming from the tap. I shake my head as if to dislodge the eeriness of how much our germ phobia matches.

With Gramps, I always had to re-wash every dish because he was sloppy in his skills, and I'd walk around after Nana returned from the store with peroxide and a cloth, cleaning everything she touched until she washed her dang hands.

"Believe it or not, I took care of you. I went to the store, changed your diaper, fed you, and played with you. I know you don't want to hear this, but your mama wasn't perfect. After she had you, she slipped into a deep depression. At the time, I thought it was just something that would go away, but I was young and had no idea about postpartum depression. I don't blame my drinking on either of you, it's my burden, but your mama losing who she has had its effects on me." He dries his hands on a towel and hands me a clean bottle.

"I came back to see you for many reasons. One of them is to tell you things about your mama. Your grandparents clearly never bothered to divulge anything remotely good about me in their continued effort to make me out to be a horrible monster."

My mouth hangs open for who knows how long until I swallow and pull it shut. Justin's hand rests on my shoulder, and I think it might be the only thing keeping me from crying. "I should feed Dixie Lynn."

Robert nods. "I should give you some space. I'll be outside, on my bed."

My father passes by me, his shoulder an inch from mine, the closest we've been since I don't know when. I press my lips together and close my eyes. Regret washes over me in the form of nausea. "I think I need to sit."

"Great plan." Justin's hand drops to my waist, and I shiver. "I'll make the bottle. You," he points at the living room, "go sit."

Normally, I don't do well with being bossed around, but it takes all my strength to stay vertical. I pat Dixie Lynn's back as

I carry her to the living room and settle into the burnt orange sectional.

Having people in the house makes me cautiously aware of how outdated everything in my grandparents', errrr, *my* house has become. I wedge two throw pillows under my arm, propping it up, so Dixie Lynn will have the best angle to take her bottle. My babysitting knowledge comes back instantly, and I've never been more grateful for a skill-set than right at this moment.

Justin appears to float into the living room like an angel with a baby bottle. "I hope this is right. It's been a long time since I last did this."

"Thank you, Justin. I appreciate your help." I lay my head back on the couch for a second. "You tested it on your wrist?"

He hands the bottle over. "Is there any other way?" He smirks and flops down on the couch next to me. I swear a cloud of dust puffs up around him.

"Don't get used to this," I warn as Dixie Lynn's lips grab hold of the bottle's nipple with such force she nearly yanks it from my hand.

"Get used to what? Us hanging out, talking, sharing the same couch?" Justin rests his head on the top of the couch and looks over at me.

"And don't do the puppy dog eye thing you do." I stick my tongue out at him.

"I'm doing no such thing." He does the puppy dog eye thing. "I'm only here to be a friend and help you out. Plus, I don't like the idea of you being alone with Robert."

"Well, that makes two of us." I watch Dixie Lynn's eyes flutter as she sucks the formula. "What am I going to do? My father shows up, and now I'm—"

"—a mama." Justin sits up and rests his leg up on the couch, facing me. "I don't think Molly's coming back."

"I don't either. Her cell is disconnected. Would you be willing to help me with my options?" I pick at a hole in the thigh of my jeans.

"Absolutely. But I didn't think you—"

"I don't want kids. But this," I gaze at the baby in my arms, "I can't hand her off to the system."

I sigh, the scent of baby and peppermint aftershave mixes in the air around me. "When I met Belinda, it was fate. Maybe Dixie Lynn is my fate. Yet, a big part of me hopes Molly comes to her senses. I don't want her to think I'm taking away her daughter. No matter what, Molly needs to know this is not finders keepers."

Justin places his hand on my leg, and I move my hand over the top. I've been in this spot before, where my emotions took over my heart despite my mind reminding me to be careful. Years and years of fighting off my feelings for him, and it has only grown harder, not easier.

"I'll be here to help you with anything you need." Justin flips his hand over and squeezes my hand.

"That's what I'm afraid of."

I hear him chuckle as I close my eyes and rest my head on the pillow.

Chapter 15 – Not that place, that one

"Goodbye, Motel 3," I said as we made our way down the city street.

"Not much better than the Motel 2, I know," Belinda said.

We picked up one of those apartment listing books last night when Belinda bought raven black hair dye. Next to the grocery store was Sally's Splendid Hairstyles, where she got a pixie cut for ten dollars. Back at Motel 3, while Belinda waited thirty minutes for the hair dye to do its thing, we circled our three top places to rent from the book.

The first place sat on Texas Street, even though we were not in Texas. A woman lived in a part of the house, and she wanted to rent out the other part. It didn't have a pool. It didn't have a dishwasher.

A pool was a must for me. Belinda's must was a dishwasher. I think all moms get excited about dishwashers. Nana had always said that household appliances were not gifts to buy for women, but she sure got excited the year Gramps got her a brand new GE washing machine.

The second place we saw was Washington Avenue. Yet another ridiculous different-state-then-the-state-you-live-in street name. It had a dishwasher. It didn't have a pool.

The third place was on Monroe Street, a good sign! It was only a one-bedroom, but it had a pool! And it had a dishwasher!

"We'll take it," Belinda told the apartment manager.

Gramps always said you couldn't have everything you want. Wrong, Gramps, I thought. Belinda and I just got everything we wanted.

It turns out running away meant apartments with other people's furniture inside.

"It's called a furnished apartment," Belinda said as she sat down on the cream-colored couch.

"It's called ugly," I said, my face scrunched in disgust. "How clean is this couch?"

"We can put a blanket on it," Belinda said, jumping up and making her way to the closet. "This should work."

She held out a midnight blue blanket.

"Is it clean?" I asked.

Without a sigh or complaint, unlike Gramps and Nana would do, she put it right into the washing machine that sat in the next closet over. Belinda knew exactly how much I hated germs of any kind.

"We'll have to share the bedroom," Belinda said.

"Okay," I told her.

I figured the more time we could spend together, the more I could get to know her.

Molly and her mom share a bedroom in their trailer. Molly said it's fun at first, but after a while, not really because she couldn't get away with anything, like reading instead of going to bed. Kind of like when you get a jumbo scoop of ice cream on your cone, and then after about ten licks, you lick too hard, and the ice cream goes rolling right off the top of the cone and onto your shoes below — fun at first, but a bummer in the end.

"We should go to the grocery store and stock our pantry," Belinda said. "My bloomers are getting tight." Belinda closed the washing machine lid. "Did you cook with your nana?"

"Sometimes, I would help cut up vegetables for supper or fruits for pies."

"A sous chef," Belinda said.

"What's that?"

She opened the kitchen cupboards. The apartment included plates, cups, silverware, pots, and pans.

"It's the second in command. The chef's helper," she said, sticking her head deep into the cupboard by the stove. "You can be my sous chef, but I can teach you how to be the chef if you want."

"I'd much rather be a chef. Nana makes my favorite raspberry cake, but never raspberry pie. Could I make French toast, raspberry pie, and chicken sandwiches with potato chips?" I asked.

Belinda stood up from behind the kitchen counter. "Yes, but not all at once." She laughed. "That would be a lot of food to eat for one meal."

I laughed, "I know."

Nana had never asked me what I wanted to bake. Maybe I wanted to be a chef. A smile grew inside, thinking about Belinda allowing me to do some of my very own cooking and baking. Chef, that sounded better the more I thought about it.

Everything with running away had turned out well so far. Yet why was Belinda still avoiding the fact that she was Mrs. Williams? My lack of secret-keeping abilities was itching to slip from my mouth like pulling off wool winter socks. They kept your feet warm but itched so badly that you couldn't stand to wear them for long.

We carried the ten bags from the grocery store to the apartment. I had three bags, and Belinda had seven. Our muscles were getting a good workout. She said the ice cream wouldn't make it in the heat. However, she let me get everything I would need to make my first raspberry pie. Belinda also bought the fixin's to make a big salad for supper. I wasn't sure about a big salad. I didn't even like little salads.

Before supper, we went down to the pool. Oddly, I didn't have an issue with germs in pools because they had chemicals in them. The stronger the pool smelled of chemicals, the safer I felt. Afterward, regardless of chemicals, I always scrubbed up in the shower, just in case.

I still had my stupid, stupid, stupid period, so I sat on the pool's edge and put my feet in. I was not ready to learn to use the cotton on a string thing. Belinda suntanned as she looked for a job in the newspaper.

"How much longer do I have with my ... you know what?" I asked.

I don't know why I called it a "You Know What," I was not fooling anyone. Any teenager could guess why a girl wouldn't be swimming on a hot day like this.

"Everyone is a little different, but it should be only a few more days," Belinda said.

"This is the longest week ever," I whined, throwing my head back and squinting my eyes from the sun.

"Oh, this one sounds good," Belinda said from the lawn chair. "Server needed for Cupcakes and More Bakery, Tuesday through Saturday, six till three."

I kicked my feet under the water, making tiny waves.

"Do you think you would get to take home desserts for free?"

"Day-old stuff, maybe." Belinda peeked around the newspaper. "You're going to be a chef in training. We may not have enough room in our stomachs for all the food."

"What did you do before, for a job," I asked, even though I knew the answer.

A mom and two kids younger than me came into the pool area. The kids had yellow floaties strapped around their arms. Their mom juggled towels and a jumbo bucket of toys as they made their way to a lawn chair.

"I was a teacher at Rimrock Elementary School," Belinda finally said.

I couldn't stand the itchy wool secret one second longer.

"Why don't you remember me, Mrs. Williams?" I asked.

Belinda slapped her hand to her heart.

"You were my first-grade teacher," I said, looking down at my feet, swishing in the water.

"Sweetheart," Belinda said, making her way over to me, the newspaper tucked under her arm. She sat next to me, slipping her feet into the pool. "I didn't recognize you at first with your new hairdo. It's true, but when we sat down to have our burgers in Little Rock, I remembered."

"Why didn't you say anything?" I asked.

"Why didn't you?" Belinda asked, bumping her arm into mine.

"I figured you didn't remember me, and I didn't want to be forgotten."

"I had a lot of kids over the years come into my classes. At times, it takes me a bit to remember, especially when you're running from something your mind is cloudy. But I never forget one hundred percent. And I could never forget a little girl who was the best hand washer and hand wash monitor ever."

Belinda put her arm around me and squeezed me close. I smiled and watched the family enjoying the pool. For the first time, maybe ever, I didn't get the sharp pain of jealousy seeing a mom and her kids. Belinda hadn't forgotten me. Even if she was also going to make me eat a big salad, I felt as happy as ever. We swished our feet in the water, just like a mom and daughter would do.

Chapter 16 –
Present Day –
2009

After I call Gail at the sheriff's office to let them know my truck is no longer missing, Justin ends up staying until my father falls asleep on the porch swing.

Now alone, I ready myself for bed. Glancing around the room with Dixie Lynn asleep in my arms, I realize I don't have a crib for the baby. This knowledge knocks the wind from me, a reminder that I'm in over my head. Crest Foods doesn't carry them, of course, so running out to get one won't happen tonight. I place the baby in the middle of my bed and surround her with pillows.

Over the years, I've developed panic attacks or anxiety attacks, whatever the medical term is, and I have them over big and seemingly little things.

My heartbeat races, and my chest tightens. Nausea washes over me as I crumple to the floor and lean on the side of the bed. Chester plops down next to my thigh. Reaching for my cell phone on the nightstand, I scroll through recent calls and hit send.

"I'm having a panic attack," I gasp into the phone when she answers.

"It's alright. I'm right here. Focus on a spot," Mom instructs. "What do you see?"

"A black and white photo of hydrangeas."

"Good, now what do you smell?" Mom has been through this with me enough times I've lost count.

"I smell a ... dirty diaper."

"Good, now, wait ... what?" Mom questions.

"I have Dixie Lynn. Molly abandoned her at the bus station."

"Oh, no. I'm on my way." I hear her mumble something, most likely to Paul. "See you in about three hours. Do you need me to bring anything?"

"I have no idea."

Chester moves and snuggles up next to my outstretched legs as tears run from my eyes. Thankfully, Dixie Lynn continues to sleep through my sobs.

"Focus on your breathing," Mom instructs. I hear her move through her house, keys jingle in the background. "You're safe, and everything will be all right. Can Justin come to sit with you?"

"No, he left. The last thing I need is him." I don't have to explain why. Mom knows my Justin dilemma.

My panic attack has subsided by the time Mom's SUV lights shine up the driveway. I've been pacing at the window like a kid waiting for it to snow for at least an hour.

My father doesn't even stir when I open the screen door. Dixie Lynn is asleep on my chest, but she's been there so long that it feels like she's now molded to me.

It amazes me how well my father can sleep through noises, but then again, he had plenty of time to perfect sleeping in a noisy prison.

It's pitch black out, and the moon is only a sliver, but I can still see Mom climb from the SUV wearing a sundress and flip-flops, carrying a bag of some sort. She pauses when she reaches the porch steps, and her eyes widen. I loudly clear my throat, and my father stirs and opens his eyes.

"Robert, you remember Belinda." I motion with my free hand. "Mom, you remember my father?"

Mom's mouth freezes half-open. "Did I mi-i-ss a phone call?" she stutters.

She glares at my father as he rises and sticks out his hand toward her. Glancing at it, she nods her head. "I'd rather not."

I hold the screen door open, and Mom enters, leaving my father with an empty handshake as he sits back down on the swing.

Mom sets the bags on the floor just inside the living room and heads to the bathroom to wash her hands. I wait in the hall for her. Once her hands are dry, she takes my head in her hand. She cups the side of my chin and runs her free hand through my hair. Then she kisses my forehead, and I feel like I'm eleven again.

She reaches out for Dixie Lynn, and I transfer her without waking her up.

"I brought you some baby clothes from when Pamela was a newborn; they should fit Dixie Lynn just fine."

I snatch the bag and pull the clothes out, one at a time. "These are adorable." My eyes focused on them, then Dixie Lynn and Mom. "Thank you."

"When were you planning to tell me about your father?" Mom rocks side to side in front of the fireplace with the baby.

Pursing my lips together, I ponder my answer. Not that I fear Mom will judge me, but I don't want my answer to make her feel unneeded. Sure, as the dust needs the rain, I need Mom. However, I wanted to see if I could handle my father myself. I'm not eleven anymore.

"Sandy?" she glances over at me with her mom eyes.

I've never known another human in my life to have motherly eyes like Belinda. They're powerful, intense eyes, yet soft at the edges. They welcome questions, while her irises pull out every secret you thought you'd never share. My guess is Pamela didn't get away with anything. Jessica always mentioned how she would sneak out late at night. And even though her dad and Belinda didn't catch her in the act, first thing in the morning, Jessica would fess up to her teenage antics to Belinda.

"I wanted to see if I had the strength to face my father and whatever came of him showing up on my own," I mumble. "But Dixie Lynn was not something I could do on my own."

"And he simply showed up?" Mom sits down with the baby and places her on her legs.

I rest my hand on Dixie Lynn's head, brushing her hair with my palm. "Yep."

Mom's face contorts. "I guess it took a great deal of courage for your father to travel here." She peers over her shoulder, probably seeing if she can make him out on the patio from the living room window.

I wrap my hands together into a ball, resting them on the baby clothes piled up on my lap. "I know if I ignored him, I would always wonder about him ... and me."

"You want to have a relationship with him?" She lifts Dixie Lynn and places the baby's head on her shoulder as she rubs her back in small circles.

"I don't know what I want." I set the clothes aside, stand up, and pace the room. "He keeps mentioning stuff here and there about Mama, and I have to at least hear what else he has to say. I mean, he's my only living link to her. Even when I had Gramps and Nana, they didn't tell me much. Anything they said came out in a tip-toe around it type of way."

"Sounds as though they were doing what they thought was best for you. But know I'm always here for you, or if you need help kicking him off the porch." Mom rests her cheek on Dixie Lynn's head.

"Thanks."

"Let's watch a movie. Pick something from your enormous John Hughes collection."

My collection's not huge, it's just well defined. I do have other movies, *Twister* and all three of the *Jurassic Park* movies. Of course, most of the items in the bookcase are books. Books are shoved in every spot imaginable throughout the house.

Because I haven't watched it in a few years, I select *The Great Outdoors* and sink back into the couch, and baby clothes topple around me.

"I think the most important thing right now is Dixie Lynn." Worry spreads over Mom's face as her lips pout at the edges. "How could Molly do this?"

"I wish I knew, but she'd been pushing me out of her life and our friendship for months. A part of me thought having the baby might bring her back to her old self, but it only made it five times worse."

"Being a single mom will be a difficult task."

"Single mom? No. Godmother? Yes." I shake my head. "I can barely manage this house on my own, besides Molly has to come to her senses and come back for Dixie Lynn. A few weeks will go by, maybe a month, and she'll realize her mistake."

"And if she doesn't?"

I place my head on Mom's shoulder, and she wraps her free hand around me while holding the baby with her other. "I have absolutely no idea."

Chapter 17 - The Album

I woke to find myself alone in the apartment. Belinda had left a note on the refrigerator.

Felicia,
I went down to the Cupcake place.
Hoping they'll hire me on the spot.
I may not be home until suppertime. Be safe!
Belinda

She signed it Belinda, not Mrs. Williams or Mom. A lump the size of a golf ball formed in my throat. Why did I even think she would sign it "Mom"? I wanted a mom, I wanted to know what the whole mother-daughter thing felt like, but I never said one thing to Belinda about it. It was all stored in the back of my mind, like a forgotten toy in the back of a closet. Yet, I expected her to understand and know that I wanted nothing more than to adopt her as my new mom. I knew the exact second we met at the bus station, but how do you ask someone such a question?

I poured myself a bowl, Powdered Sugar Squares, and turned on the television. Cable had been included with our apartment, but not a phone. I clicked through the channels until I found the morning news, I wondered if I would be on it. Did Nana and Gramps finally report me missing?

I held the bowl in my lap. Not one single mention about me. I flipped through the channels again until I found MTV. "The Right Stuff" video by New Kids on the Block played in the background as I went to change out of my jammies. I put on my new jean shorts and a black long sleeve Led Zeppelin shirt.

A beaten-up six drawer dresser sat under the bedroom window. Belinda had the three drawers on the left, leaving me with the three on the right side. I'd already wiped down the knobs. Opening the first drawer, I put away my clothes.

"What's that?" I asked the empty room.

In the bottom drawer sat an album. With my sleeves over my hands, I took it out and crossed my legs with it in my lap. It had a blue cover, and there were several gold-colored squares around the edges. Daringly, I rubbed my fingers over the soft cover before opening it with care.

The first picture had a woman cuddling a baby in her lap. The baby held onto the woman's fingers. The woman looked down at the baby, not at the person who took the photo. I went page by page through the photo album. In each picture, the baby grew older and older. Each picture had the same woman and the child. A man was only in two pictures. Below each picture, it read: Sharon and Theresa, with the age of Theresa. The first photo, Theresa: six months old. In the last photo, Theresa: ten years old. Love was captured through their smiles.

"Who would leave such a special photo album behind?" I asked.

I wished I had a photo album of Mama and me, or at least more photos of Mama. Nana said taking photos of Mama wasn't her thing, whatever that meant. When I asked where my baby photos were, Nana didn't know, like they'd been misplaced and no one cared but me.

Theresa and her mom must be missing this album, I thought, opening it again. I desperately wanted Belinda and me to make a photo album. The disposable camera with the pictures from the zoo rested on top of the dresser, waiting to be developed. As soon as Belinda came home, I would ask her about making our own.

I took the apartment key left on the kitchen counter, locked the door, and made my way down the steps to the office building by the pool. A bell chimed when I opened the door with my sleeve-covered hand.

"Hi, may I ..." the apartment manager said. "Oh wait, you just moved in with your mom, didn't you?"

The words hit my heart, spreading warmth down to my toes. I smiled. My mom. I repeated her words in my head again, my mom. We had to tell the manager that or else she may not have rented Belinda the apartment. It was a big lie, and we knew it.

"I found a photo album in the dresser and wanted to know who used to live there so I could give it back to them."

"I'm sorry, but I can't give out that information."

There it was again, "sorry"—what a useless word.

"You can't?" I asked. "They must be missing it."

"If they come by the office, I can let them know. You can leave it with me."

I didn't want to leave it with her. I wanted to find the mom and daughter myself.

"No, that's okay," I said.

Defeated, I turned and moped out of the office. The bell sounded less welcoming on the exit.

Back at the apartment, I sank into the couch, staring at Reba McEntire's "Is There Life Out There" video playing on CMT. Even though it was only ten o'clock in the morning, I munched on two cookies.

The apartment felt cold and dark. As Billy Ray Cyrus's "Achy Breaky Heart" played next, I didn't dance or sing along. I missed Mama. I missed Belinda. Maybe I even missed Gramps and Nana. Then I thought of the ocean. How quickly I'd forgotten. I couldn't think of a better reason to find it immediately.

I let my toes sink into the white as sugar sand as I clutched my flip-flops in my hand. The salty air surrounded me. Tall beach grass swayed and whispered in the breeze. I'd finally made it to the glorious ocean! As Molly would say, "plumb right glorious!" I wished she was here with me to see it too.

I found a spot away from others and sat with my legs stretched out. Had Mama touched these same grains of sand?

I could see why she loved the ocean. I think I loved it too. I watched the waves come back and forth along the sand.

Every thought disappeared from my mind as I stood up and made my way towards the water's edge: The ocean and I.

The first splash of water rolled up to my feet and sucked my toes deep into the wet sand. I closed my eyes and let the gentle waves go in and out over my feet. I pictured Mama standing next to me doing the same thing. I finally made it to the ocean, Mama, I thought. Did Mama ever stand here and do this too?

I'm not sure how long I stood there, taking in each wave, but I didn't care. Until I grew weak in my legs, and my chest felt like it was pinching my heart. I stumbled backward and flopped onto the sand. Why did my heart hurt if I'd accomplished what I wanted? Did I have it all wrong?

Tears formed, and I let them fall. I didn't want to go. I didn't want to leave Mobile. Each wave that crashed the shores sent another thought into my mind. My father. I couldn't shake the lingering questions about him, for him. Why did he do what he did? Could he really be such a horrible person?

I moved my toes, feeling the sand between them. Leaning forward, I dug my fingers into the sand too. A part of me wanted to bury myself deep underneath and forget all the questions I had. Do I stay with Belinda? Do I go try and visit my father? Do I go home?

I flopped back onto the sand, making a sand angel, staring up at the clouds as they traveled without a care in the blue sky.

Chapter 18 -
Present Day -
2009

The scent of bacon pulls me down the stairs. I find Mom and Dixie Lynn in the kitchen. Mom's still wearing her jammies, and it transports me back to the special memories of us together in Mobile. The baby wiggles her feet in her car seat, sitting on the kitchen table, farthest from the sizzling cast iron pan.

"Morning," I announce.

Chester stares at the back slider door handle, and I let him out.

"Good morning, sweetheart." Mom peeks over her shoulder at me. "I hope you're hungry."

The last time someone cooked me a full-on breakfast would've been the last time I was at Gabriella's restaurant, about two months ago. Justin's mom's muffins didn't count as a full breakfast unless I'd eaten three of them.

I lean over the car seat and grab hold of Dixie's bare feet. She produces a smile and kicks them.

"I'm starving." My stomach aches with emptiness as I hadn't eaten since breakfast yesterday. "Did you see my father this morning?"

"I heard him pacing about when I woke." With tongs, Mom removes the cooked bacon from the pan and places it on a plate lined with paper towels. The grease spreads through it like watercolor on a wet canvas. "Do you want to invite him in for breakfast?"

I pick at the dry skin on my lower lip with my top teeth. "I should." A twitch of guilt towards how cold I've been to him makes me quiver. "I suppose so. I have him doing a lot of work today." I look down the hall.

"Well, go on then. These eggs will be ready in a minute." Mom wipes the grease from the cast iron and proceeds to crack blue and brown eggs on the side of the pan.

The eggs are from Bob and Mary next door. The couple has supplied me with them since I got rid of the hens I had after Nana and Gramps passed. I love the blue ones the most. The way they taste, pure and simple. There's not an adequate way to describe an egg, but if I ever figure it out, I'll use it for the blue ones.

As I open the screen door, I find my father leaning over the railing, gazing out in the distance at the prairies beyond the property.

"Good morning." He nods in my direction. "Have you ever watched a sunrise so closely you can make out the shadow changes across the land?"

"I'm not sure I have." My body frames the doorway.

"You should. It's rather wonderful."

"Would you like to come inside for breakfast?" I take a step closer to him, thankful I'm wearing the flip-flops I left at the entry.

He turns and straightens himself. "I'd enjoy that, thank you."

I move out of the way as Chester trots up the front porch steps. Robert passes me, heading inside. As he walks down the hall, I notice a limp in his stride and wonder what caused it.

"Good morning, Belinda. Thank you for breakfast." My father approaches the kitchen island and rests his hand on the back of the bar stool.

Mom faces Robert. They stare at each other for a few seconds until I step in front of them, breaking their concentration. "I'll get the plates."

After removing three plates from the pantry, I collect an empty mug and hand it to Robert, watching my finger placement. "Coffee's in the pot." I point.

He takes the mug from me, our hands don't touch, but our eyes meet. His eyes glisten with something unexpected, a softness I've not noticed before. Suddenly, Dixie Lynn fusses, and Chester taps his paw on his food bowl. The universal signal they both want breakfast.

I open the dog food bin and scoop out Chester's morning allotment of dry kibble. Next, I hurry to make a bottle for Dixie Lynn before her fussing turns into a full-on crying fit.

Mom and Robert serve themselves, piling scrambled eggs, strips of bacon, and English muffins onto their plates. They sit across from each other at the table; a vase of dying antique blue hydrangeas blocks their view from one another.

"I'll feed her, if you'd like," my father states with a fork in his hand.

I balance the readied bottle and my plate full of breakfast essentials and make my way to the kitchen table. "Thank you."

Handing off the bottle to Robert, I put my plate down and turn the car seat, so it's facing him. With his left hand, he takes a bite of bacon and holds the bottle for Dixie Lynn with his other. I watch my father in disbelief of his ability to parent like he's done it his whole life.

The table remains silent, minus the scrapping of forks and the slurping of coffee. Clouds form outside the kitchen windows, causing the light to darken coming in.

"Supposed to storm today?" My father places the empty bottle down next to his plate.

"Hard to say. I haven't watched the weather report in a few days." Scooting out my chair, I carry my empty plate to the sink and scoop up Dixie Lynn. I go to the slider, the baby's head on my shoulder, and I burp her.

"Best get started then. Still lots of scraping to tackle on the siding." Robert's chair slides back, and he takes his plate and mug to the sink. "Want me to wash these?"

"No, I'll handle them." I rock Dixie Lynn while Chester looks on, annoyed his meal didn't include bacon scraps.

"Thank you again." Robert exits the kitchen.

As I move in his direction, I notice he's paused at the entry to the living room.

I hide behind the wall with the phone. After a few seconds, I peek around the corner into the hall. My father is nowhere in sight. Taking Dixie Lynn, I head into the living room and spot Robert in front of the fireplace mantel.

"Outside of the few inside one of Gramps and Nana's photo album, those are the only photos I have of Mama." I step up behind him.

The mantel holds four framed photos. The one farthest to the left is of Mama holding me, all bundled up on what I was told the day I came home. Behind her, there is hideous blue floral wallpaper. In the next photo, Mama has me sitting in her lap on the floor, the person taking the picture looking down from above. The third photo is of me, the day Gramps and Nana brought me to live with them. My cheeks are puffy, and my eyes red, obviously I'd been crying. In my arms, I clutch a Cabbage Patch doll. And the final photo on the mantel is my favorite. Mama has me in her lap, my hair as naturally bleached blonde as they come. I must've been about one. Mama's eyes were fixed on me, not the person taking the photo. I'm looking up at her with such admiration you can feel it coming through the photo. Mama never smiled much, as far as I know from the limited photos I have of her.

As I turn to my father, he glances away and wipes at his eyes. Then without making eye contact with me, he hurries to the front door. "I'll be outside if anyone needs me." His voice cracks as though his words are held back by a lump in his throat.

Dixie Lynn burps, breaking any sadness sinking into my heart with a chuckle. "Excuse you." I pat her back.

Mom comes into the living room. "Let's go shopping for some essentials, a crib for starters."

"Great idea."

The sound of scraping outside against the walls echoes in the room. Robert doesn't waste any time for sure.

"He does seem rather equipped with baby parenting basics." Mom nods at the noise.

"There've been a lot more surprises from him than I ever expected."

Mom wraps her arm around me and glances at the frames. "Your mama was so beautiful, just like you." She kisses my head and squeezes my shoulder. "I'll go get ready."

I press my eyes closed. The smell of bacon lingers in the air and mixes with the sweet scent of the baby. I could nestle my nose right up against Dixie Lynn for hours.

As I glance at the photos one more time, my heart aches. How could Molly do this to her daughter? Even though I'm not typically a praying type of person, I say one right there and then. Molly has to overcome whatever is going on with her and return to Dixie Lynn.

Chapter 19 – Neighbors

When I woke in the morning, my questions still didn't have answers. And there was another note stuck to the refrigerator.

Felicia,
Off to work.
Make some friends today.
We'll talk when I get home.
Belinda

I finished my cereal and dressed in a pair of jean shorts and a lime green long sleeve shirt. Being already hot and sticky in the apartment, I put an extra layer of deodorant under my arms.

Locking the apartment door, I hurried down the steps, hoping another day at the beach would be enough to answer my questions somehow. Making my way past the office, I noticed the pool area was empty. My horrible, nasty, awful period had finally stopped, so I could go swimming if an adult was around.

Maybe a lifeguard on duty at the beach would offer me half of their lunch. The sound of a ball bouncing in the distance, followed by yelling, caught my attention. I left the pool area and headed around the building. The apartment complex had a basketball court in the back.

"Stop stealing the baalllll!" the little boy screamed.

"I'm not stealing it, Miles," the girl said. "It's called winning."

The girl framed herself with the basket and tossed the ball. It swished through the net.

"I'm telling Daddy! You're mean!" the little boy screamed.

"Hi!" the girl called out as I walked closer to the basketball court.

"Hi," I said.

The girl was tall, skyscraper tall, and thin as a fence board. The little boy was the opposite, short and plump. They had matching brown hair the color of wheat. The girl's was straight and cropped at her chin. The boy's buzzed with spikes like a porcupine.

"I'm Jessica, and this is my little turd of a brother Miles."

"I'm nooot a turd!" Miles yelled.

"I'm Felicia," I announced, using my new name with confidence.

"Do you want to play?" Jessica asked.

"I'm not very good, but I'll try." I moved my sleeves over my hands as Jessica tossed me the ball.

"Can't be any worse than Miles," Jessica laughed.

"I'm telling Daddy!" Miles took off running.

He reached the first door in the building labeled B and flung it open. "Daddy!"

"Oh, don't worry about him," Jessica said. "He tattles on me at least twenty times a day."

I made every fourth shot I attempted. Jessica made every shot.

"It would be easier to shoot if you touched the ball," Jessica said, pointing at my sleeves.

"I kind of have a thing about germs," I replied.

"Oh, okay. You're new here, right?" Jessica asked. "Because I haven't seen you around."

We both sat on the grass at the edge of the court, sweaty and tired.

"Yep, I moved here," I paused, "with my Mom."

"It's my dad, Miles, and me. My dad is off work for the summer because he's a teacher. He's home all ... the ... time. Does your mom let you stay home alone?"

"She works at Cupcakes and More Bakery."

"You get the apartment all to yourself; how cool."

"Yeah, I guess."

"Is your dad here too?" Jessica asked.

I wiped the sweat from my forehead with my fingers.

"He lives in Tallahassee," I sort of lied.

After all, he did live in Tallahassee.

"Okay, I have to ask, did you lose a bet with your mom?" Jessica pointed at my hair.

I touched my tumbleweed, realizing I had forgotten my cap. "No," I said, thinking fast. "I wanted to see what it would be like to look like Annie Warbucks. The blonde version, of course."

Jessica laughed. "Come on, let's get something to drink," she said, jumping up.

I followed her to into her apartment and closed the door behind me with my hand tucked inside my sleeve. Miles sat in front of the television with a box of juice. Jessica's dad washed dishes in the kitchen.

"Hi," he said. "Grab a juice box, girls, and go cool off."

"This is Felicia," Jessica said.

"Nice to meet you, Felicia. I'm Dad, but you can call me Paul."

"Nice to meet you, Paul," I said.

Jessica handed me a cold juice box, but I didn't take it.

"Can I use your restroom to wash my hands?" I asked.

With my hands now cleaned, I punched the straw into the tiny silver circle and took a sip. Jessica grabbed my arm and pulled me into her bedroom. Aerosmith and *Beverly Hills 90210* posters covered her bedroom walls.

"Do you watch *90210*?" Jessica asked, flopping onto her bold yellow beanbag chair.

I thought before I answered. Nana didn't let me watch it, but I watched it once when I stayed over at Molly's house.

"Of course I watch it," I lied.

"My dad lets me, but he watches it with me, and at commercials, we have to talk about what's good and bad. It's soooooooo embarrassing."

Jessica covered her face with her hands and leaned back in her beanbag chair.

"Do you watch it with your Mom?" she asked, uncovering her eyes.

Another pause. "Umm, yeah, of course."

"Lucky."

I remained standing in the middle of her room because I didn't know where I should sit. "Do you watch *MacGyver*?"

84

"Yes, at least my dad and I don't have to discuss that one. Miles even gets to watch it."

I stop myself from telling her that it's Gramps and my favorite show. Instead, I looked around her room some more. Jessica's bed had a pink daisy comforter. Her nightstand had stickers on it.

"Never put stickers on anything," Jessica says, pointing to them. "Can't remove them no matter how hard I try."

I grinned, thinking about the stickers I had on my dresser back home.

Jessica's dresser had an oval mirror attached to it. On the dresser sat a picture of a woman holding a little girl.

"Is that your mom?" I pointed at the frame.

Jessica shook her head yes.

"You don't live with her?"

"She died. She had MS. Are you going to sit down?" Jessica asked as though she wanted to change the subject. "I promise I don't have cooties. And my bed is clean. Miles is not allowed in here, at all.

Laughing, I made my way over to her bed and sat on the corner.

"What are you doing this summer? Camp?" Jessica asked, taking a sip of her juice.

"No camp."

"I've done nothing all summer," Jessica said, "It's been sooooo boring."

Jessica jumped up, as best as anyone could from a beanbag chair, and plopped onto the bed next to me.

"But you're here now. Maybe it won't be so bad. We can hang out together. Miles will have to tag along sometimes. He is pretty good if you promise him a chocolate ice cream bar to not be a turd."

Paul appeared in the bedroom doorway, wiping his hands on a kitchen towel.

"You girls want to go swimming?"

"I do," Jessica said.

"Yes, please," I said.

"As long as it's okay with your Mom," Paul stated.

"Yes, she said I can, as long as a parent is supervising."

I ran to my apartment and changed into the swimsuit Mom bought me. A hot pink one-piece suit with a purple stripe around the center. I dashed down to the pool as fast as my flip-flops would flop. Jessica and I cannon balled in at least ten times, sending water splashing on Miles.

"Meanies!" Miles screamed as he drifted by with his orange arm floaties holding him up.

Paul made us jelly and marshmallow crème sandwiches for lunch. We had to eat three baby carrots before we could eat the sandwiches, though. Baby carrots tasted just as gross as adult size carrots. Paul also made us drink water to stay hydrated. He put a thing called a mint sprig in each glass. It made the water taste delicious and not like boring water.

I looked down at my fingers. The skin was as wrinkled as those dancing raisins on television.

"Felicia," Paul called. "You put on sunscreen, right?"

Sunscreen? The white lotion stuff that I didn't have? The stuff that keeps you from burning in the sun? The stuff I didn't put on!

I pressed my fingers into the skin on my arm. "Ouch."

⁂

When Belinda opened the front door, I laid on a towel in the middle of the living room floor. The box fan pointed at me as I spread out like a snow angel. A pinkish-red snow angel.

"Oh, my word for all that's pink." Belinda dropped her purse on the floor and rushed to me.

"I got a little burned today," I said, not moving at all.

"Sunscreen!" Belinda blurted. "I bought you a bathing suit and forgot the sunscreen. Wait, who watched you at the pool?"

"My new friend Jessica's dad, Paul."

"Oh, that's great, sweetheart, but why did Paul not check that you had sunscreen?"

"He did, at the end."

"Where is he?" Belinda asked, scowling as she made her way to the door. "I need to speak to him about this. As a parent, he should know to check if a child is wearing sunscreen."

"Please, don't."

Belinda stood at the door, hand on the knob. Her eyes fixed on me.

"Building B," I moaned. "Number 20."

I ADOPTED MY MOM AT THE BUS STATION

Belinda was going to embarrass me. I guess that is something moms do to their daughters.

Chapter 20 – Present Day – 2009

Mom left a little bit after we unloaded her SUV full of Dixie Lynn's new baby essentials. She, Paul, and Pamela had a trip planned for the following day, and she needed to get back home.

The remainder of the dust settles in the driveway as the SUV disappears into the distance. Robert has been busy in our absence and greets me along with Chester, who's grown a liking to my father over his few days. Around the entire front, east, and backside of the house, the remains of paint strips rest like snowflakes on the ground.

"Probably would've been easier to pressure wash this." A ladder rests against the siding, as my father stands at the base of it. He readjusts his cap and squints at the house as the sun starts to lower over the roofline.

I approach. "I tried, but it kept tripping the breaker."

The clouds continue to puff up in the distance as Robert looks in my direction. "If you need help setting anything you picked up for Dixie Lynn, let me know."

Sweat has formed under his arms and around the base of his shirt. Gramps's shirt.

"Come inside. It's been a hot day."

His feet shuffle behind me, a clear sign it's been a long day of work for him. By the time we make it up the porch steps, an all too familiar Chevy rumbles up the driveway.

"Want me to take her so you can have some time with him?" Robert cranes his neck toward the Chevy, now parked next to my Toyota.

My arms twitch as I hand Dixie Lynn over and then hesitate. The backs of my hands brush up against my father's chest, and warmth radiates through the shirt.

"I promise I won't drop her. I only dropped you a few times." Robert laughs and then straightens his lips. "Joking. I never dropped you."

Sliding my hands out from around Dixie Lynn, I chuckle a sigh and take a deep breath as my father and my temporary baby girl head inside.

"Hi," I holler at Justin as he climbs from his truck. "What brings you over?"

"I came to talk to you about Dixie Lynn." Justin skips a step, and suddenly, he's in my personal space. I can smell the wintergreen gum he has tucked in his cheek.

"And to check on me." I blink hard.

Justin reaches his hand out and wraps it around my arm. "I don't have to come here to check on you. My binoculars work rather well."

"Thank goodness I know you're joking." I squirm from his grip and smack him in the chest. My hand practically bounces off it. Hard as a rock.

He wiggles his eyebrows and plops onto the porch swing. "How's everything with your father?"

"Better than I expected," I whisper. "Mom just left."

"I thought I saw an SUV coming out of here. I wish I'd been a few minutes earlier to say hi to her."

I sit next to him, our jeans touching. "She makes everything okay. It's hard to describe. It might be a mom thing, and I simply don't understand, but I feel safe with her. I'm strong with her, but also, I know it's okay if I'm weak."

Justin focuses on his boots, scuffed and stained. "I think you described it perfectly." He tilts his head in my direction, the sunset in the distance. "The reason I came over—"

"—besides to see my beautiful self." I lean into him and then pull back.

"Of course." He blushes. "It's about Dixie Lynn."

89

My posture straightens, and my hands clasp together. "We have to find Molly."

"Exactly." He rubs his palms on his jeans. "I looked into the laws, and the state will do what they can to find the biological mom before they'll allow any adoption. They'll most likely also reach out to any family members to see if they want to adopt the baby over non-family."

"I want nothing more than to see Molly and Dixie Lynn together again, but something is not sitting right in my gut."

"You don't think Molly will change her mind?"

I shake my head and grind my teeth. "Not the Molly I know now."

Justin leans back and pushes the porch swing into motion with the heels of his boots. "I know Molly's mom moved to Nevada."

"It was so sad how she completely disowned her as soon as she got pregnant out of wedlock. Heck, Molly's mom has the exact same backstory."

"Probably didn't want to witness Molly making the same mistakes. Plus, her mom could want her grandchild. The courts will at least try to contact her."

"I doubt she'd even return a phone call."

"Does Molly's mom have siblings?"

"Maybe, but I have no idea where they're located." I sit back in the swing and tuck my legs to the side.

"What about the Dixie Lynn's daddy?"

"There are at least five different possibilities, but not the current boyfriend, Mark." My lip wrinkles like Elvis at the thought.

In many ways, Molly and I are different, but the most obvious one is her dating life. Or more like her jump in the sack life. "Can the dad step up and want the baby?"

"Most certainly, but we could fight in court if we needed to. Especially if the man doesn't even know he's a dad."

I glance at the living room window; shadows move around.

"You have a stable life; it would look good to a judge," Justin states.

I turn to him, my vision resting on his eyes, trying to avoid staring at his lips. "I think most people in this town do, in some way or another. Look at you, you're stable. Not to mention the nicest and most down-to-earth guy I know." As the words leave me, I'm reminded how cozy being around Justin makes me.

"And yet, I can't get the most wonderful woman in all of Oklahoma to date me."

If he only knew how much I want to date him. How being close friends all these years pulls my heart in two different directions. How his father's role in my father's life is something I've struggled to shake.

"I appreciate you helping me with Dixie Lynn." I catch the last of the sun disappearing over the ridge and refocus on Justin.

"Do you want to keep her? Be her mama?"

I press my lips together and stretch my feet out in front of me. "Is it wrong if I say I do? Or I don't."

"Either way, absolutely not. If yes, you'd be amazing." Justin nods his head, and a smile forms. "Looks like your relationship with your father has taken a shift." His eyes go to the living room window.

"He's not the man I thought he was, but we have a long way to go."

Chapter 21 - The Truth

"What is MS?" I asked as I continued to rub slime green Aloe vera gel on my burnt skin. "Jessica said her mom had it, and that's why she died."

"Multiple sclerosis is a disease that causes nerve damage. People with it usually struggle with walking and end up in a wheelchair. As the disease progresses, a person might struggle with talking and not be able to feed themselves."

"Is it contagious? Will Jessica die too?" I asked.

"Oh gosh, no, it's not contagious."

"Good," I said.

Belinda worked on supper as I sat and watched CMT. I tried to sit as still as possible. Every time I moved, it hurt. Belinda finished cooking and brought my food over to me. She placed a glass of plain milk on the coffee table in front of me. I rolled my eyes.

"I wanted to talk to you about the bruise on my face," she said, sitting down next to me.

"My husband, he developed a drinking problem. He became incredibly controlling and didn't allow me to do anything I wanted. My dad didn't approve of my marriage. I didn't see the issues until I stepped back from the situation. Mike, my husband, hadn't hit me until the day before you and I met at the bus station. It had always just been yelling and telling me that I belonged at home. He told me, as a woman, I wasn't supposed to work. Men were to make the money. Women were to cook and clean. His thoughts were from a world many centuries ago and didn't allow me to follow my dreams."

"Gramps always told me I could do anything I wanted," I said. "Well, I can't do drugs or go to the moon. Gramps has a thing about the moon. He says it's too far for me to travel. He told me I could go anywhere, even to Australia, but not the moon."

"Sweetheart, your Gramps gave you excellent advice. Minus the moon. I think if you want to go to the moon, you should."

"Why didn't you divorce Mike?" I asked, taking a bite of chicken.

"It started slow, one little thing here and there. You're right, though. I should've divorced him a long time ago. It got to the point where I was too afraid to leave. Plus, I love him, or I think I still do, and divorce was something I never wanted."

"I don't know anything about divorce, but I know about wanting your dreams to come true," I said.

"Besides the beach, what is your dream?" Belinda asked.

"I've always wanted to know what it would be like having a mom," I said. "To be normal."

Just letting those words slip off my tongue made my chest tight, as though my heart was pushing the tears up and out. But, I held it in.

"Even for one day, anything to fill the pain in my heart," I added. "What did you want to do, your dream?"

"I wanted to be a dance teacher. To teach others to dance like what we saw on *Girls Just Wanna Have Fun*. I want to take what I liked about teaching and what I liked about dance and mix it."

"Why couldn't you? What's so wrong about teaching dance?" I asked.

"Mike saw it as a waste. He thought dance was inappropriate for a lady to teach to children. He saw it as not ladylike to be jiggling all around."

"Will you do that here? In Mobile?" I asked.

"Maybe, I need to make sure my teaching credentials are accepted here. I'll figure it out."

"Figuring things out is the best part of life," I said.

Belinda placed her plate on the coffee table. "You're a brilliant girl. Figuring out life is the best part of who you are and who you'll become."

A commercial came on for a Polaroid camera, and I remembered the photo album.

"I found an album in the back of the dresser drawer yesterday. I forgot to tell you."

"Show me," Belinda said.

Where had I put it? I carefully stood up, moving like a Transformer around the apartment, retracing my steps from yesterday. Belinda got up and helped me look.

"I think I found it," she called.

We flipped through the pages of Theresa and Sharon.

"Can we make one like this?" I asked.

"Of course! We have the camera from the zoo. It has a few pictures left, but we'll get another camera. I used the rest of the money from the envelope on the deposit for this apartment and getting those few extras."

"My clothes?" I asked, lowering my head.

"Now, don't get all pouty. I wanted to get you those clothes. We'll do the scrapbook, promise."

"I want to find Theresa and her mom and get this back to them too."

"What a great idea. I bet Jessica could help you too. Maybe she knows who they are?"

I hadn't even thought about asking Jessica, but I didn't tell Belinda. I wanted to remain as brilliant as she thought I'd been five minutes ago.

"What's on television tonight?" Belinda asked, flipping through the TV Guide.

"*Beverly Hills 90210*," I said.

"Have you watched it before?"

"Well ... I watched it at Molly's house."

Belinda looked at me, deep in thought. Her mouth moved in a "hmmm" motion back and forth.

"I'll let you watch it, but we'll watch it together."

It turns out, moms and dads were a lot alike.

Chapter 22 - Present Day - 2009

I'll never admit it to Justin, but I didn't want him to leave. I never do. He may notice it, though, even if I don't want him to. The way I leaned over the door of his truck as he put on his seatbelt. I might've given it away when I waved at him as he backed out of the driveway, my lip pouted. As soon as I realized it, I fixed my mouth into a smile, but I think it was too late.

Entering the living room, I find my father swaying Dixie Lynn and humming. I clear my throat, and he turns around. There's something to be said about seeing your father holding a baby, especially when you have a limited connection to either of them, but know it might change in a second. Just because the blood in me is half my father's doesn't mean I need to claim it. I've spent my life trying to disown him completely. Yet, the baby is a different story.

"Justin take off?" Robert asks.

"Yeah."

"You've noticed he looks an awful lot like a young Andrew McCarthy, right?"

"I see they gave you some great movies to watch in prison." Of course, I've noticed this. I'm an '80s movie fanatic. I know where my father is heading, and I jump in to lead him off course. "I'm hungry. You?" I shove my hands into my jean pockets.

"Incredibly." He smiles at me, and I see myself in him.

We have the same smile—the same ugly nose. Our lips, both fuller than lips ought to be.

"Great, chicken 'n' dumplings alright with you?" I hurry toward the kitchen, my stomach already set to eat. "I know it's summer and all, but I've been craving it for weeks."

"I think any time is a good time for chicken and dumplings." He takes a seat at the kitchen chair, Dixie Lynn resting on his shoulder.

I remove a whole chicken from the refrigerator and then move the robin's egg blue Dutch oven to the sink and fill it with water. "Did you ever make it in prison?"

"Never, far too expensive to make something with whole chickens. Not to mention the time it takes to cook."

I move through the familiar process of putting on plastic gloves. Next, I remove the bird from the wrapper and submerge it into the Dutch oven. Then, I remove the gloves like a doctor and set them inside the trash. I turn on the water with my elbow and wash my hands, twice.

After setting the Dutch oven on the burner, I wash my hands a third time to be extra safe. While I hate to be environmentally cruel by wearing plastic gloves for all of five seconds, the thought of having raw meat on my hands is horrifying. Usually, I can pick up the raw meat with a fork, but a whole bird proves impossible. I've made many attempts to go vegan and avoid it altogether, but without any success.

A question itches at my throat, although I fear asking it. There are so many questions I want to ask, but at my age, they all seem immature. I clear my throat, hoping it'll pass.

"You know, your Mama loved chicken and dumplings. But she refused to say 'n.' She insisted it should be 'and.'" Robert chuckles and rests his hand on Dixie Lynn's back. "I guess it stuck with me after all these years."

I swallow the lump. "Did she cook it often?"

My father stands and hands me Dixie Lynn. "She had to. I couldn't stand to handle a raw chicken." His face lit up like the Fourth of July. "She'd laugh at me, called me ridiculous." His eyes wander as though lost in a memory he's trying to relive in the kitchen.

96

He removes his cap and plays with the bill. "I miss her." His vision goes to the ceiling and then back at the cap. "You know, your voice, if I close my eyes and you speak, it's identical to hers."

"It is?"

Gramps and Nana should've mentioned that fact.

"Yes, you're her daughter." Robert approaches the Dutch oven and leans over it. "It smells just like I remember."

"Don't all chicken 'n' ... and dumplings smell the same?" I check the oven clock. Dixie Lynn should've had her bottle thirty minutes ago.

"Maybe. But I only remember your mama's." He turns to me. "I guess it's a plus of being in prison. It allowed me to sit with every memory I had of her. No escape."

The ache to hug my father engulfs me with the fury of a tornado's wind and sucks the breath from my lungs. It's hard to move, but I push myself to ready the bottle for Dixie Lynn with my free hand while I cradle her with the other. Robert stares at the Dutch oven the entire time as though it's a window into the past.

"Tell me something else about Mama." I take a seat at the kitchen table, the baby in my lap, as she sucks away at the bottle.

"She loved storms. Nothing scared her. A tornado could be coming right for our house, and I'd have to grab her by the shoulders and nearly drag her to the cellar."

Finally, he looks up from the stove and makes his way to the slider. Outside, clouds dot the sky, visible by the full moon. "Thunderstorms, dust storms, anything involving dramatic weather, and your mama would be out on the porch. Better yet, she'd be where she shouldn't be, out in the open."

He folds his hand over his chest. "I remember shortly after we married, I'd fallen asleep watching something on television and woke to a loud clap and rumble. I called for your mama all over the house, and when I was just about to panic, I spotted her through the living room window. She was standing in the middle of the yard, hands outstretched, her head tilted back and her tongue out like a child, drinking in the raindrops falling from the sky."

A smile forms on my face, big enough for my eyes to narrow as my cheeks press upward. "I love storms too."

I can picture Mama, from the images in the few photos I have, standing out there in a storm. What I wouldn't give to stand out there with her. The sudden reality hits me in my heart as the realization that my father is standing in my kitchen, and he's the reason I can't.

"Do you mind if I shower? I don't want to smell stronger than supper."

I nod and stare at Dixie Lynn. Her eyes, her nose, her chin. The hurt I have after all these years makes it so very hard to fathom why Molly left her daughter behind. In a million trillion years, I'd never do such a thing after everything I've been through. Heck, even if I hadn't lived the life I have, I could never imagine leaving an infant so helpless and so pure.

Nausea rose in my esophagus, and I swallow it back down. As I hear the water running upstairs, déjà vu washes over me. Unable to explain the moment, I allow it to happen, taking over my thoughts. I have to be confusing a memory from the past, maybe with Gramps, when Nana was showering.

The first time I wandered off to see Mama's grave. Gramps had a baseball game on the television and was focused on it to the point a tornado could've knocked on the door, and he would've remained seated.

Without a second thought, déjà vu or not, I fill up a water bottle and carry Dixie Lynn to the front door. Chester sits while I slip on my flip-flops and click on the porch light.

The moon's glow shows the way as Chester, Dixie Lynn, and I head to the end of the drive and onto the main dirt road. I can walk this path with my eyes closed if I need to. A perfect breeze fills the air and provides a cooling effect to the summer night's warmth hanging around.

"I'm taking you to meet the most important person in my life." I glance at Dixie Lynn as we continue down the road. A car can't be heard for miles, but lights from the highway outside of town are like fireflies in the distance.

"Whenever I'm scared or worried, sometimes even when I need a sign, I go out to visit Mama." Dixie Lynn's eyes are wide, looking up at the night's sky. "Maybe, Mama can show us the answers we can't see."

As the cemetery comes into view, Chester's stride lengthens, and he goes from next to me to several feet in front of me.

Mama's gravesite rests just to the right of the entrance. Black walnut trees line the small cemetery, naturally fencing it in. The light pink hydrangeas I left after my last visit have been baked by the sun and dried up. I leave them as they still add a loving touch and will replace them with the next bunch of flowers I bring out.

I face Mama's tombstone and sit crossed-legged, resting Dixie Lynn against my chest, her bottom in my lap. Chester lies like a sphinx next to me, and I stroke his smooth coat.

"Hi, Mama," I sigh. "I brought Dixie Lynn to meet you."

I press my lips together and glance around. I always feel immature and foolish coming here, let alone talking to a tombstone, but it doesn't stop me. Tears start to form on the rims of my eyes, but I let them be. I know I don't have to be strong around Mama, and this is a safe place to cry and not be judged.

Chester springs up and licks at my cheeks as the tears fall. "It's okay, Ches. I'm okay." But I know it's a lie.

"Mama, I'm so scared. Robert is back. Or maybe it's that he's home. Can he really be back when he's been gone for so many years, or is he really home if he's been gone for so long? And now I'm a ..." I kiss the top of Dixie Lynn's head.

Chester lays back down but leans against my now outstretched legs. "I loved Dixie Lynn before she was born, but this is so very different. Molly left her, and I'm struggling to wrap my mind around it all."

I listen to the wind dance through the trees' limbs. Crickets chirp in conversations. And I close my eyes, paying attention and hope for an answer. I've lost track of time, as I often do when I visit Mama. The sounds of nature at night time surround me as I open my eyes.

"I'm going to try and find Molly. Bring her Dixie Lynn. Help her understand she can do this. I can help her face whatever caused her to leave her daughter behind."

The only problem being, I have no idea where to start the search, but I have an idea where she might be, and I'll need both Justin and my father's help.

Chapter 23 - The plan

In the morning, Jessica knocked on the door, smiling as though she'd won a trip to Disneyland.

"Hi, you want to come over and watch movies?" she asked.

"As long as I don't have to move too much," I said, wincing.

I carefully changed out of my jammies, trying not to let the fabric touch too much of my burnt skin. I cradled my bottle of aloe vera gel as though it was a grand trophy. A trophy for the pinkest skin in all of Mobile, Alabama. Jessica pulled me nearly the entire way to her apartment.

"Hi, Paul," I greeted.

"We rented a bunch of movies." Jessica pointed at the stack on the counter. "We have all three *Back to the Futures*. Plus, we have *Kindergarten Cop*, because Miles picked it out, and *Look Who's Talking*, 1 and 2."

They all looked like awesome movies. Diamond City had Bob's Video Rental, which meant movies from the 1900s. If they even made movies then. Bob had movies from 1900 to 1980, but anything newer, and Bob didn't have it yet.

"I haven't seen any of these," I said.

"Really?" Jessica asked. "I think we should start with *Back to the Future*."

Jessica snapped open the Hollywood Video box and placed the tape into the VCR. I eased myself down onto the couch, clutching my Aloe vera trophy.

"I want to watch it too!" Miles called, running out of his bedroom.

He threw himself onto his blue beanbag chair, which sat to the right of the couch.

"Okay, Miles, but no talking. I mean *no* talking," Jessica warned him.

Miles squeezed his thumb and finger together, put them to his lips, pretended to lock them, and chucked the imaginary key across the room.

We finished *Back to the Future* and had started *Back to the Future 2* before Paul announced he made us lunch.

"I wish I could travel back in time," Jessica announced. "Do you?" she asked.

"Yes, so that I could ..." I stopped myself. So that I could remember more about Mama before she died, stop my father, I thought to myself. Of course, I couldn't say that aloud to Jessica. Jessica didn't seem to notice that I didn't finish my sentence. Then, out of nowhere, I remembered the album.

"I found a photo album in the dresser drawer of my apartment."

"Here you go, kids," Paul said, placing our sandwiches and juice on the coffee table.

"A photo album?" Jessica asked.

"Do you know who used to live in my apartment? The album only says Theresa and Sharon under the photos." I headed to the kitchen sink and washed my hands.

"Theresa," Jessica said, taking a bite of her sandwich. "Theresa and her parents moved to Florida. Not really moved, more like one day here, the next day gone. Her mom's sick, and there's a hospital in Florida that said they could help make her better."

"What kind of sick?" I asked, easing back onto the couch.

"Cancer," Jessica said, frowning.

Why was everyone having mom issues? I didn't like hearing about it, but I didn't feel so alone either. "Do you have Theresa's mailing address?" I asked. "We could mail it to her?"

"No, last time I saw Theresa, she waved goodbye to me from the truck as her dad pulled out of the parking lot. She'd been my best friend before she up and left me. And, I haven't heard from her since."

"I can be your best friend," I blurted.

I don't know why I said it. Everything Jessica knew about me was a lie. My name wasn't even Felicia.

"I would like that!" Jessica said, putting down her sandwich and coming in for a big hug.

"Ouch, ouch, ouch!" I cried.

"The sunburn, right." Jessica pulled away, a smile still lit up her face. "Best friends." She took her pinky and held it up to me.

My mind went to Molly. Could I have two best friends? Would I see Molly again? When did Molly get back from camp? The first or fifth of August. I'd forgotten.

"Felicia?"

Jessica's pinky was still alone in the air. I took my pinky, wrapped it in my long sleeve, and locked it with hers.

"Best friends," I said, half smiling.

Everything in my body was weighed down at that moment, as though I had on a heavy jacket. A part of me was starting to miss Molly and Gramps. Even Nana, a small, crumb-sized bit. My thoughts of Mama were still on my mind, but not in the front as much as they used to be. Mobile was turning into home. And being here, I felt closer to Mama. It was her birthplace and all.

After *Back to the Future 2*, I dashed over to my apartment to grab the photo album. When I returned, Jessica started the next movie as we sat together on the couch, just like Molly and I usually did.

"I want to see. Move! I can't see," Miles whined, trying to sit between us.

"You can see it from there," Jessica informed him.

"Daddy!" Miles hollered, stomping down the hall.

"How do we find Theresa and Sharon?" I asked.

"We have a phone book, but it's only for Mobile," Jessica said.

"What about calling the operator?" I asked.

"I don't know if they'd be listed since she went to the hospital," Jessica said. "I think she's going to be there a long time. Maybe, her dad will be listed."

"What hospital?" I asked.

Jessica shrugged her shoulders. "I don't know."

"What's her dad's name?" I asked.

"Richard. And there must be a thousand Richard Collins in Florida."

"We need a plan," I told her. "We need to find Theresa and get this back to her," I added, gripping the photo album.

"She hasn't written me a letter or called. Best friends do that stuff," Jessica said.

Jessica crossed her arms and focused on the carpet.

"Maybe she lost your phone number or forgot the address. Maybe she doesn't have a phone hooked up yet, or doesn't have a stamp for the envelope."

Jessica glared at me.

"Maybe ..." I stopped myself. I shouldn't go there yet, and I know Jessica knew the words I'd stopped from exiting my lips. The word Jessica and I knew. The word that affected us both, but that Jessica only thought affected her. Something that shouldn't happen until a mom is wrinkled like a prune, carrying butterscotch in her pocket and using The Clapper to turn the lights off and on. I couldn't let the word slip from my mouth.

"If, maybe, *it* happened," I said, "then Theresa definitely needs the album back."

"What if we call the operator, and they don't have her listed, then what?"

"We call the hospitals and find Sharon."

"Together," Jessica said, "as best friends."

But, this time, we didn't smile. We must have been thinking the same thing, afraid of what we might find in Florida. I hoped for one thing, that this was not a sign from Mama about going to see my father.

Chapter 24 –
Present Day –
2009

"Where have you been?" My father hollers as he hurries down the front porch steps. His arms flail about as though he wants to fly. "I come out of the shower and can't find you, the dog, or the baby! And you left the stove on!"

At this point, I'm grateful the neighbors' houses are at least a few acres away in all directions because Robert is making a rather big scene. It seems that way to me anyway, because why should he care? It's not like we have a normal father-daughter relationship.

"I went to see Mama." Sweat beads at the edge of my forehead. "Plus, supper needed to simmer."

Carrying a baby creates a whole new workout I've never thought of before. "And," I step onto the porch, and my flip-flops flop firmly as though it's a judge's gavel, "I don't have to answer to you."

Robert's face is red, and his eyes are flustered. "Correct, you don't have to answer to me, but it's a common courtesy to notify people if you're leaving. Unless, common courtesies aren't popular anymore."

"Because when you stole my truck you let me know?" I remove my cell phone from my back jean pocket and wave it at him. "I had my phone with me. Could've called."

"Because I know your phone number?" His arms go out like bird wings.

I roll my eyes. "I haven't had to answer to anyone for years now."

My father crosses his arms. "Supper smells ready."

I nod and pass him, heading inside the house. "We need to go find Molly. Justin left me a voicemail when I was on my way home; he was able to dig up the information on where she might be. I don't think I can travel alone with a baby and Chester."

Robert's footsteps follow behind me as we enter the kitchen. The aroma of chicken and dumplings fill my nose with delight. After placing Dixie Lynn into her car seat and handing her a soft set of baby keys, I hurry to the stove.

"I shredded the chicken and dropped in the dumplings while you were gone." Robert leans on the island with his hands. "You want me to go with you? To find your best friend?"

"Thanks for helping with supper." As I remove the lid, steam rises from the Dutch oven. "I'd use the term 'best friend' lightly right now. Do you have something else you need to do with your time?"

"Yes." He stands up straight. "This house for one. Besides, I would think maybe Justin would want to go with you. Him being a lawyer and all might be a better plan."

Stirring the chicken and dumplings, I realize Robert does have a point. But, being alone in a car with Justin for any length of time might prove too much for me to handle. If I could turn my feelings for him off, I would flip that light switch as fast as possible. Keeping our distance is always a safe bet.

"No, Justin ... is too busy. I mean, as you said, he's a lawyer ... cases and such." I take out two miss-matched bowls from the cupboard and ladle in the chicken and dumplings.

We sit at the table, Chester's at my feet, as the sound of our spoons tapping against the bowl echoes through the kitchen.

"I'll go with you if that's what you want." He eyes the baby and gives her a grin. "Do you have any other friends you'd rather take?"

"Mom's step-daughter, Jessica, she moved overseas about two years ago. Her brother, Miles, is still in the states, but is always out adventuring."

The thought of how few friends I have to rely on smacks me. Some of it's my fault. After Gramps and Nana passed, I sort of shut out the world minus Justin, mostly because he would never let that happen. And Molly had been in her own world for a while. Everyone else from college or high school started families, and we drifted apart. All the teachers at school were spending time with family or vacationing. Looking back, growing up sucks.

"I guess we have ourselves a little road trip then." Robert raises his spoon toward me like it's a glass of champagne.

"We'll leave first thing in the morning," I say without smiling.

※※※※ ※※※※

In the morning, just after the sun rises over the plains, Justin climbs from his Chevy. He has two coffees in hand, and a white paper bag as I shove my backpack into the extended cab of my truck.

"Road trip?" Justin's forehead wrinkles, and his eyes squint as though he's figuring out a complex mathematical equation. "Wait, you're going after Molly?"

"Yes." I place my hands on my hips and face him.

"Is Miles in town?" He glances over the top of my head toward the house.

"Nope." I reach for one of the coffees.

"Is Belinda back?"

"Nope, she left for a vacation. My father, Dixie Lynn, and Chester are coming with me."

Justin's mouth drops open. "No, that's not why I dug up the info on Molly's boyfriend for you." He shakes his head. "I did it so we could contact the authorities. No. No."

I sip the hot black liquid. It nearly burns my tongue. "Yes."

"I don't think that's a safe idea. Shouldn't you be focused on Dixie Lynn?"

"I am. That's why I'm going. To find Molly." My vision goes to the bag, still wrapped in his hand. Grease stains dot the lower half. "What else did you bring?"

Justin glances at the bag. "Donuts." He hands the bag over. "I knew I never should've told you about Mark's parent's house."

Once I set my coffee cup on the hood of my Toyota, I un-roll the top of the paper bag and peek inside. My shoulders relax with delight.

"Raspberry glazed with rainbow sprinkles." I reach inside and remove one of the donuts.

In order to eat donuts in Diamond City, one has to make them in their kitchen or drive twenty minutes to the next town.

Closing my eyes, I take the first bite, it's soft and sweet. The dough nearly melts on my tongue.

"I don't know how I feel about this." Justin takes a long sip of coffee.

"Yes, you do. I love raspberry glazed donuts, and you know to always get me two."

Justin pulls this coffee cup away from his lips as they form a straight line. "Not the donuts. You and your father."

"Well, I can read a map, but I can't travel alone with Dixie Lynn and Chester. I need help." I take another bite of the donut as a few sprinkles fall onto the dirt driveway.

"I'll help. Let me come too." Justin reaches his hand out, and I lean back, his thumb too close to my lip. "Chill, it's only a sprinkle."

Our eyes find each other's, and everything around me blurs. Justin's hand rests on the crook where my neck and shoulder meet. Thank goodness I have a donut in my right hand and the bag in my left, or I would have set my hand over the top of his to keep it there forever. Instead, I stare into Justin's perfect eyes until my vision falls to his lips.

"About ready to head out?" Robert's voice breaks up my daydream.

I step back toward my Toyota, and Justin's hand falls to his side.

"Oh," my father says. "I didn't mean to interrupt anything."

I take a larger than needed bite of the donut.

"Sandy was just telling me about her road-trip to locate Molly." Justin takes his hand and wraps it around the other side of his coffee cup, locking his fingers together where they met.

"Yes, I guess you were busy with work." Robert puts Dixie Lynn's diaper bag into the cab of the truck.

"Thanks, Justin, for stopping by." Using my free hand, I push Justin toward his truck. "Watch the house while we're gone, please."

He twists around. "But I'm not busy."

"Of course you are. You're a lawyer." I pop open his driver's side door.

Justin places his boot onto the running board and slides into the seat. "No, I'm—"

My eyes widen in a warning fashion, and he glances at me and then my father.

"Fine. When will you be back? Will you call me and let me know how it's going? I mean, you need my help to proceed forward if you can't find Molly. Or if it doesn't go as planned."

All I can think about as I stare at Justin, my hand resting on the door of his truck, is kissing him. I want to reach out for him, wrap my arms around his neck and press my lips to his. God, I want it more than all the donuts in the world!

"I'll call you." I force myself backward. "Thanks for breakfast."

Spinning around, I swipe the coffee cup off the hood of my truck and head toward the house, meeting up with Robert as the Chevy starts up in the background. I run my hand through my hair, knowing that one of these days, I might not be able to walk away from Justin.

Chapter 25 - Pie

This was the day I'd make my first ever raspberry pie! I didn't know why I was excited. It's only a pie. A glorious mouthwatering raspberry pie, at least I hoped it would be. Outside, the rain came down as though there was a cry fest going on within the clouds. It pinged off the windows and thumped on the roof.

"Felicia," Belinda said. "Focus. We need to roll out the crust."

I'd made the crust a half hour ago and placed it in the refrigerator to chill.

"Put a little bit of flour on the counter and a little on the dough ball."

I followed Belinda's instructions as she handed me the rolling pin.

"Now push real hard and roll it back and forth. Then go left to right, so you roll it in a circle."

"I know. I have seen this part before."

"Okay," Belinda said, putting her hands up in defense.

I pushed firmly, rolling the pin back and forth and then left to right, but the crust looked more like a big egg than a circle. I kept trying, rolling left to right, back and forth. Finally, it turned into a circle.

"This is the trickiest part," she said. "Do you know how to get the crust into the pie dish?"

"No."

"Take the rolling pin and roll the dough over it halfway, then lift it into the dish."

I placed the rolling pin in the middle of the dough and rolled the dough over it, then lifted the pin. I started to move it to the dish when the dough slid off the rolling pin and flopped onto my bare toes below. Belinda and I both looked down at the crust over my feet and laughed.

"I guess you could make the first-ever tootsie pie," she said.

I repeated the first steps and put the new ball of dough into the refrigerator to chill. A half-hour later, I went back to rolling out the dough and did a better job making the circle. This time I got it in the pie pan without creating another foot pie.

Following her directions, I mixed the raspberries with sugar, cinnamon, and cornstarch. I poured the mixture over the pie crust.

"Please show me how to do the fence thing on top," I said, my hands pressed together as though I was going to pray.

"The lattice?" Belinda said, raising her eyebrow in confusion. "Oh, cause it looks like a fence." She laughed. "Okay, roll out the other ball of dough into a circle."

I rolled it out, and then I cut it into strips as Belinda instructed. Together we laced the top of the pie and brushed it with egg wash.

Egg wash was not soap and eggs. It's the same as when you scramble the egg before you put it in the pan to make scrambled eggs. I thought making the pie would be the hard part, but waiting for it to cook and then waiting for it to cool before you could taste it, that was the hardest part.

I flipped on CMT, but I checked the timer every two minutes. My sunburn had healed for the most part, which meant I didn't have to spend every hour rubbing Aloe vera gel on myself. I moved the blinds in the living room window to see if Paul's car had returned with Jessica and Miles. The spot remained empty except for the puddles of rain.

"What happened with the photo album?" Belinda called, coming into the living room.

"Jessica and I want to find them. The mom has cancer and is in the hospital. Theresa is, or maybe was, best friends with Jessica. We made a plan."

"A plan?" Belinda asked, flopping next to me on the couch.

"We're going to call around as soon as she gets home today," I said. "Since we still don't have a phone."

"We'll get one soon. Tell me about the plan?" she asked.

"To go to Florida and find them," I said, checking the pie timer again. "As long as Paul says she can, and you say I can."

"How will you get to Florida?"

The timer dinged. I put on two oven mitts, and I pulled the hot, bubbling pie out of the oven.

"We didn't think that far into the plan," I said, concerned.

One thing about moms is they remind you of the obvious—the obvious problems in your plan. I looked at my pie. Belinda came over and put her arm around me.

"Looks delicious," she said.

I stared at the red sauce bubbling from between the lattice. Being caught up in all things pie and photo album, my mind had glossed over, yet again to what else was in Florida. And I didn't think I had a plan for that either.

Chapter 26 –
Present Day –
2009

Chester and Dixie Lynn are both buckled into the extended cab of the truck. And, even though the front seat is a bench, my father sits as close to the passenger side door as humanly possible. If he moves an inch closer, he'll be sitting on the door handle.

"That's the plan?" Robert gazes straight ahead at the I-40.

I hand him the folded up map from the corner of the dashboard. "Molly's boyfriend is from Memphis. I've highlighted our route." I point at the map. "My thought is maybe that's where they went. If they were anywhere in Diamond City, we would've known."

Hickory and pine trees line both sides of the highway. The grasses between the east and westbound lanes are lush and popping with tiny white buds. Rolling hills appear in front of us as we continue toward Little Rock. We head south as the highway switches from two lanes to three.

"Hungry?" I ask, the first words spoken in over two hours.

"Yes, if you want to stop."

I click on the blinker and take the South 65 to Little Rock. "I remember a great place for milkshakes, if I can find it. Hopefully, it's still there."

"Did you and Belinda stop here on your way out to Mobile?" My father cracks his window, the sounds of the highway filters in the air.

I nod and glance at Dixie Lynn's car seat in the rearview mirror. "We had such a wonderful time together. Looking back, I'm pretty sure if I was in Gramps and Nana's position, I might've lost my mind over what I did."

"Sometimes leaping is all you can do. Just because it's wrong doesn't mean you don't need to do it. It's how we found out what we want."

"What do you want?" The words slide from my tongue without caution.

"Sandy, I don't even know where to start." Robert fidgets and rests his elbow on the door handle.

"How about when I was two? No, what about when I was ten or twenty?" I squeeze the steering wheel until my hands ache for me to loosen my grip. What I wouldn't give for a tornado to come dipping down from the sky right now. Something strong enough to take away all of my thoughts for at least five minutes. Have them sucked up and spun around because they're swirling in my head already.

Dixie Lynn fusses, and Robert reaches his hand back to her car seat, trying to comfort her.

"We're almost to the River Market. There should be outside seating for us."

I drive over the Arkansas River, the sunlight reflecting off the pale brown water. Moving to the right lane, I get off the highway and take Second Street. Nothing looks familiar, but then again, the last time I was here, I was eleven.

After we find parking, I check the concrete for heat with my palm before letting Chester out of the truck. Then I pump some hand sanitizer on my hands.

"I can't imagine what your journey with Belinda was like." Robert carries Dixie Lynn's car seat as we walk down River Market Avenue.

"Amazing, life-changing, and a little bit nerve-wracking. I think if I'd been any older, or wiser, I would've never done something so bold. But, at the time, I didn't have a great deal of fear holding me back."

"As long as you don't or didn't regret it, that's all that matters." Robert glances over at me, and I catch his smile.

I take a deep breath in the moment as the realization of the fact that my father and I are heading out to lunch together. I never imagined this would happen, and I most certainly never wanted it to. And on top of it all, we're not going to just any place for lunch, but the restaurant Mom and I first went to—a place where we viewed the map of our trip. The trip I went on because I missed Mama's history so much. And now I'm with the man who caused me a lifetime of missing.

"River Grill." Robert points. "That's the place, right?"

As I look ahead, the sign hangs just as I remembered it. I nod my head. "That's it."

"I'll stay outside with Chester and Dixie Lynn. You head in." He switches the car seat to his right hand and takes the leash from me.

"What do you want me to order for you?" Anxiety pulses through me, and I miss having the leash around my wrist for comfort.

"A cheeseburger is fine and something to drink. I'm not picky."

The situation presses heavily on my heart. I gasp for a few breaths before forcing my feet to take me inside, away from my father, but toward the memory of my childhood visit with Mom.

Inside looks exactly as I remember it. The booth where Mom and I sat is occupied by a teenage couple sharing a chocolate shake and making lovely eyes at one another. On the wall, over the counter, is the menu written in chalk.

After ordering two lunches, I allow my mind to continue to wander back to the memories. I have no idea how long I've zoned out, but a waitress taps on my shoulder, bringing me back to the present.

"Thank you." I take the to-go bag, grease already blotting through the sides.

The waitress hands me two milkshakes, and my outstretched fingers struggle to balance them in my palm. I open the door with my back and locate my father and Chester at a nearby plastic table with the car seat occupying a chair.

I sit the milkshakes down and peek at Dixie Lynn, who's still asleep. Robert removes the food from the bag.

"I got us both cheeseburgers and fries. You have a chocolate shake because I figured who doesn't like chocolate? You like chocolate, right?"

My father's face goes solemn.

"Oh no, you don't like chocolate?" I lean back, actually feeling bad.

Robert chuckles and shakes his head. "Of course, I like chocolate."

"Funny." I sit up straight, rub hand sanitizer on, and unwrap my cheeseburger. "I didn't imagine you as a joker." I suck on the straw of my raspberry milkshake.

"There's a lot we don't know about each other. And I hope that'll change, Sandy." He places his elbows on the table, squirts on hand sanitizer, and then proceeds to shove a handful of fries into his mouth. "I hope you know, regardless of how you feel about me, I want to learn all the things I missed while you were growing up."

"Did you expect Gramps and Nana to send you updates in prison?" I return to my milkshake, sucking it up so fast my brain tingles. My words are sharper than I expect, but he and I are adults. I don't have the patience to sugarcoat anything, especially with him.

This time his face stays solemn, and he focuses on his cheeseburger. The honesty I doled out suddenly causes the pit of my stomach to ache. I grab a fry and fold it in half.

"I hated the dark. Still do actually." My eyes meet his.

"Do you sleep with a nightlight now?" Robert asks.

"I keep the bathroom light on and crack the door."

When my father glances down and back up from his meal, I notice tears resting on the bottom of his lids. A wave of something I've never felt before for him wells up in my throat. Hurt, pain, maybe a little reflux from the cheeseburger.

"Your mama used to make me leave a light on in the living room or kitchen. Said she could see if someone was creeping around in the shadows that way."

The tears in my father's eyes make sense. I'm a constant reminder of Mama. But I can't understand why if I despise him, how I allowed him in my home, and now on this trip, with my best friend's baby.

"Do you think we have time to make a stop?" He sips his chocolate shake.

"Okay, where?"

"Briscoe, a small town between here and Memphis. I wanted to stop on my way to you, but I had limited money to get to Oklahoma. And that was my priority."

I shrug. "What are we stopping for?"

"A photo album of your Mama."

Chapter 27 – The phone call & the fountain

Jessica had her pink pad of paper and pen in hand, prepared to call the operator. Last night, Paul's car had a flat tire, and Jessica didn't get home until way past her bedtime. This morning we were more than ready.

"You call," Jessica said, shoving the phone at me.

"Ohhh, no," I said, pushing it back at her with my sleeve-covered hand.

"Fine," she said, reluctantly taking the phone. "I'll call."

Jessica pressed zero and waited for the operator.

"Hi, yes, may I please have the number for Sharon Collins in Florida?" Jessica asked. "Umm, the city ..." Her eyes widened, and her face panicked.

I thought back to school social studies.

"Orlando," I mouthed.

"Orlando."

I waited. Jessica waited. She shook her head, no.

"Miami," I mouthed.

We waited. Jessica shook her head no.

"What about a Richard Collins? Okay," she said, "thank you."

Tallahassee dropped into my head like a piece of hail falling from the sky. But I wouldn't say it aloud. If Theresa and Sharon were in Tallahassee, then I would need to make a decision. Maybe the album was a sign from Mama that I had to face my fear.

"No one listed in either Miami or Orlando." Jessica hung up the phone.

I found it strange that not one single person in either city had the last name, Collins. Even Diamond City has four Smiths. Four!

"Maybe they are ... unlisted," Jessica chimed in. "They might not have a phone yet."

"If she's in the hospital, then she wouldn't be listed."

The word hospital had shot from my mind, down to my mouth, and out my lips without a thought. Theresa's mom was sick. Jessica's mom had been sick too. I glanced at the framed photo on her dresser. I could see Jessica looking at it too. The word appeared to float between us. Every letter was enormous and separated as though it were individual clouds: HOSPITAL.

"Let's get out of here," Jessica said.

"Where are we going?" I asked as I followed her out of her room.

"I don't know, just out of here." Jessica swung the front door open.

I had trouble keeping up with her as we made our way out of the apartment parking lot and down the oak-lined streets. Most of the trees had moss draping from them. It helped block the sun's light, but unfortunately, not the heat and humidity. Sweat formed in places my deodorant didn't cover. I think I even had sweat behind my ears.

Jessica slowed her feet enough for me to catch up and keep rhythm with her. We walked in silence. The only noises were the hum of cars going by, the sound of birds, and our shoes on the pavement.

The houses and short white fences were now in the distance as the streets began to line with shops and tall buildings. We made our way into the park, following a path. Trees appeared as though their branches were holding the branches of the nearest tree, drawing us forward. In the center, a tall and wide fountain with a green sign read: Bienville Square.

Randomly placed trees and curved deep green iron benches circled the fountain. Jessica took a seat on one bench, and I sat next to her. Music drifted over from the decorative ironwork gazebo just outside the fountain's circle. Behind us, a grand, but plain concrete cross stood with flowers surrounding the base. The soft sounds of a guitar weaved its way around the fountain's cascading water.

"My mama used to take me here," Jessica said, soft enough that I could barely hear her.

"She would reach into her pocket and pull out a penny and place it in my hand," Jessica said, her eyes locked on the fountain. "I would make a wish and toss it in. It was the same wish every time."

"Did it come true?" I asked.

"No, she died."

We sat there in silence, my shorts sticking to the bench and my legs. Lines of sweat crossed my back from where my shirt pressed up against the slats of the bench. I wanted to run home and shower the germs, which were seeping through my shirt and shorts, off me.

"I think we should call the hospitals in Florida and see if we can find Sharon," Jessica said, breaking the silence.

"Yeah," I mumbled. "It's the only way to find her."

"But how will we pay to get there?" Jessica asked.

I looked at the crowd of people gathering around to listen to the music at the gazebo. A possible plan came to me.

"We could have a bake sale. They did one at my school to earn money," I said. "My ... mom is teaching me how to make pies. We could bring them there." I pointed at the gazebo. "And sell them. With enough money, we could take the bus to Florida."

"That might work, as long as our parents agree." Jessica turned to me. "Can I help you make the pies?"

"Yes, we can make more that way," I said. "Oh, wait, how will we pay for all the ingredients?"

"You don't get an allowance?" Jessica asked.

"No."

Jessica shot up. "Come on, let's go see how much money I have saved up."

We raced back to the apartments, a poor plan, as it was far too hot. When we came around the pool area, Paul and Miles were splashing about. Jessica grabbed my hand, and before I could yank it free, she pulled me through the gate door and up to the edge of the pool.

"Cannonball!" Jessica yelled.

Clothing and all, we leaped into the water.

I pushed myself up to the surface, now free of Jessica's hand, laughing once I took a breath. A look of shock spread across Paul and Miles's face before turning to laughter. The kind of laughter where your stomach hurts, and you can't breathe. And, for a few minutes, my fear of germs disappeared beneath the water. A free feeling soaked my entire body.

After the cool off in the pool, I went and changed into dry clothes and washed my hands twice, just in case. I grabbed my pastel notepad and a purple pen Belinda had bought me and headed to Jessica's.

"I'll call the hospitals; my dad said I could call long-distance," Jessica said, sinking into her beanbag chair. "You work on the pie list."

First on my "To Make" list, raspberry pie, followed by strawberry, blueberry, and peach. I wanted to stay with fruit pies because I knew how to make them. I hadn't attempted to make complex pies such as key lime or chocolate mousse. Fruit pies were easy. As long as you put enough sugar in it, no one could tell if it was not perfect.

"Did you put strawberry rhubarb pie on your list? We need to have strawberry rhubarb," Jessica insisted.

I added strawberry rhubarb pie on the "To Make" list and reminded myself that strawberry rhubarb must be Jessica's favorite, and I should remember that as a best friend would.

"I forgot to tell you, your mom came over yesterday to use our phone," Jessica said.

"Do you know who she called?"

"No," Jessica said. "She whispered the whole time."

I thought about who Belinda might be calling. She called someone outside River Grill, and now she'd called someone that she needed to whisper to.

Jessica punched in the numbers and held the phone to her ear.

"Yes, can you please tell me if Sharon Collins is in your hospital?"

I sat frozen with my pen in hand, waiting.

"Okay, thank you."

Jessica glanced at me and shook her head no. One down.

I focused on my ingredients list while Jessica called the second hospital. Each phone call ended the same, with a headshake no.

"Yes, can you please tell me if Sharon Collins is at your hospital?"

Hospital number five.

"Really?" Jessica's eyes opened wide, and she smiled. "Thank you. May I please have your address?"

Jessica's pen moved rapidly over the paper.

"Thank you, thank you so much!" she said before hanging up the phone. "Sharon Collins is at the Tallahassee Cancer Hospital."

"Tallahassee?" I asked.

My breathing became shallow, and my heart pulsed up to my ears.

"Dad, where's the map?" Jessica hollered as she made her way out to the living room.

She returned and spread the map out on her bed.

"There it is," Jessica announced, pointing to Tallahassee.

My arms and legs tingled. Of all the places, why did Sharon have to be in Tallahassee?

"How many pies do you think it'll take to get there?" Jessica asked.

I tried doing the math in my head, but the numbers floated around without a care in the world. Jessica pulled out her Wonder Woman wallet from her jean purse and started counting.

"I have thirty-two dollars. How much will it cost to make one pie?" she asked. "Felicia?"

"Maybe we could mail her the photo album," I suggested.

"I thought we were going to take it in person. What changed?" Jessica questioned.

I shrugged my shoulders, not wanting to admit the truth.

"We have to take it to Tallahassee," Jessica said. "The postman could lose it or damage it if we mail it. The album is an in-person kind of thing. Hey! Your dad lives in Tallahassee! We could stop by and see him. I'm sure he misses seeing you in person."

"Yeah, in person," I mumbled.

In my mind, the math numbers disappeared. They were replaced with the words: IN PRISON.

Chapter 28 -
Present Day -
2009

My heart doesn't know how to react to my father's news of the photo album, but my mouth does. I shovel the rest of my burger and fries into it like it's an eating contest. The fact that I've always wanted to see more photos of Mama, and now that I'll be able to causes a lump in my throat and tears to well up in my eyes. However, I push past it because I want to focus on getting to this album.

I eye Robert as he continues to eat like a teenager with a plate of broccoli. "How far is this place from here?"

"It's probably an hour."

As I stand up, the metal from the chair scrapes the concrete below, causing an ear-piercing noise. Dixie Lynn goes into a crying fit. My father stands, brushes his hands on his jeans, and lifts the baby from the car seat.

"There, there." He bounces Dixie Lynn in his arms.

Chester wraps himself up with his leash attached to the leg of the table. After untangling him, I'm ready to leave but find Robert has returned to his chair, Dixie Lynn in his arms as he eats one-handed.

I glance around. There's no way I can sit when all I want to do is run back to the car and floor it to Briscoe. "Wait, why is a photo album of Mama in another state?"

"They didn't allow me to bring anything into prison. I worried your grandparents would never give it to you. So before I was arrested, I handed the album off to my friend, Tony, who at the time lived in Diamond City. He's kept it safe all these years."

"So, you've spoken with Tony lately?" I can't recall my father using my phone, and I know he doesn't have a cell phone.

"Right before my release, I called him up, and he's expecting me, but doesn't know when."

"So Tony could've called me, at any time, and told me he had something I'd find utterly important?" I snap.

Robert's cheeks droop, and his mouth hangs open. He rubs a hand over his eye and drags it down his chin. "Have you thought about what I went through for one second? Or is everything always about you?"

I gasp.

My father digs through his basket of fries as though he's looking for the perfect one. "This photo album was all I had left of both of you. I didn't know what to expect when I knocked on your door a few days ago. She might have been your mother, but she was my wife. And regardless of what occurred, I never stopped loving her."

I focus on my breathing to keep it from spiraling into a panic attack. Candy, I focus on the sweet taste of candy. I wonder if that candy store is still here. "You can watch them both, right?"

He nods, fries in hand.

I'm far too aggravated to sit at the moment. "I'll be right back." I spin around and start on my search. I need to get away from him, from this new information.

My feet speed through the River Market; everything has changed from my memory of the brief walk-through with Mom. However, I know the candy shop has to still be here. Candy never goes out of style. After a few turns, the scent of sweet sugar fills my nose and pulls me in the direction of the store.

I open the door with my pinky to avoid as much contact with the germy handle as possible. Inside, the store is exactly as I remember it—the cases brimming full of confectionery treats. Thankfully, I have self-control to keep my face from suctioning to the case like a toddler.

A poof of pearly white cotton candy hair appears from the back room.

"Oh, gosh, I remember you." I step forward. "You're still here."

"Of course, dear, where else would I be? But refresh my memory," her elderly voice squeaks and strains.

"I wandered in here, lost when I was a kid." My eyes observe the chocolates in front of me.

"I wish I could recall, but many children come in here lost or not." She slides on food handler's gloves. "I probably should've named this place The Lost and Found Candy Shop."

I gently laugh and smile. "What do you recommend? They all look like winners."

She tilts her head. "Tell me, what's your favorite color?"

"It used to be a tie between purple and pink, but it's been blue for years." I fold my arms.

"And what's your favorite flower?"

"Same as my Mama's favorite, hydrangeas."

She picks up a tiny cardboard box and eyes the candy in the display. Sliding the glass door open, she goes around and places different chocolates in the box. "I'm sending you off with a blueberry truffle, a raspberry truffle, and a strawberry cream."

"Do you have anything for a man who was recently released from prison?"

The lady pauses, her gloved hand in the box. "Family member or friend?"

My eyes squint, and I glance out the nearby window. "It's complicated."

Her right eye raises, and she moves to another section of the case and slides the door open. "Caramel Apple and Wine Nugget." She folds the lid on the box and moves to the register between the cases of sweets.

"How much?" I ask, watching her wrap a ribbon around the box and securing it into a bow at the top.

"It's on the house. Since you're a returning customer." She hands the box over.

"Oh, I can't accept it without paying you. When I was little, you gave me candy for free."

She wiggles the box at me, and I take it.

Removing her gloves, she says, "And did you find your way?"

I glance at my shoes and bite my bottom lip, embarrassed by my age that even a stranger recognizes I may not know the direction my life is going. "Thank you."

She and I make eye contact.

"I'm Sandy." I reach my hand out towards her—something which takes all the courage I have at the moment. Shaking the hand of a stranger has been done only when the occasion called for it. And only when I knew I could immediately go and wash my hands. However, something about this elderly lady pulls me in, making me feel safe with such an offer of hand-to-hand germ contact.

"Nice to meet you, Sandy. I'm Patricia."

My hand squeezes around Patricia's hand, and the shake lasts longer than I plan. But I don't want to let go of her soft, bony hand.

"Patricia, it's a lovely name. My mama had the same name."

As I exit the shop, I spot From Bark to Book and make a beeline for its glass doors. I spent a lot of time thinking about what the inside of this store looked like during my teenage years, guilt-stricken that I never went inside.

Using the bottom of the handle, I pull the glass door, and it opens as smooth as butter on a hotplate.

The scent of pine and paper fills my nose, and I look past the fact that I must wash my hands. I haven't made a trip to Borders in Oklahoma City for a few months, meaning my stack of new books is in need of replenishing.

I'm tempted to run my fingers over the embossed covers of the New Release section near the entryway. I snatch up the newest book by John Grisham and John Saul and set them in the crook of my arm.

The store isn't huge, but I locate the bathroom to wash my hands before I find the children's book section and pick out several board books for Dixie Lynn.

As the cashier rings up my total, a display rack of bookmarks catches my eye. I take the bottom of it and rotate it with my pointer finger. One bookmark causes a lump in my throat. It reads: Books are printed memories.

Going into this store has thrown me off, and suddenly I'm reminded of my own memories. The ones I've yet to see in the photo album of Mama that Robert mentioned.

I snatch the bag of books from the cashier and run from the store without getting my receipt. Books have always caused my mind to forget about things, and that's why I love them. But right now, I'm on a much bigger mission.

It's all I can do to focus on finding my way back to Robert, Chester, and Dixie Lynn. I see Mama on the faces passing by, and I scold myself under my breath because, at my age, it's ridiculous.

When I find my way back to the River Grill, I pause and hide in the shadow at the edge of the building. As I watch, Robert appears like any other person to strangers. The picture-perfect man taking care of a baby and a dog. Since his arrival, I've found myself in these moments, seconds, when my brain forgets what he did all those years ago.

I saunter toward the table and stand at the side.

"About earlier," Robert mentions.

I hold my hand up to stop him from saying more. "While I had every right to be upset about the album, you did too."

My father's Adam's apple shifts when he swallows. "Looks like you found something delicious."

I hold up the box in response. "Yes, the candy store I wandered off into when Mom and I were here."

Chester pulls his leash, and my father drops it as my dog trots over to me. Bending down, I wrap my arms around Chester, taking comfort in hugging his soft fur. "Ready to go?"

Chapter 29 – Things to avoid

I woke to the smell of bacon and sprung from the bed. Belinda had two days off work, which meant goodbye Powdered Sugar Squares, hello homemade breakfast.

"Good morning, sweetheart," Belinda said. "I meant to wait for you to wake so you could be chef, but I was hungrier than a bear coming out of hibernation."

I know it's not something girls my age did. Most of us were probably too old for it, but I gave Belinda a long hug anyway. Since she started working at the bakery, she smelled of cinnamon bread. If a mom had to smell, I'm sure cinnamon bread is one of the best smells to have.

"Bacon," I said.

"And ..." Belinda said, opening the oven door. "French toast. I'm just keeping it warm until the bacon is done."

I set the table without being asked. Nana would bug me to do it when I was in the middle of something important, like reading the next book in R. L. Stine's *Fear Street* series.

I placed the maple syrup in the middle of the table next to the stack of napkins. Belinda brought over the French toast and bacon. I poured us both a tiny glass of orange juice.

"Did you find Sharon and Theresa?" she asked, pulling out a chair.

I wanted to tell Belinda all of this the previous night when she got home from work, but she crashed on the couch from exhaustion. We ate fast food while watching *Home Improve-*

ment on TV. She was so tired she nearly fell asleep with a fry in her mouth.

I nodded as I poured syrup over my French toast. "She's at a cancer hospital in Florida."

"Is that what you were trying to tell me about last night before I fell asleep?"

"Yes, Jessica and I made a list of pies," I said. "But I don't know if we will make enough money to get us to Florida and back."

"We'll work it out. Besides, I'm going with you, so I need to pitch in."

"But, the ingredients will cost money."

"We already have most of what you need to get started, and we can afford to buy fruit."

I smiled, a concerned half-smile. The thoughts of Tallahassee went racing through my mind. They swallowed up the joy of getting the album back to Sharon and Theresa.

"Thinking about your dad?" Belinda asked.

I nodded but remained focused on my plate of bacon and French toast. Then Belinda threw more thoughts my way. One I'd tried to avoid but had failed.

"I'm guessing Jessica doesn't know the truth?"

The truth, I thought, was that my father doesn't live in a house. That my name is not Felicia, and my Belinda wasn't really Mom. My once delicious bacon and scrumptious French toast now tasted like salty tires and syrupy sponges.

"I don't think I can tell Jessica now," I said. "I thought at first I might have to worry about her finding out if she saw the news, but I'm not on the news. Nana and Gramps don't care that I am gone."

"Why do you say that?"

"I haven't seen anything about me missing."

Belinda's fork was midway to her mouth when she paused and returned it to her plate. "Just because you don't see yourself on the news doesn't mean they don't miss you. Plus it's only been a few days, those things probably take time." She winked.

I pushed my toast around the puddles of syrup with my fork. "You think so?"

Belinda reached her hand out and placed it over mine. "Of course, sweetheart. I know they miss you."

"What am I going to do?" I dropped my fork on my plate. The noise echoed off the walls.

"What do you want to do?" Belinda asked like all moms probably do.

"Will I have to tell the truth to Jessica? What about all my clothes and books back home, will I get those? And what about my father, should I see him?"

"Do you want to see your dad?"

I'd tried hard not to think about it at all.

"I don't know. I'm scared to see him, but something inside is nagging me constantly that I need to, that I should see him. It's confusing me and all my thoughts. They're all jumbled around."

I pushed my French toast around in the syrup. The pain in my stomach felt like I stuffed a whole Thanksgiving turkey in there.

Belinda took a sip of her juice. Her silence made me worried. I thought of Gramps and Nana, and I wondered if Molly missed me. I don't have a phone number, so she couldn't have called. I had her number memorized, so I guess I could've called her from Jessica's phone. But, I didn't know what I would say to her.

"Do you think I should see my father?" I asked.

"Why don't we focus on your pie bake sale first, okay? Then we'll focus on all those really hard questions." Belinda's words warmed my heart. She knew just what to say to send my worries away.

"Thank you, Belinda. There's something else, though."

"What would that be?" she asked and picked her fork back up.

"Jessica's dad, Paul, invited us over for supper tomorrow."

She choked a bit on her food and took a sip of juice to settle it. I think she liked Paul. The day she went over to yell at him, she came home all flustered, but she had a slight smile.

"Why did he invite us over?" Belinda's cheeks were rosy.

"He said that you two needed to start off on a better foot than when you first met."

I'm not sure what moms did when they liked someone, but I was pretty sure it was what Belinda was doing.

Chapter 30 – Present Day – 2009

Tony's trailer sits about sixty feet from the main gravel road. The yard around the yellow-painted vinyl siding showcases more Worley-gigs than ten garden stores combined. A tan SUV is parked under a carport surrounded by oak trees brimming with shamrock-green leaves.

Robert and I didn't speak a word the entire hour drive to Briscoe, but we both devoured the chocolates from the candy shop. Patricia had matched our tastes perfectly because I've never tasted candies that feel more personal than those. Not to mention much better tasting than anything from the grocery stores.

I leave my truck running, needing the air conditioning on for all four of us. "I'll wait here with Chester and Dixie Lynn." The truth is, I want nothing more than to jump from the truck, bang on the trailer door, and demand the photo album. Then, I'd sit on the weather-damaged wood steps and look through the album.

Robert pops open the passenger door. "Alright."

The trailer's door swings open, and a man wearing overalls and a cowboy hat fills the doorway with his massive stature.

With the truck's windows rolled up, I can't hear anything other than mumbling voices.

Robert waves at the man I assume is Tony as he staggers off the steps, his stance wide.

My father weaves his way around the massive Worley-gig collection, and Tony pulls him in for a hug. They continue to pat each other's backs for such an extended amount of time that I lean forward in awe. Finally free, my father follows Tony up the steps and into the trailer.

Fiddling with the radio, I find the local country station, close my eyes, and rest my head back on the seat. I need time to hurry up so I can see this album myself.

A knock at the driver's side window causes my eyes to pop open as I let out a squeal of surprise.

Outside the truck's window stands a woman in her sixties with wavy fire engine red hair. She waves and smiles at me.

I roll down the window. "Hi."

"What are ya doing sittin' here? Come on inside." She motions for me to get out of my Toyota.

"Thanks, but I've got my dog and a baby in the back." My fingers rest on the window controller of the door's armrest.

"Nonsense, bring them inside. We don't bite. Where are my manners?" She shoves her hand inside the window. "I'm Jewel. It's nice to meet you, Sandy."

I press myself back into the seat.

"How do you know my name?" I pivot and face her.

Jewel withdraws her hand. "How do I not? Your Daddy and us were old friends, we knew you when you were born." Jewel's eyes pinch at the sides as she smiles. "Come in, bring everyone, please." She steps back from the truck and waves at me to come on.

I glance at Jewel, the trailer, and the open farmland full of sprouting cotton through the windshield.

"I made a pineapple upside-down cake, fresh from the oven," Jewel mentions as though she knows I have a sweet tooth.

"Alright, sure." I open the driver's side door with my knee.

"We can't believe we finally get to meet the grown-up Sandy."

I lift Dixie Lynn from her car seat, wanting and needing to be able to hold her against my chest for comfort, even in the muggy July air. Chester springs from the truck and proceeds to mark his territory at the base of each and every Worley-gig.

Jewel holds the front door open, and I enter with Chester now at my heels. The single-wide makes for a narrow living room. My father and Tony are directly in front of me, seated on a brown and orange couch that I'm pretty sure is from the '70s, along with the shag olive green carpet. Oddly enough, it smells delightful inside, like warm pineapple and sugar.

Tony stands up from the couch. "Sandy. You look just like Patricia." His voice crackles like a teenage boy as though I caused some type of emotional reaction.

I wrap my arms tighter around Dixie Lynn, preventing any idea of Tony shaking my hand or hugging me. Chester locates Robert and sits at his feet. Jewel slices up pieces of cake at the kitchen counter.

"Well, Sandy, hon, sit, sit." Jewel motions with the knife toward the kitchen table wedged between the end of the couch and the hall.

I follow instructions and sink into a brown chair with wheels.

"Your Daddy here was tellin' me y'all are heading to Memphis to find the baby's mama." Tony walks up to Jewel and places his hand on her back.

"Yes, Molly." I don't like the term "baby mama." It makes Molly sound like someone not worthy of having a child or being a parent. "Once she and I talk, I know she'll see she needs to come back home and raise Dixie Lynn." I kiss the baby on the forehead.

Jewel places a plate of upside-down pineapple cake in front of me, and everyone pulls out chairs, joining Dixie Lynn and me at the table. I spot what appears to be a photo album. It's hunter green, maybe vinyl or leather, on the coffee table within my view—the only thing between it and me are my manners.

I move the baby to my left shoulder and proceed to devour the dessert. It's easy, as Jewel's baking is sheer perfection. The cake is light and airy on my tongue, followed by the tang and stickiness of the pineapple and caramelized sugar.

"Tell us, Sandy, what've you been up to all these years?" Tony inquires. The fork in his hand seems toddler-sized as his gigantic fingers wrap around it.

"College, work, keeping the house somewhat maintained." I don't know Tony and Jewel from any other stranger and don't feel like I need to extend my conversation beyond being polite.

"Well, we sure know your mama would be proud of you. Especially caring for someone else's baby." Jewel sips her tea.

A piece of cake wedges on the side of my throat as I try to speak too soon. I swallow a couple of times. "You were close with my mama?"

"Yes, all four of us used to go paint the town together." Tony holds up his fork. "Rob here would pick the worst movies."

My father chuckles. "Not all of them were bad. Patricia enjoyed them."

"They were pretty bad." Jewel winks at me.

"We loved to go off on adventures," Robert continues. "Horseback riding, rafting, hiking, storm chasing, and sometimes just resting in the bed of the truck, watching the sky fade into nighttime."

The notion that this couple, Jewel and Tony, have pieces of Mama that I never knew about causes the cake to flop around in my stomach.

Jewel's hand reaches for my arm, but since I'm holding Dixie Lynn, I can't move it away. Her fingers graze the outside of my thin, short-sleeved blue and white striped shirt.

"Tony and I desperately wanted to visit and reach out to you." Jewel glances at Tony and my father. "But your grandparents ... they refused our calls and visits."

Chester senses my anguish as he stands from his prized food-catching spot and rests his chin on my knee. The bottom of my chin starts to quiver, and I bite my lip in an attempt to stop it.

"Sandy, your daddy isn't the man you think he was." Tony scoots his chair out and picks up the photo album from the coffee table.

Jewel stretches both arms out and wiggles her fingers toward Dixie Lynn. I hand the baby over, and Tony places the album in my hands.

As I open the cover, I can feel everyone's eyes on me, even Chester's. It's my first time seeing any of these photos. Tears fill my eyes, and I take the back of my hand to wipe them away.

Photos of Mama and my father fill the pages. Mama's smile is like looking into a mirror. As they cuddle, I can feel the love seeping right through the photograph like tie-dye ink soaking a shirt. I flip through the pages and glance at each photo before moving onto the next.

Mama goes from winter jackets to shorts and blouses to dresses, and then the picture that takes my breath right from my lungs is a photo of Mama pregnant. My father has his arm wrapped around her shoulder and a hand on her enlarged belly. Mama's vision is glued to Robert. Knowing I'm in that photo, inside of her hits my heart so hard I think it just broke.

I take a deep breath and continue flipping. Then I notice it. The emotion of Mama conveyed in the photos changes. Her spirit weakens, her smile is gone. It's like the photos on the mantel back home. I'm sitting in Mama's lap, and Mama appears distant.

When I look up from the album, Robert has turned away, his eyes no longer on me. "Something happened," I whisper as though she might hear me.

Jewel touches my arm again, and I catch her wiping a tear from her cheek.

"What happened? How did she go from this vibrant, happy soul to ..." The depression seeps from the remaining photos.

"I tried, Sandy." My father's voice weakens with the words. "God, Sandy, I tried to get her help."

"Help? You said she was depressed."

"We didn't know what it was at the time, but she suffered from severe postpartum depression." My father places his fork down on his empty plate and closes his eyes. "She tried to take her life and yours several times."

As I launch myself out of the chair, the album crashes to the floor. All I see are spots as I grasp for my breath that I can't find. Staying here, next to my father, who is causing my memories to spin out of control, is too much to handle. Running away is my only answer, as it was when I was a kid.

I stumble to the trailer door and nearly trip going down the steps onto the grass. I run past the truck, out onto the gravel road, and keep on going.

Chapter 31 –
Fancy old house
& supper

"It'll be fun. We'll take pictures for our scrapbook," Belinda said.

I slipped on my new flip-flops and grabbed our disposable camera. Belinda tried to convince me that visiting some fancy old home would be fun. It wasn't working.

We were able to walk to the old fancy house, or its official name, the Oakleigh Complex. Unfortunately, the tree roots had pushed up the sidewalk, making the pavement uneven down the street. I tried not to step on a single crack but found it impossible.

"Arlene, from work, told me the mansion is haunted." Belinda pretended the sidewalk had a hopscotch pattern on it.

"You're trying to trick me into thinking this isn't going to be borrrring," I said, kicking a pebble along the way.

"No, it's true," Belinda reiterated, still playing imaginary hopscotch. "Arlene said people have seen shadows. Moving figures to be exact."

I loved it when she said "exact." Maybe it's a sign this mansion won't be boring after all. Maybe Mama had even seen it when she was my age.

As we came around Selma Street to the Oakleigh Complex, all I could see were the tips of two chimneys. The trees made it hard to see the entire house until you were directly in front of it.

The white two-story mansion had pitch-black shutters. Belinda stopped, and we read the historical plaque outside. The mansion was built in 1833. Surprisingly, the house hadn't burned or fallen down. Gramps couldn't even keep up with the house repairs back home, and their house had been built long after 1833.

Belinda made me stand next to the sign and take a picture with it. I hoped she captured my eyes rolling in the photo.

As we strolled up to the mansion's front, I noticed a spiral staircase on the outside. It seemed like an odd place to put something that belonged inside. The house formed a T-shape, as a fountain trickled to the right of the house. Mobile sure loved their fountains.

Belinda opened a side door on the first floor, and we joined a group of older adults with silver hair. I wanted to point out to her that I was the only kid in the group, but she grabbed my sleeve-covered hand and smiled.

We followed the twelve sets of gray Velcro sneakers shuffling up a set of worn stairs. At the landing, a chill shimmied up my spine. Something made me feel uneasy, as though I was being watched. The tour guide gave a history of each room as we walked the hallways.

The rooms had either floral wallpaper with dainty flowers or landscape murals covering the walls. Canopy beds filled the center of the rooms with plush quilts folded at the ends. Wooden dressers rested against strips of railings, which sat midway up the walls. Thick curtains hung long and low, piling up on the floor around the windows.

I held Belinda's hand tight through my sleeve as we made our way down the narrow hall. Out of nowhere, Belinda started to clear her throat. When I turned to check on her, she had the camera out and snuck a photo of me. She was trying to cover up the sound of the camera click.

"Ah-hum." Click. "Ah-hum." Click.

"For the scrapbook," she mouthed.

I smiled, Belinda, a rebel, because the tour guide and the signs plastered all over the house read: NO PHOTOS.

We turned down another hall, and the uneasy feeling hit me again. I had it almost every time I went to the cemetery to visit Mama. Nana and Gramps didn't know I went at least once a week after school instead of going to Molly's house. I would pick wildflowers along the way and place them between Mama's name and the dates of her birth and death. Then I would lay down with my head resting just under her name. Sometimes I cried, but sometimes I didn't. I would look up at the clouds and wonder if she could see me from heaven.

Nana had said heaven is real and that all good people go there. Gramps had said heaven is a bunch of hogwash and that heaven was right here, right now. Of course, I'm not sure what a hogwash had to do with any of it. It could be a sheepwash or a duckwash, for all I knew.

"Any questions?" I heard the tour guide's voice breaking through my thoughts.

"Did anyone die here?" I blurted.

"Why yes," the tour guide stated. "Corinne Irwin died of typhoid fever just two weeks before she was to wed."

Maybe that explained why I felt uneasy. Maybe Arlene from the cupcake shop was right. The spirit of Corinne Irwin might haunt this place.

Belinda thanked the tour guide, and we made our way out of the mansion. The uneasy feeling disappeared as we headed towards the street. We were going a different way home, but I didn't care. My thoughts were busy thinking about Mama. For as long as I could remember, this had been the most time between visiting Mama's grave.

As we headed down Common Street, every step was hotter and stickier than the last. Belinda stopped dead in her tracks, and it took me a minute to realize I'd been walking alone. When I turned around, Belinda was ogling a different white mansion. While I found this one more beautiful than the Oakleigh Complex, it appeared more dilapidated.

Before us was a two-story rectangle house with forest green shutters. The columns were similar to the pictures of The Parthenon in Greece that I'd seen in my social studies book.

"Oh, I wish we could go inside!" Belinda exclaimed.

I was glad we couldn't. I didn't want to risk feeling uneasy again. Belinda stood like a mannequin, staring at the white Parthenon house as though it was the world's largest ice cream sundae.

"Look at this one too," I said, pointing at the two-story brick home across the street.

Belinda grabbed my hand, hidden under my sleeve, and squeezed hard. "You can't find this in Oklahoma."

I'll give her that. We didn't have houses with towering pillars and lanterns strung from the porch roofs. We had a lot of wheat. Field after field of golden wheat, pumpjacks, beige houses, and falling down porches. Belinda sighed at the beauty of the old homes as we dragged our feet in the heat.

It started to drizzle when Belinda turned to me. "Why is having a mom important to you? I know you mentioned early that your dream was to have a mom, but you never went into why."

I dropped my hand from her grasp and swallowed hard.

"I don't want to sound harsh, but I'd like to know. I think it's important for you to understand why we are here together," Belinda said.

"We're here together because I ran away from home," I said, crossing my arms. "And I wanted to know what a Mom felt like, because ... I miss what I've never had before. I wanted to know what normal felt like. And don't tell me I can't miss something I never had. I can because I know what missing feels like. Only with missing a mama, it's a trillion times harder than missing anything else, ever."

The rain came down faster as the sky turned a darker gray. Thunder clapped in the distance. All the rain hid my tears.

"What's so great about being normal?" Belinda asked.

"Normal feels like home. Having a mom is like having a home in your pocket wherever you go."

"But your Mama is always with you." Belinda spun in a circle, her hands raised and out. "And here, not in your pocket, but here." She tapped her finger on my heart.

"What's wrong with wanting to feel home in person, in real life?" I pushed my wet tumbleweed of curls off my forehead. "Even just for a short time."

Belinda wrapped her wet arm around my sopping wet shirt as we made our way home.

Belinda smelled of magnolia flowers when she came out of the bedroom. She curled her hair and wore a peach-colored sundress.

"You look beautiful."

"Thank you," she said and took a deep breath. "I'm ready."

We carefully made our way across the damp grass. I knocked on Jessica's door, watching the doorknob turn a few times before it swung open.

"Hi, Miles," I greeted.

"Felicia!" he screamed, wrapping his arms around me. "Daddy and Jessica won't play trains with me. Please play trains with me, Felicia. Please!"

Before I could say anything, Jessica came up behind him.

"Miles, let them come in," she said, opening the door all the way. "Felicia doesn't want to play trains with you."

"Daddy!" Miles screamed, running off towards Paul.

Paul smiled at Belinda. "Hi."

"Hi." I saw Belinda's cheeks turn a rosy pink color, and I could tell they liked each other.

Jessica could tell, too, because she rolled her eyes at me, and we tried not to giggle aloud. If Belinda wanted Paul to be her boyfriend, then I guess it was okay, as long as they didn't get all kissy face.

Chapter 32 –
Present Day –
2009

My legs burn as I seek shelter under an oak tree somewhere in Briscoe.

I weave my hands through the grass blades around me. Every thought of Mama, or who I believed Mama to be, has been stripped from me, and I can't stop crying.

Betrayal courses through my veins, and as though a sign from Mama, the sky shifts from pale blue to gray angry clouds.

I ponder being upset with myself, which feels like a great place to start. I've always held Mama on such a high pedestal, but everything that happened in the last thirty-some minutes makes me wonder if I'm a good judge of anything or if everything is a cotton-picking lie. This entire time I've been a fool or fooled.

I reach into my back pocket and realize I've left my cell phone in my truck. How desperately I need to speak with Mom, Jessica, or Justin. They have to tell me this is all a dream, that nothing since my father knocked on my front door, is real. That Mama didn't try to end our lives. This horrible knowledge is something my feet can't outrun. And I realize I can't keep running from things, but I don't know how to face them either.

The sound of a vehicle comes down the gravel road and mixes with the developing thunder overhead. I wipe my tears as a tan SUV creeps along. Its brakes squeal when it stops in front of me.

The driver's side window eases down, and Jewel leans her head out. "Sandy, hon, come on back. Let's talk."

"I don't want to," I whine like a kindergartner.

"It's gonna start dumpin' buckets of rain any minute." Jewel glances at the clouds.

"Then I guess I'll just sit here and get wet." I yank a blade of grass free.

"Sandy, you're acting like a child," Jewel snaps. "Now get in here right this instant."

With a blade of grass wrapped around my pointer finger, I push myself off the ground. The sound of hail smacks the SUV. A quarter-size ball of hail slaps my right shoulder, and I dash to the SUV and throw open the door.

My shirt and hair are wet but not soaked through. And I make a note to myself I need to wash my hands of the SUV door handle germs, plus the trailer door.

Jewel's hands rest in her lap and not on the steering wheel as she places her head back against her seat. The hail lessens and soon turns to rain. The wipers throw water like paint across the front windshield.

I focus on my hands, wrapping them together in my lap.

"You're exactly like your mama. Stubborn, beautiful, and emotional."

My head cranes toward Jewel. "It's rude to call someone emotional."

Jewel throws up her hands. "Only if you perceive it as such. There's nothing wrong with being emotional. It means you feel more than others. I wish I could be a little more emotional. Then maybe I wouldn't feel like an outcast during book club when all the women talk about is how much a book made them cry."

She turns to me. "I know you grew up with this perfect vision of your mama based on your grandparents. And it's okay to keep such a vision, but you need to understand the truth. Your daddy deserves that much."

"Are you trying to excuse what my father did?" My mouth gapes open in disgust.

"Have you bothered hearing his side of the story?" Jewel looks straight ahead.

I shut my mouth and swallow. The sound of rain hitting the SUV intensifies, and the sky grows darker. The thought of Mama causing this storm seems like the right fit for the moment.

"I've heard the story from my Gramps and Nana." The sky thunders so loud I think it might shatter the SUV's windows.

"No," Jewel declares. "You heard their version of it." She shuts off the windshield wipers, blurring the rain-soaked world in front of us. "Your mama will always be your mama. Hearing your daddy's side of the story won't change that. But it will, I hope, change the relationship with you and him."

She grips the steering wheel and uses it to pull herself more upright in the driver's seat. "Your mama loved your daddy, and they were such an amazing couple. His love for her never once wavered. Everything that happened ..." Jewel rings her hands back and forth over the steering wheel. "It was an accident, a horrible accident."

Chapter 33 –
Baking & pie sale

Felicia,
> *Have a wonderful day! I can't wait to see all the pies you and Jessica make.*
> *Mom*

I read those three letters on the note again. M-O-M. She didn't sign it Belinda, but Mom.

Last night, right before my eyes closed, I'd let the word "mom" come sliding out. I hadn't meant to say it aloud, especially after our talk in the rain.

Seeing this note meant she'd accepted being my new mom. Even though I'd adopted her at the bus station, it was real now.

I took the note to my clothes drawer and slid it under my shirt before heading over to Jessica's for the day.

Jessica, my sous chef, assisted with rolling out the dough for the pie crust. She'd even been kind enough to wash her hands without me asking.

Miles ran back and forth between *Tom & Jerry* on TV, and the kitchen, while Jessica and I worked on the pies. Mom said it would be best to bake the pies over at Jessica's since Paul could supervise.

"Miles, go away!" Jessica yelled for the fifth time. "We're baking, and people don't want your dirty boy hands in their pies."

Miles stomped out of the kitchen and went to tattle on us for the millionth time.

"I think my dad likes your mom," Jessica whispered as I stirred the sugar into the bowl of cut strawberries and rhubarb.

"I think my mom likes your dad," I whispered back.

Paul didn't know the truth about Mom and me, or at least I don't think he did.

"If they get married, then we would be stepsisters," Jessica said, smiling. "We could be step-sister best friends."

How could I tell Jessica the truth now, I thought. If Mom signed papers to be my mom legally, then it wouldn't be a lie after all. The word "if" floated over my head in rotating stars like when Tom bopped Jerry on the noggin. A warm feeling filled my chest; it felt comfortable, like a blanket on a cold night.

We moved on to the next pie. Peach pie worked best with ripe and juicy peaches. But, this meant they were really hard to grip without them slipping from your hands. Once the peaches were peeled, they needed to be cut.

I cradled the peach and cut it like an apple, but it was just too slippery. I squeezed it to prevent it from slipping, and I ended up with a pile of mush in my hands. I wiped the mush into the bowl and started on another peach. Maybe this pie will be for those without teeth. Come get your no-need-to-chew pie!

"We make a great team," I said.

"Best friends should make a great team," Jessica stated.

Every time Jessica mentioned something about best friends, my heart had a sharp pain. Best friends always tell the truth.

I returned my focus to the bowl of peaches and mixed in a few spoonfuls of flour like Mom taught me to soak up the extra juice when it baked.

We had four pies cooling on the top of the counter next to the refrigerator, two blueberries, and two strawberries. We were finishing up with two strawberry rhubarb and two peaches. Jessica and I decided to make a total of eight pies for our first sale. It would be enough, but not too many, if they didn't sell.

"Wow, your lattice is pretty," I said.

"I learn quick. Say, we need a name for our pie business."

"Like?"

"Best Friend Pies."

"I like it," I said, trying to ignore the sharp pain.

Miles galloped behind the cherry red wagon containing our pies as we headed towards Bienville Square. He had the job of a supervisor. This meant he had to make sure the pies were safe in the wagon. It also kept him in the back and away from Jessica and me so we could talk about who's better, Aerosmith or Led Zeppelin.

We parked the wagon at the gazebo steps and handed the homemade sign we made to Miles. Paul said we had to take Miles with us so he could go grocery shopping without having to buy the whole store.

"Hold it up high, Miles," Jessica instructed. "We want people to be able to see it over by the fountain."

"I am!" Miles whined.

Jessica and I stood on opposite sides of the wagon. There weren't any musicians playing in the gazebo to draw people in today.

"Pies!" Miles hollered. "Pies!"

Miles reminded me of a movie I watched where a peddler stood next to his stagecoach selling bottles of elixirs to the community. He yelled out the miracles of what would happen if someone drank a sip of the concoction.

"Come get your pie!" Miles hollered.

The hollering seemed to work. People were looking our way.

"Great job, Miles," I said.

Strawberry and peach were the first four pies to go, followed by two strawberry rhubarbs. We had two blueberry pies left to sell.

Jessica handled the exchange of money. Every time a buyer tried to hand me the money, I shoved my hands into my pockets.

We had guzzled over half of our water supply during the hot and sticky afternoon. Every minute that passed, the sign Miles held drooped closer and closer to the ground.

"Smile, girls."

I looked up and saw Mom with a disposable camera.

Jessica and I smiled at the camera and hugged, our faces almost touched. Click.

"Mom, what are you doing here?" I asked.

"I took a late lunch. I wanted to see how it was going. Of course, I needed to get a picture of you two on your first business adventure."

"Do you like our business name?" Jessica asked, pointing at our sign.

"Oh, I love it," Mom said.

"Thanks, Belinda," Jessica said. "We sold six of the pies in about an hour."

"That's great, keep at it. I'm sure the blueberry ones will go soon."

"Pies," Miles yawned.

He plopped onto the grass, picking dandelions and blowing the white fuzz everywhere.

"Looks like more shoppers," Mom said, stepping back as the couple came in our direction. "I'll see you at home later."

"Bye, Mom." I waved.

We sold the last two blueberry pies, and Miles climbed into the wagon.

"Let's go, girrrrrrls," Miles nagged, with a smirk on his face.

Jessica and I rolled our eyes in unison but were too tired to argue with him.

She pulled the Wagon-o-Miles for the first three blocks. I pulled the last three blocks. He weighed more than eight pies. Yet, with Miles, we didn't have to slow down over the sharp bumps on the sidewalk. Every time the wagon hit a bump, his body levitated in the wagon.

"Woohooo!" Miles screamed.

Having a little brother didn't seem as bad as one might think, but I'm glad he wasn't mine.

Chapter 34 - Present Day - 2009

I need a few minutes to myself.

Jewel runs inside, trying to keep as dry as possible. On the other hand, I don't care as I meander to my truck. The sky continues to dump, and by the time I've climbed into the truck, my clothing is soaked, and I've caught a chill.

I can't get over the audacity Jewel and Tony have making it sound like Mama was anything but amazing. However, the mention of Mama wanting to take our lives is beyond comprehension. I don't want to believe it's true.

"Mama, if you were here, you could straighten this all out."

The rain pounds on the truck as I slather on hand sanitizer and then pick up my cell phone. Three missed calls, three voicemails, and two text messages. Both texts are from Justin, wondering why I haven't answered the phone. I go to the voicemails. The first is from Justin.

"Hey, Sandy, call me. I'm getting worried."

The second voicemail. "Sandy, hello, please call me back. I need to know you're okay."

While I appreciate Justin's concern, I'm not in the mood for it at the moment. I listen to the third voicemail.

"Sandy! It's Miles. I'm going to be in Diamond City in probably two hours. Let's do lunch, or supper, or both! Call me. We need to catch up."

A smile, although weak, grows on my lips. I miss Miles so very much. He outgrew his annoying little brother vibe mid-way through his teenage years, and his energy is contagious. And I need it. I need to soak it up from him.

I pull up Miles's number and punch send.

"Hey!" Miles answers. "I'm an hour from you now."

"I'm not in town." I sink further into the driver's seat as though I need it to hold me.

"What? No, you have to be. I miss you."

I blush. Miles always makes me smile. "I miss you too, but I'm in Briscoe right now and heading to Memphis."

"Is Justin with you?"

"No, why would ... never mind. No, my father is with me, Chester, and Dixie Lynn."

"I heard about Robert and the baby from Mom. Justin should be with you."

I tuck my wet hair behind my left ear and yank down on my lobe.

Miles has been a member of the Justin and Sandy relationship club for some time. The level of forgiveness Miles showcases always astounds me. Not that I need to forgive Justin for anything; he's been an amazing friend. The fault only lies within his father—guilt by association.

"Did I lose you, Sandy?" Miles's voice breaks through my thoughts.

"No, I was thinking."

"What's going on? I pulled off the road. You have my undivided attention."

I glance at the trailer through the rain-soaked driver's side window. "These long-time friends of Mama and my father have a photo album. Pictures I'd never seen."

"Sandy! That's amazing. But wait, then why do you sound down?"

"The photos ... the photos capture Mama's postpartum depression. It's so bad, photo after photo of a woman who doesn't look like the memories I've collected all these years. And seeing them all makes me realize the photos at home are the same, yet somehow I've overlooked this."

The line is silent as I wrap my hand around my stomach and rest my forehead on the steering wheel.

"Miles, she wasn't well. They said she wanted to ... kill us." Tears welled up on my lids. "She wanted to commit suicide and take me with her. They're saying my father isn't this bad man I made him out to be—who Gramps and Nana made him out to be." I press my eyes closed and listen to Miles's breathing, calm and soft.

"My father still did what he did, but maybe this whole time, I've pushed him away for the wrong reason."

"Sounds like you need to have a long talk with your father."

"I don't want to," I whine.

"Well, I don't want to spend time in Diamond City without you in it, so we're even."

I roll my eyes. "That's far from even. Diamond City is a great place. You should feel lucky to be there." Sitting back in my seat, I wipe my eyes. "Where are you headed too?"

"Colorado. Figured I'd swing by and see you, then take the I-40 west and make it a straight shot up to Boulder on the I-25."

"How was Corpus Christi?" A bolt of lightning strikes in the distance, and thunder claps.

"Same as always, lots of surfing, too many tacos, and probably too many drinks." Miles chuckles.

"So what's in Boulder? It's not ski season."

Usually, Miles travels to places he can surf and see women in bathing suits.

"Hiking. My buddy, Nick, Air B&B'd a cabin for a week."

Miles somehow manages to make enough money by working weekly jobs in every city he is in. In Corpus Christi, he waited tables at a restaurant in the evenings. In California, he teamed up with a landscape company. In Washington, he taught ski lessons at Mt. Baker. His home base is his van.

"Sounds fun, but everything in your life is, isn't it?"

"It's the only way to live, Sandy. Hey, you're off work for the summer, come up and join me."

"While it sounds awesome, I have a baby and a father to figure out. Plus, I'm old. You and your friends would drive me nuts partying at all hours of the night."

"You're not old, just not any fun."

I laugh. "Chester thinks I'm a blast."

"Chester thinks lying on the patio is a blast."

"I'm scared, Miles."

"I know." He pauses, and I wish I could see his face right now, his comforting eyes. "You owe it to yourself, if not your father and your mama, to hear him out. You'll regret it if you don't. Heck, you welcomed Robert into your home when he was released, and now you're traveling with him to find Molly. It can't be all bad."

I rub my hand over my face and lean my head on the side of the window—the sound of rain taps against my ear.

"Have you spoken to Jessica lately?" My eyes lock on the cotton field in front of me.

"No, I tried to reach her a few times, but I don't think she has cell service."

When I glance over at the trailer, someone peeks through the blinds. With the rain, I can't see who, but I know one of them is keeping an eye on me.

"I better let you go. I can't sit in this truck forever. Drive safe, Miles."

"Thanks, you too. And good luck with Molly and your father."

After ending the call, I locate Justin's number to send him a text.

I'm okay. Made an unplanned stop. I will explain later.

Before I can set my cell phone back into the cup holder, it alerts me of a text.

Justin: Criminy! There you are! I was about to put out an APB!

I reply: I haven't been gone that long!

Justin: It feels like a lifetime.

I can't deny my heartbeat fluttering at his concern: **I miss you too, Justin.**

My cheeks flush as I re-read what I typed. But it's not a lie. I miss him.

Justin: Be safe. Call me when you make it to Memphis.

The rain continues to beat down on the earth as I make my way up the two steps to the trailer door. It swings open before I can knock. Once inside, I don't move from the tiny spot of linoleum square at the door. Water drips from my clothes and hair.

My father holds Dixie Lynn, and Chester sits at his feet. Tony's in a recliner, and Jewel observes us all as she holds a mug in her hand.

"We should probably get going," I suggest.

"You can't be driving around in this weather," Tony states. "Wait until the storm passes."

Chapter 35 –
The truth in
Tallahassee

Over the next two days, Jessica and I baked sixteen pies. We decided the blueberry pies weren't popular and switched them out for apple pie. While the pies baked, we watched MTV, trying to guess which music video they would play next. Paul didn't know this since he took Miles out to shoot some baskets, giving us a well-deserved little brother break.

Paul didn't allow Jessica to watch MTV. He said the videos were too mature, so we had to listen for noises outside the apartment door. There were many false alarms when the neighbors came home, and we clicked the channel over to cartoons like *TaleSpin* or *Chip 'n Dale Rescue Rangers*.

"We have eighty-nine dollars," Jessica said, counting our pie sale money one more time. "That should be enough money to get us to Tallahassee and back. How long is the bus trip?"

"I think my mom said about three hours."

"We'll go there, drop off the photo album, and stop by to see your dad." Jessica waved her hand in front of my face. "Felicia?"

"My father is in prison," I blurted.

Jessica's face had frozen, scared, and worried, like when you notice lima beans on your supper plate.

"Your ... dad is ... in ... prison?" Jessica finally asked. "Why?"

Tears formed in my eyes, and a lump the size of a ping-pong ball formed in my throat. There was no way out of this now. I should tell her all my truths, but judging by her face, one truth at a time might be best.

"He killed ... someone in the family," I said.

My mama, he killed Mama, I finished saying in my mind. My father killed Mama, that's why she's in the ground, and he's in a Tallahassee prison.

"Your dad ... is a ... murderer?" Jessica asked.

Jessica hugged me so hard I thought she might break a bone, but I didn't care. I didn't care about anything, not even germs. All I wanted to do was cry. Maybe I wasn't ready for Tallahassee.

Chapter 36 –
Present Day –
2009

Jewel and Tony take Dixie Lynn into the back bedroom of the trailer after I change into dry clothes from my backpack and wash my hands. Sitting next to my father on the couch, we both face the front door, the photo album between us like an elephant in the room.

I clear my throat. "I'm not sure how to approach this discussion."

My father turns to me, and I copy. His eyes move around the room before focusing on me. "The postpartum grew worse every week. Your mama refused to get out of bed other than to use the restroom. Even getting her to take a shower was a fight. She wasn't eating much and started to lose weight. Diamond City wasn't and probably still isn't full of the latest medical expertise. And my focus was on keeping you safe, healthy, happy."

Robert ran his hands back and forth over his jeans. "She'd be up all night watching television and sleep off and on during the day. I was working two jobs to pay the bills, and that meant most of the time, you were lying on a blanket on the floor or in your crib. She stopped wanting to hold you. I'd get home from work, and your face would be red from crying for who knows how long. Your mama would be in another part of the house with the television turned up, trying to avoid it all."

Tears fall from my eyes, streaming down my cheeks, and Chester presses his body against my leg. "Why didn't you get help for her? She wasn't well."

"Sandy, I ask myself that question all the time, but I was alone. I had no family around me. And I naively had no idea what was really going on with her. Your grandparents didn't want to open their eyes to the problem, and none of my friends knew what to do to help."

Robert ran his hand through his hair, pausing on the back of his shoulder. "I needed to find a way to cope. Drinking became my best friend."

He glances down the hall of the trailer. "I pushed my friends away, including Tony and Jewel. I thought your mama would get over her depression once you started walking and talking. I figured an infant who was dependent on her was too much, but once you were a toddler, it would be better."

"But it didn't change." I push myself back into the couch pillows.

Robert shakes his head no. "You started walking and talking, but Patricia stayed in bed. My drinking increased, and I lost my jobs. Your mama became irritable, and I didn't know how to cope." His watery eyes met mine. "Do you want to know?"

No, I don't want to know the details of the night my father killed Mama, but I needed to know. I press my lips together and close my eyes. Then, when I open them, I nod, yes.

The scent of pineapple upside-down cake continues to fill the room, mixing with the dampness from the rain, and I know I'll never be able to eat it again.

Rain batters the trailer's siding. I pray I can handle a future rainstorm without thinking of this moment.

"Your Mama and I'd been arguing about the money we didn't have and the things you needed. You were napping in your bedroom in a crib that you'd outgrown sometime before. She kept going on and on about how unhappy she was and how much she hated me. Every word from her cut into me. For two years, the hatred had grown, first from her, then from me. I'd turned into a monster right along with her. I was naïve to think time would make it better for her. That she would wake up one morning and be her old self again. The Patricia I loved. The Patricia who loved herself."

I reach out and run my palm over the photo album. Chester has moved over to sit next to my father.

Robert pets him and continues. "Our arguing grew loud. We screamed at each other. She put her face inches from mine and cursed me out. She said horrible things about being a mom, about you, about me."

My jaw clenches.

"God, I didn't mean for it to happen. But she pushed me with both hands, hard. Harder than I thought she had strength for. She kept shoving me. I stumbled backward over the coffee table and landed on my knee and hip wrong. The pain was excruciating. She picked up something, a glass or a picture frame. I don't remember. It flew out of her hand and sliced my cheek."

I remember his limp.

He buries his head into his hands. "I lost it. She didn't even care that I was bleeding. I only meant to get her attention. Shake some sense into her. I pulled myself up and grabbed her by the shoulders. She fought me, moving her body like I was going to harm her. Like my touch made her sick. You walked into the room, stood there, crying. Patricia lunged for me, and I fought back. She pushed, and I pushed, hard. She fell backward. Her head hit the edge of the fireplace. Then it was over. All I remember was blood. Blood on me, on her. It was an accident. When I turned around to where you stood, you were gone. I didn't have the strength to search for you."

My father rests his elbows on his knees, no longer making eye contact with anything other than the shag carpet. "The neighbors found you. I knew my fate. I knew a judge or jury wouldn't believe my story. So I left you with them. I never got to say goodbye." He uses his thumbs to wipe his tears.

Our jeans touch as I place my arm around his shoulder. I'm touching him for the first time. My fingers press into his arm, pulling him toward me as we both cry.

Chapter 37 –
The Tallahassee
Cancer Hospital

I'd cried all I possibly could when I told Jessica about my father, so later that night, I was tearless when I told Mom the whole truth about him.

In the morning, Mom placed the legal papers, allowing me to see my father, into her purse. I didn't know how she obtained them or what they said as she kept them inside a sealed envelope.

The bus left at six-thirty in the morning, which had been fine with Mom, but Jessica and I always slept until at least nine a.m.

I'd wrapped Theresa and Sharon's album in a plastic bag to keep it protected. Jessica brought a bag of snacks to keep us from getting too hungry along the way. We ended up sleeping the entire ride to Tallahassee. I figured this was a good thing in case I started to cry. I couldn't cry if I was asleep.

"Girls, wake up; we're here," Mom said.

Tallahassee didn't look much different than Mobile. Shiny buildings and the blue sky. But the knots in my stomach knew we were not in Mobile.

"I don't feel good, Mom," I whispered as we stepped off the bus.

"It is just nerves, sweetheart. Remember, if you don't want to see your dad, you don't have to."

"Which way to the Tallahassee Cancer Hospital?" Jessica asked.

"Let's see," Mom said.

She unfolded the city map and turned it a few times in a circle.

"I'm bad with directions, so I have to put myself into the map," she said.

Jessica and I giggled, throwing our heads back as though it was the funniest thing ever.

"Ha, ha, very funny, girls," Mom said. "Okay, we need to go down South Magnolia Drive to Park Avenue, and then it'll be on the corner. Can't miss a hospital building, right?"

"Can't miss a big, tall building for sure," I said, raising an eyebrow.

I clutched the album tight enough that my knuckles were white. It helped distract me from my stomach knots. As we made our way down the congested city street, sweat beaded across my forehead. Not only was my mind focused on my father, but I had no desire to enter a building of germs.

We'd finished our juice boxes by the time the towering white building appeared against the skyline on the corner. The cold air-conditioning hit our sweaty skin as we entered through the automatic sliding glass doors.

"Can we please have the room number for Sharon Collins?" Mom asked the hospital receptionist.

I shifted the photo album from one hand to the other, the plastic stuck to my sweaty arm.

"Sign in, take a visitor sticker," the receptionist instructed. "Take the elevators to your left, go to the sixth floor. Get off the elevators and go right. Then take your first left, then another left. Room 624 will be on your left side at the end of the hall."

I hoped Mom remembered all those directions because I lost her after she said to get off the elevators.

Mom signed us in and stuck the sticker on my shirt for me.

As the elevator doors shut, and I looked at Jessica. She played with her slap bracelet, pulling it off and slapping it back on, pulling it off, and slapping it back on.

"Everything alright?" I asked, placing my hand on her shoulder.

"It's weird, being here, going to see them. I'm nervous," Jessica whispered.

We exited the elevators and followed Mom through the maze of halls. Ladies in scrubs with metal-type clipboards scurried about. The thick smell of Pine-Sol plugged our noses.

"Look, girls, room 604, 605," Mom said, pointing.

In the distance, a man burst into the hallway.

"Help!" he hollered.

Two nearby nurses dashed into the room.

The numbers continued to increase as we neared the room with the hollering man. 619, 620, 621.

"Do something! Help her!" the man cried out from inside the room.

Mom held out her arm, blocking Jessica and me from stepping forward any further.

I squeezed the album. My heartbeat pounded in my chest as though it was trying to fight its way out. Out of the corner of my eye, I saw the number 624. The man cried inside the room.

Jessica's eyes filled with tears. My excitement to meet Theresa and Sharon faded like a hyper color T-shirt. Mom guided Jessica and me by the shoulder to the couch in a room made of windowed walls. But I didn't want to sit. I stood like a lone candle, clutching the album as commotion filled the halls.

Jessica stared at her shoes as she wiped tears from her eyes with her arm. We were too late. Exactly too late.

"Here, girls, drink some water," Mom said.

She handed us each a tiny blue-flowered paper cup. I sipped mine, but Jessica just held it in her hands as one would a cup of hot chocolate on a snowy day when your hands were freezing.

A girl meandered into the room. Her eyes focused on the view outside the soaring windows. Tears ran down the girl's face, and her eyes were puffy. I recognized her from the photos. I tapped Jessica's arm and pointed.

"Theresa?" Jessica asked.

Theresa turned around and faced us.

"Jess?" Theresa asked.

Jessica stood and made her way over to Theresa. They hugged like best friends do after one has been away for a long time.

"She's gone," Theresa softly cried. "She'd been breathin' and then stopped. The machines were beepin', and Daddy was yellin'. Jess, she's gone. My mama's gone."

Had I cried like Theresa when Mama died? It's hard to remember anything from when you were a toddler. I don't remember Nana and Gramps showing me my bedroom. I don't remember what happened before Nana and Gramps, or what the house I came from looked like. I remembered one thing only, black garbage bags with the red drawstring tied in bows.

"Theresa, this is Felicia."

Jessica pointed to me.

"Hi," I said.

I didn't want to say sorry about her mom. Everyone says sorry, but what will sorry do? Nothing, it won't bring her mom back. All sorry does is make the other person have to say thank you, or it's okay. And why would anyone want to hear those words when their mom dies?

"We came here to give you the photo album," Jessica said.

I held it up for Theresa. "I found it in the dresser. I knew it must be important."

Theresa took the album as though it was an egg balancing on a spoon.

"We were looking everywhere for this," Theresa said, wiping tears away.

"We sold pies to make money for the bus tickets," I said. "We came as soon as we could."

However, we didn't make it in time. We failed. If I end up with cancer, I'll remember not to come here. They didn't help cancer at all.

"Daddy, look who's here," Theresa said.

Theresa's dad shuffled into the room.

"Jess and ..." Theresa looked at me. "Sorry, I forgot."

"Felicia," I reminded her.

"They came all the way here to bring us the album we'd been missin'," Theresa said.

"Sorry for the inconvenience this must have caused you," Theresa's dad said, looking at Belinda.

"The girls wanted to hand-deliver it," Mom said.

A woman with her hair in a ponytail entered the room. Her pearl white coat read: Faith Hines, M.D. in cursive blue lettering over the pocket.

"I don't mean to interrupt Mr. Collins, but we have some," Faith Hines, M.D. said, then looked around the room, "personal matters to discuss."

"Thank you for bringing us the album," Theresa's dad said.

"Oh yes, of course," Mom said, "This is not the time for visits. We're sorry, your wife ... about your wife."

I couldn't believe Mom said "sorry." So many sorries were being used.

"Thank you," Theresa's dad said.

There you go, I thought, the mandatory thank you reply. He didn't mean, "thank you." He meant "this is a horrible, horrible day," a day where sorry didn't mean anything other than ugly, dirty charcoal letters put together.

"Theresa, why don't you give Jessica our new address so she can write to you."

Theresa wrote down her address, and we said our goodbyes before heading back out into the Tallahassee humidity.

Chapter 38 - Present Day - 2009

Gramps had always said the rain brought out the worst drivers like cockroaches after a storm, everywhere and always in the way. And as I change lanes on the highway trying to avoid an accident, I remember his words.

After about an hour of driving, classic country music fills the silence in the truck. My father and I haven't said a word to each other since we left Briscoe. There's not much to say anyway. The truth is out there, and I think it shook both of us in different ways.

As we cross over the Mississippi River, the sunset reflects off the pyramid in downtown Memphis. I flip my visor down. "Okay, Molly's boyfriend's parents live on Macon Road."

I feel my father's eyes on me. "Seems like rather specific information."

"Justin knew someone who knew someone and did a little investigating." I flip on my blinker. "It's no guarantee that Molly is there, but from what I've gathered about Mark, he seems close to his parents. A real mama's boy."

"And what'll you say to her if she's there?"

The light turns red as I glance over at my father. "Great question. I wish I knew."

I spot a bumper sticker that reads: Two Milkshakes Are Better Than One.

As I snicker, I point it out to my father. He laughs.

"I don't disagree," I say between laughter, "but I don't know why it's so funny."

My father's laughter grows, and then mine does too. As the light turns green, tears from laughing so hard blur my vision. I wipe them away, but we both continue to laugh as though we'd been saving it up for a lifetime. My stomach muscles hurt as I try to catch my breath. I can't recall the last time I'd laughed this much. However, it comes to a halt when I pull up in front of Mark's parents' house.

Three cars sit in a narrow driveway leading up to a one-car garage on the side of the brick house. A pearl-colored sedan is parked closest to the garage, directly behind it a blue hatchback, and then Mark's hunter green Jeep.

"Stay here with Dixie Lynn and Chester." I pop open the driver's door before he can say anything.

I step onto the concrete steps with an iron railing. After pushing the doorbell with my elbow, I step back. The door swings open, and behind the screen door stands Mark.

"Hi, Mark."

His mouth falls open. "Sandy? What the hell?"

"Is Molly here?"

Mark steps closer to the screen door. "Where's the baby?"

I motion to my Toyota. "Dixie Lynn is with my father."

"Molly doesn't want to see anyone."

"I gathered that since she left her daughter all alone in a bus station."

A female voice, not Molly's, drifts into the room. "Who's at the door, Marky?"

"Marky?" I lift my hand in a slight wave. "Hi, I'm here to see Molly." I lean forward. "I have her daughter with me."

"Marky, what's she talking about?" the woman inquires, her hand on Mark's arm.

"Nothing, Mom." He starts to close the door.

"It doesn't sound like nothing. Molly!" Mark's mom hollers. "Molly, come out here!"

Mark grunts. "Mom, I said it was fine."

Molly appears. "Sandy." My name comes out as though she sighed it.

"Hi, Molly. We need to talk."

163

"I can't." Molly stands between Mark and his mom. "Not right now."

Anger creases my face. "Molly."

"I can't. I'm sorry."

She knows better than to use that word. She did it on purpose.

"My father's in the truck with Dixie Lynn." I point.

Molly pushes past Mark and Mark's mom, flinging the screen door wide open. I step back, barely escaping getting smacked by it.

"Why is she with your father?" She glares at the truck.

"Because he came to live with me after he got released from prison."

Molly's face contorts at the news.

"Why didn't I tell you? That must be what you're wondering." I cross my arms. "Well, because you've completely disregarded our friendship. Every month you slip further and further away, and when I tried to tell you, you were too busy with Marky here."

I press my fingers to my forehead, massaging it. "Molly, you need help. I think you might be suffering from postpartum depression." My hands fall at my sides. "Your daughter needs you."

Molly glances over my shoulder at my truck and then back at Mark and his mom. Her short blue and purple-dyed hair appears un-brushed. The clothes she's wearing hang off her skinny frame as though she can't afford a meal. It doesn't take me being her best friend to see she doesn't look healthy at all.

"How dare you make such accusations?" Molly's voice cracks. She hunches over as though the sky is about to fall on her. "You don't know what you're talking about."

"Sure, Molly, let's not discuss you leaving your baby in a bus station."

"I left her with you," Molly mutters softly, so only I can understand her.

"No, you left her with a note for me. If I hadn't checked my phone, who knows how long she'd have been alone in that bathroom."

"Someone would've seen her. There were people there. She wasn't alone."

My hands shoot up in the air. "Do you hear yourself?" I throw my head back and scream at the sky.

164

"You're making a scene," Molly hisses.

Mark and his mom come down the steps. They stand on opposite sides of Molly. My father has stepped from my truck and leans against the door.

"Molly, your daughter deserves the very best, and you're treating her like garbage." I rest my hands on my hips. "You're coming back with me to Oklahoma."

Molly shakes her head and wraps her arm around Mark's waist. "I'm staying here with Mark.

"You have a baby? Is it Marky's? My son is a father?" Mark's mom asks, concern emphasizing her words.

"No, Mom, there's no baby." Mark glares at my father and then back at me. "This woman's only here to cause trouble."

"Mark, you know Molly has a baby. Her name is Dixie Lynn." My face scrunches with confusion. "You were with her when she delivered it in the hospital."

Mark eyes his mom, whose eyes dart between everyone. "Molly lost the baby."

"What!" I shout and lunge at Mark.

Molly jumps back. Mark's mom jets out of the way. My father reaches me by the time my fist makes contact with Mark's chin. I step backward, Robert's hands around my arms as he stands behind me. Wiggling out of my father's grip, I shake out my right hand. My knuckles burn.

"You hit a law enforcement officer!" Mark bellows, his hand on his chin.

The bottom of my lip quivers as I look at Molly. She's not the friend I used to know, and admitting it causes my ribs to tighten and constrict my breath.

Molly points at my truck. "Go, okay. Mark won't press charges. Just Go. Please."

"Dixie Lynn needs her mom," I choke on my words.

Without hesitation or even a glimmer of sadness, Molly says, "I don't want her." Then she mouths, "she's yours. Forever." Molly turns around, places her hand on Mark's back, and heads for the house.

"Don't come back here again," Mark calls out without turning around.

Mark's mom hurries after them, and I collapse to my knees in the damp grass. My father kneels next to me, his hand softly presses against my back.

"What happened?" I press my hands on the tops of my thighs and suck in air. "I ... I ... d- -don't understand."

"I think you're hyperventilating. Sit on your bottom and put your head between your legs," he instructs.

I do as I'm told, and after a bit, I'm calm, and my breathing is back to normal. My father helps me to my feet, and we walk a few feet to the Toyota.

After backing out of the driveway, I drive a few houses down and pull over. Resting my head back, I close my eyes. The truck feels like it's spinning. When I open my eyes, tears fall from them.

"I'd say she has postpartum, but I'm not a doctor." My father glances in the side mirror. "Are you alright to drive?"

I grip the steering wheel with both hands. "If I weren't, I wouldn't let you drive. Did they even have cars before you went to prison?"

"No, it was still horse and buggies back then." He smirks. "You're probably right."

"Shoot, I was supposed to get a hold of Justin when we got here." I pick up my cell phone from the cup holder. Thankfully, no missed calls or texts. I pull up Justin's number and press send.

He answers before the second ring. "Sandy, everything alright?"

"Hey, Justin. No."

"Are you okay? Is Dixie Lynn with you?"

"Yes, we're safe. But, Molly." I glance in my rearview mirror. "She ... she refused to even talk about her daughter, and Mark had the audacity to say that Molly's baby died at childbirth."

Justin mumbles and curses. "I'm befuddled that it would come to this. You must be exhausted."

"I am, but we're going to head back home."

"No," Justin's tone is firm, as though he's in court. "You're in Memphis still, right?"

"Yes, but—"

"From what it sounds like, you had a horrible time, and it's not safe for you to drive back tonight. I'm worried about everything you've been through in the last week. You need a break."

"I guess." I don't want Justin to know that inside, I'm crying with joy over his caring for me and that he recognizes how hard everything has been lately.

"Great. Go grab a bite to eat, and I'll call you with the hotel location before you can finish your last fry."

"Thanks, Justin." I press my palm on my forehead. "It was horrible. Seeing Molly act that way, saying those things about Dixie Lynn."

"I know, baby doll. I hate that you're dealing with this, but you're not alone."

My desire to reach through the phone and hug Justin courses through my hands, and I squeeze the steering wheel with my free hand.

"I wish I was there with you. I should've gone."

I bite my lip. The words I'm about to say are the truth and not for flattery's sake. "I wish so too."

Chapter 39 – The Tallahassee prison

An hour had passed since we said goodbye to Theresa and her dad. And now, I trembled with nervous fear in the prison lobby. I'd decided to face my father but was not at all ready.

Mom instructed me to sit with Jessica while she went over the paperwork with the correctional officer behind the thick glass. I couldn't sit, so I stood, my legs just an inch away from the chair. Mom slid papers through the slit and spoke in a whisper to the guard.

"You're shaking," Jessica said. "I don't think I would be brave enough to do this."

"I'm scared," I said. "I feel sick."

"If you want to leave, just tell your mom."

"I must do this, even if I am scared."

"Closure?" Jessica asked.

I shrugged. Maybe I needed closure and a puke bucket.

"Ready?" Mom said, turning to me.

My legs were weak, and my feet were heavy. Thoughts of Mama's headstone helped push my legs forward.

Jessica waited in the front waiting room with a guard they sent out. Mom and I made our way through the thick metal doors. Each time they slammed shut and locked into place, I jumped.

Two more metal doors were unlocked and slammed closed as we made our way into the visitation area. Inmates sat on one side of the table, visitors on the other. My trembling increased as we made our way around the tables. My heart raced, sweat formed anywhere it possibly could. The room appeared to sway. Maybe we were having an earthquake. Did Florida have earthquakes?

I'd expected to meet my father with a glass window between us while we talked on the phone, like in the movies. I didn't think he would be able to reach forward and possibly touch me.

I grew dizzy, even though I was sitting down. I pulled my sleeve up so Mom could hold my actual hand, so I could feel her heartbeat rushing down her hand into mine. Mom squeezed my hand tight as if she knew. I focused my vision on the guard across the way, trying to calm my nerves.

"Sweetheart, do you want to leave?" Mom asked. "We can. We can get up and leave this second."

"I'm going to do this, Mom. I don't want to give up."

"It's not giving up. I think maybe it's too much for you."

"Mom," I said, keeping my eye on the guard. "I have to do this for me."

A man entered through a metal door across the way. He wore a baggy orange one-piece pajama-looking thing. He had sandals on his bare feet and choppy cut shoulder-length hair. A smile grew upon his face when he saw me, and I noticed I had his nose.

"Hi, Sandy," he said, sitting across from me.

I leaned back. He felt too close even with the steel table between us. My father felt too close for someone I hated. My name, Sandy, coming from him, echoed through my ears and sent goosebumps across the backs of my arms. I couldn't bring myself to say hi.

"I'm Belinda. I have ... Sandy for the summer," Mom stated.

I attempted to open my mouth. Dizziness hit me again, and without a thought, I grabbed the side of the steel table to try to make it stop. Once the dizziness subsided, I let go of the table. Thoughts of soap and a scrub brush filled my mind.

"I'm so happy to see my little girl. The last time I saw you, you were so tiny. You're all grown-up."

My father's words appeared to slither from his mouth as though he were a talking snake.

"I hate you." My voice was a whisper of fear.

"Please don't hate me," my father said. "I sent you letters, asked for pictures of you, and explained what happened. You must know I'm sorry."

Stupid *sorry*. My father reached his hands across the table towards me. I leaned into Mom and held tight to her hand.

"I never got any of your letters," I choked out.

"You're Nana, and Gramps must've thrown them away. Look, Sandy, I'm real, real sorry about your mama. Although it was an accident, I can't go back and fix it. I wish I could because I would. All I can be is sorry."

There's *that* word again. Sorry, sorry, sorry. Plus, he was calling it an accident; how dare he.

"Sandy, what made you come here to see me?"

"Even if a daughter hates her father, she should at least know what he looks and sounds like."

"Is there anything you want to know about me?"

"I know everything I need to know about you. I want to know about Mama."

My father hung his head.

Tears formed in my eyes. I blinked ten times in a row to keep them from falling. I wouldn't let him see me cry.

"Why are you here and not in Oklahoma?"

"Change of venue for my trial and then everything after that. I think your grandparents might've paid off someone to get me shipped out of the state. Prevent you from seeing me."

My eyes appeared to eat back up my tears, and I sighed with relief.

"Sandy, your mother, was beautiful, smart, and she loved everything and everyone. Until she ... she ... she loved raspberries the most."

"What?" I asked, wiping the welled-up tears before they fell onto my cheeks. "She did?"

"It was her favorite. She loved everything that had raspberries in it. Milkshakes, pies, jams. She'd even eat them fresh, right out of the green little cardboard carton as we walked through the grocery store."

Mom squeezed my hand. She knew without letting my father know that I'd just discovered something Mama and I had in common. Gramps and Nana had not told me this before. They rarely spoke of Mama.

"You look so much like her. Your hair color. Your eyes. Sadly, I see you got my nose." He chuckled.

I'd always hated my nose.

"Did Mama have any favorite music and movies?" I asked.

"She loved the beach, oh, did she ever. She loved Elvis, but everyone loved Elvis back then. She was also a Beach Boys fan. And she loved scary movies, like *Jaws*."

I took mental notes. I added *Jaws*, Elvis, and The Beach Boys. I wanted to listen to all their music and watch *Jaws*, which Nana said I couldn't watch because I would have nightmares.

"For years, I've sent you letters. You didn't get any of them?" my father asked.

I shook my head no but remained scrunched up against Mom.

"That's disheartening to hear. Your Mama's parents, Nana and Gramps, blamed me for many things and never liked me much." He picked at his fingernail with his thumb. But when he looked back up at me, his eyes were sad.

"It's nice to see you, though." He smiled. "Very nice. Thanks for comin'. I never expected I'd be so lucky. I do need to ask you something. Somethin' I've wanted to ask you for many years."

He cleared his throat. "I realize you're too young to comprehend what happened. I understand that now, but I want to know if you can forgive me ... for what happened?"

I peered around the room, which was now swaying slightly less than before. Men were talking with people on the other side of their tables. Some were smiling, some laughing. The word "forgive" floated around the room with locked metal doors and cold steel tables. FORGIVE.

"I can't. I know that in school, they tell us to forgive but not forget. I can't. I can't forgive you for taking away Mama. Maybe I can stop hating you, that I might do, but forgiving you, I'll never do that.

My father lowered his head. When he looked back up, tears were in his eyes.

He stood. "Thanks for coming, Sandy," his voice choked. "It was nice to see you after all these years."

He made his way to the guard by the door.

I stood. "How long are you here until?" I hollered after him.

He stopped and turned around. "I have about sixteen years left."

171

Mom and I left in the opposite direction of my father. He would never be "dad." A dad was someone like Paul.

"When we get home tonight, let's rent *Jaws*," Mom said as we headed back through the locking metal doors. "After you wash all the germs off you, of course."

Mom always knew just what to say.

Chapter 40 -
Present Day -
2009

My father and I unload Chester and Dixie Lynn from the truck and enter The Peabody Memphis.

"Justin went all out." My father's eyes open in delight as we move through the automatic doors welcoming us into the lobby. "I can't believe they allow dogs in here."

"They allow a flock of ducks." I shrug.

My father's neck cranes up at the interior veranda circling the lobby. Oversized chandeliers reflect light all around. Chairs are organized in tiny sitting groups, and the famous inside water fountain-pond sits to the left. The wood trim shines with polish, and tanned marble columns showcase the two levels in the lobby. On the ceiling is a strip of gold and green stained-glass windows.

I leave my father and Dixie Lynn to ogle the fancy hotel as I check us in under the reservation Justin just made. Once I pick up our keys, Chester and I locate my father in the same spot.

"This place is beautiful." My father's head continues to look up as we gather into the elevator to head to our rooms. "Justin likes you."

I punch the number nine button on the elevator with my elbow. "Justin is just being Justin."

My father switches Dixie Lynn's car seat to his other hand. He rocks on the balls of his feet, and the corner of his mouth twists up. "How sweet."

I catch a witty response at the edge of my tongue and bite my cheek to avoid saying it.

"Here is your room key." I hand it to my father.

"Justin got us separate rooms? This has to be costing a small fortune." My father slides the key into his pocket.

"I learned a long time ago that when Justin offers something, you accept it, no questions asked." I eye the elevator counter as we continue to climb to the ninth floor. "Let's just say it was a two-week battle the first time, and I don't have the energy for it anymore."

The elevator dings, and the doors open. My father follows me to my room and places Dixie Lynn's car seat on the bed.

"Thanks." I let go of Chester's leash and shove my hands into my jean pockets.

He nods, removing the key from his pocket.

"I can't recall the last time I slept in a hotel." I sigh. "But you, gosh, I bet you slept in a few from Florida to Oklahoma."

My father flips the hotel key between his fingers. "No, actually, I slept on the buses. My goal was to get to you, and money to pay for anything more was not available."

I squeeze my hands together, unsure of how to respond.

"I'm going to let you settle in." He backs up. "I'll be in my room."

"Do you have money? I mean, if you need anything like a midnight snack or something?"

"Don't worry about it." He turns to the door. "Enjoy your night. I'll see you in the morning."

I step forward, unsure of what to do. Wave, pat him on the shoulder, or perhaps nothing. "Thanks for today. I mean, it's not what I thought it would be. And I appreciate your support."

"Happy to be there for you and Dixie Lynn." Chester trots over to him. "Yes, Chester, you too."

My father pets Chester and then opens the door. "See you in the morning. If you need anything or help with Dixie Lynn, feel free to ... " He steps into the hall, holding the door. "Call or stop by. I'm sure even after all these years, they still have hotel room phones."

I give him a half wave as the door shuts. I sigh at the thought of the day and Molly's behavior.

I remove the container of sanitizing wipes and go to work. I wipe down the doorknobs, remote, light switches, sink handles, toilet handle, and hotel room key. Then, I go to the baby and lift her out of the car seat.

"You must be so tired of sitting in that thing." I press my cheek to her head.

Chester hops up onto the bed, does a circle, and curls up. "Great idea." I join him after preparing Dixie Lynn's bottle and changing her diaper. Then, a half-hour into a movie, someone knocks on my hotel room door.

The baby is wide awake and babbling as we go to the door. Chester growls from the bed. "It's okay. It must be Robert."

With Dixie Lynn in my arms, I swing it open and gasp. "Justin?"

"Hi, Sandy."

His tie hangs loosely around his neck. His five o'clock shadow is approaching ten o'clock. *Dang, he is handsome.*

"What are you doing here?" I step aside and motion him in with my head.

Chester bounces off the bed, his tail wagging as he hurries over.

"Hi, buddy." Justin bends over and gives Chester a scratch around his ears. "Well, I tried to focus on this case, but by lunchtime, I realized it was useless. I couldn't stop thinking about you, worrying if everything was okay."

"It ... it wasn't good." I sit at the edge of the bed, snuggling Dixie Lynn to keep from snuggling Justin. But I know right now it has to do with an emotional day and not because I like him—not only because I like him. "You didn't need to drive out here. I mean, it's a long drive, and you have cases for work that need attention."

Justin sits next to me on the bed, and it sinks under our weight. We tilt into each other, our arms and thighs touching. He smells like wintergreen.

"I needed to be here with you." He wraps his arm around my shoulder, and I allow myself to lean fully into him. My head rests on his upper arm, and I feel his lips kiss the top of my hair. "I—I didn't mean to overstep." He pulls back and removes his arm.

I sit straight up. "You didn't. I needed you; I still do."

His arm returns, and I turn my face to his. "Thank you. For everything." I bite at my lower lip and stare at his mouth.

"You don't have to thank me," he whispers, his lips moving closer to mine.

I close my eyes. I want the kiss as much as I want to breathe. When Justin's lips feather mine, all the blood leaves my upper body and shoots into my toes. His hand moves to my back and pulls me closer. Dixie Lynn, between us, keeps things from getting out of hand. When we part, we're both out of breath. Justin smiles, and I lick my lips.

"That's not why I came here." His hand remains on my back. "I don't want you to think I'm using this as a—"

I grab the front of his shirt and tie with my free hand and pull his lips back to mine. The kiss is firm, and my heart races even after it ends. "I didn't think for a second you did." I release his clothing from my grasp.

"Good." He smiles and glances at Dixie Lynn. "You have plenty on your plate, and I don't want to complicate anything. I've never wanted to make things messy for you—for us—but I can't move past my feelings for you."

"I think a lot of things are about to change. Today was enough information for a lifetime." I sigh and rub Dixie Lynn's back. "But for tonight. Can you hold me?" A single tear falls, and then another.

Justin wipes each tear running down my cheek with his thumb. "I can't think of anything in the entire world I'd rather being doing."

Chapter 41 – Discoveries

"Look at this great picture," Mom said.

In an hour, Ray's Camera Hut had developed the twenty-four pictures from our disposable camera. The picture had Mom, Jessica, and me eating ice cream cones in Tallahassee. There were pictures from everything we'd been doing since the Jackson Zoo. We added glue to the back of the photos and stuck them on the album paper. At the bottom of each picture, I added a note of the date and where it'd been taken.

I attempted to focus on the scrapbook, but my mind wandered to my father. A part of me was actually happy I met him. The other part of me was still shaken up by not only meeting him but being in prison. I kept thinking about my father saying "accident" and wondering about forgiveness. I thought once I saw him, all my questions could be answered, and I could move on. I guess it wasn't that easy.

"It'll get easier," Mom said, as though she could read my thoughts.

"Do you think I was wrong to see him?"

"I can't answer that, only you can."

I slathered glue on the back of a photo taken at the Oakleigh Complex and pressed it on the paper. I stared at the photo, wiping my hand over it as if something had smeared on it. A dark shadow stood behind me in the picture. I blinked a few extra times and wiped the photo again with my hand.

"Mom?" I asked. "What's that?" I pointed to the dark shadow.

Mom took the scrapbook in her hands and pulled it close to her eyes. Then she pulled it back and then close again.

"Mom, is that what I think it is? Is that a ..."

"A ... ghost," Mom replied.

"The ghost of Corrine Irwin."

The dark shadow hovered behind me in the picture.

"Is that why they didn't allow photos to be taken?" I asked.

Mom laughed. "It might frighten people for sure."

"I have to show Jessica!" I exclaimed, picking up the scrapbook. "I'll be right back!"

I pounded on Jessica's apartment door. The door flung open, and I looked down.

"Hi, Feelissaas," Miles said.

He'd lost his right front tooth the other day and therefore had trouble pronouncing words.

"Hi, Miles," I said, holding back my laughter.

Paul stood hunched over the kitchen sink and waved me in with a soapy hand. "Let her come in, Miles."

"Hi, Paul." I made my way to Jessica's bedroom.

"Jessica," I called, knocking on her closed door.

The door creaked open just enough for me to squeeze in before she slammed it closed. Jessica marched back to her bed and flopped down as though she were doing a belly flop in the pool. Something was not right. Jessica always had a smile on her face.

I put the scrapbook on her nightstand and sat down next to her.

"What's wrong?" I asked.

Jessica rolled over and sat up, crossing her legs. Tears were in her eyes and running down her cheeks.

"I miss my mama," Jessica whispered. "The trip to Tallahassee with your mom made me happy and sad. You're so lucky. Not about your dad, of course, that sucks."

Jessica's words made my heart sink to my belly button. How long could I keep my truth from her? I wanted to tell Jessica I understood what it felt like.

"It sucks. It just sucks," I said to her. "You miss your mama, and it sucks."

Jessica wiped her tears. "It does suck."

It sucks that I'm lying to my best friend, too, I thought.

"Is that your scrapbook?" Jessica asked.

"Yes, I came over to show you the ghost," I said.

"The ghost?"

I opened it up to the page and pointed at the dark shadow behind me.

Jessica gasped. "That's spooky!"

A knock at the door startled us.

"Jessica, we have to get going," Paul announced through the closed door.

"Dentist appointment." Jessica rolled her eyes. "I'll come over when I get back." Jessica wiped her tears.

I closed the scrapbook and tucked it under my arm.

When I returned, Mom was in the shower.

"Mom, do you have any gum?" I called through the bathroom door.

"Yes, in my purse," she called back.

I plopped her purse on the couch and dug through it, looking for the package. A white ripped open envelope was in my way. What was it with Mom and envelopes? I pulled it out and set it on my lap, and then returned to digging. I found the gum and opened the foil wrapper, folding the piece onto my tongue. When I went to place the envelope back into Mom's purse, the return address caught my eye: 478 Graham Lane, Diamond City, OK 74945

I took the envelope in both hands and read the return address again. The address I'd called home since I was little. I opened the envelope. There must have been two hundred dollars in it.

"Did you find the gum?" Mom asked, standing in the hall.

I glared up from the envelope. Mom froze when she saw what I had in my hands.

"I should have told you. I'm sorry, sweetheart," she said.

"Don't say *sorry*! I hate that stupid word!" I hollered. "Don't ever say you're sorry!"

I bolted from the apartment. I didn't know how far I could run, but I wasn't going to stop until my legs were too tired to go any further.

Images of the return address flashed in my mind as my flip-flops smacked the pavement. I imagined Nana and Gramps's house, myself running down the road to the bus station. Running away from home again. Running away from Mom. My mind flashed back to Diamond City. Running from the house with my bedroom on the second floor. From the bedroom with a picture of Mama on my dresser.

Chapter 42 – Present Day – 2009

The squeal from Dixie Lynn jolts me out of my deep sleep. Justin's arm remains wrapped around my waist as I sit up. Before we fell asleep last night, I'd put her to sleep in the playpen.

As I ease myself to the edge of the bed, Justin stirs. Peeking back over my shoulder, I can't help but stare for a moment. The soft morning sunshine presses against the closed curtains, muting the room's light.

"Good morning," Justin states without opening his eyes.

I smack his arm with the back of my hand. "Oh, goodness, you startled me."

He smiles and opens his eyes. Dixie Lynn continues to cry, and I scoop her up in my arms. The scent of a warm baby drifts up to my nose, and I hold tight to it. I close my eyes and hum as I rock her.

"I thought it might be nice if you and your father spent the morning together." Justin stretches as he sits up in bed. "Go out and do something."

"You want to hang out with a baby and a dog?" I take Dixie Lynn to the window and open the blinds. "I'm sure you need to get back home for work."

Justin swings his legs off the bed. "I need to do some work here too. For Dixie Lynn."

Dizziness washes over me, and I sit down with the baby next to Justin. "I don't know about this. Yesterday was rough seeing Molly, and you'll have Dixie Lynn and Chester with you. I'm not sure it's safe to take her back to that house."

Justin reaches out and rubs my back with his hand. "I would never put Dixie Lynn in danger."

I rest my head on his shoulder. "I know, but maybe it's best if my father and I take her with us."

"I might be able to remind Molly that she's a mom." Justin reaches out for Dixie Lynn. "Approach the situation impartially."

What I want is for life to be less complicated. I lift my head off him and hand her over. It's my emotional state that causes my guard to fall around Justin, and I need to pull myself together. Last night was nice, but had I not been distraught by such a roller-coaster day, I never would've needed him to hold me. Sure, I'd enjoyed it and slept well, but anyone would after a day like mine.

"Right now, I want a shower." I grab a change of clothes from my backpack.

"I've got the kids," Justin smirks. "I'll get us breakfast."

I step into the bathroom. "With a baby and a dog?" I lean around the door frame.

"Well, Chester has to do his morning business. You know, I can juggle a few things at once, Sandy."

I raise an eyebrow because, even to me, it seems like a fair bit to handle with only two hands. "Alright, I look forward to seeing the results when I get out." As I close the door, I can't help but smile.

Twenty minutes later, when I swing open the bathroom door the built-up steam and I emerge as though I'm on a concert stage. "Do I smell bacon?"

I find Justin sitting at the tiny dining table near the window. Chester is at his feet, and Dixie Lynn is in his lap with a bottle. "And you didn't think I could do it." Justin waves a piece of toast at me.

"This is room service." I toss my dirty clothes onto the bed.

"Breakfast is breakfast. It doesn't matter where it came from, only that it's here."

I pull out a chair and join him, removing the cover from my plate. Scrambled eggs, toast, and bacon greet me. My eyes roll back into my head at the sheer delight of the smell. "I guess you're right." I shove a piece of bacon into my mouth and take a long sip of black coffee.

Justin glances down at the infant in his arms. "I hope today has a better outcome than yesterday."

I spread raspberry jam over my toast. "Me too."

Justin tosses Chester a piece of bacon.

My mind flashes back to yesterday and Molly. The complete shock of the situation is fresh. "I don't understand her reasoning. Maybe without me there, you can make her see that she's wrong to disown her daughter. Maybe I'm a reminder of something bad."

"I don't think you're the issue."

"Well, either way, as you said, you'll be an impartial third-party. Besides, you're a lawyer, it's your job to convince others."

He nods yes, his eyes glaze over.

"Justin." I wave my hand in front of him.

He squints and shakes his head as though doing so would bring him to the present. "I'm trying to wrap my mind around the situation too." Justin sighs as he puts the coffee mug to his lips.

"I refuse to let Dixie Lynn go into foster care." The scent of scrambled eggs, jelly, and coffee fills the silent air between us. "Honestly, I want my best friend back. I want the Molly I grew up with back."

"Some things are meant to change." Justin presses his lips together. "Some things are not."

A knock at the hotel room door causes me to jump. Maybe Molly has come to her senses and found us. I shake my head at the impossible thought and open the door.

"Robert, morning." I yank the door open all the way. "Come in."

A shift has occurred between my father and me during those hours in the truck together, with Molly's outburst, and undoubtedly, after the photo album of Mama. In no way is it forgiveness but an understanding. A shift on the path we're on.

"Justin?" my father states as he spots him. "When did you get in?"

"Last night. I figured you both might need some assistance." Justin moves Dixie Lynn to his shoulder and rubs her back in tiny circles.

Robert shoves his hands into his pant pockets after petting Chester. "Mighty nice of you."

Justin eyes me as if he needs permission to speak. "I thought if I took Chester and Dixie Lynn, then you and Sandy can do something fun."

"Fun?" My father's eyebrows arch.

"Can you think of anything you want to do in town?" I return to my plate and munch on my final piece of toast. But before I can allow him to answer, it hits me. "Graceland!"

Justin's, and Robert's eyes widen at my excitement.

"How could I possibly forget?" Both of my hands go up.

"You've had a lot on your mind," Justin reminds me.

"Elvis's house would be fabulous. I can't believe I didn't think of it right away either. Your Mama always wanted to go, but we never made it." My father's eyes shift to me.

"We must go then." A smile breaks across my face, and my shoulders rise near my ears in excitement.

Chapter 43 –
More truths

I stopped to catch my breath. I had run as fast as I could, nearly slipping and falling on my butt through the pouring rain. My shirt and shorts were soaked with rain and sweat. The Teen Spirit couldn't help me now.

I wished I could time travel like Marty McFly in *Back to the Future*. If only I could get my feet to go eighty-eight miles per hour, the speed the DeLorean needed to time travel. Then, poof, I would disappear back in time and fix everything. I could have stopped my father from killing Mama. Then I wouldn't be here in Mobile. I wouldn't have needed to adopt a mom at a bus station. I could make raspberry pies with Mama. And watch *Jaws* with Mama, and listen to Elvis and the Beach Boys. We could do it all without lies. Exactly no lies. Instead, I'm here with a fake mom who lied to me.

I collapsed onto a bench, leaning my head back on the curve. Germs be damned.

Boy, I was thirsty. For a second time, I ran away from home unprepared.

Why didn't Mom tell me about the envelope of money from them? How did they even know our address? Maybe they were paying her to keep me.

The sound of footsteps sloshed through the rain behind me.

"There you are!" Mom stammered between heavy breaths. "Mind if I sit for a spell?" She plopped on the wet bench before I could say no.

The cascading noise of the water fountain filled the air between the sudden lighter rainfall.

"Here." Mom smacked a water bottle on my arm. She twisted off the lid on her bottle, and I did the same. "I should've told you," Mom said, putting the lid back on.

"Why didn't you?"

Mom crossed her legs at her ankles. Visions of the bus station came flashing from my memory.

"I wanted you to have a fun summer. For you to have a mom again." She took a chug of water. "I know George."

"George, as in my Gramps?" My voice squeaked with confusion.

"My dad is Hank, your Gramps and him are—"

"Best friends."

"I called your grandparents."

"All those phone calls. Outside the River Grill, Jessica's. Did you make a call when you went to get ice at Motel 2?"

Mom nodded, yes.

That's why it took so long to get ice, I thought. "Have you been calling them every day?" I asked.

She nodded yes again.

"The bus station," I said, my voice harsh, "it was not a sign from Mama. It wasn't fate."

"Oh sweetheart, that was exactly fate," Mom said, placing her hand around my shoulder. "I ran away that day myself, but I noticed you, outside of school, of course. Your Gramps carries a picture of you in his wallet. He showed me your photo when he was over playing poker with my dad a long time ago. Your Gramps even pulled me aside one day and told me about your Mama."

"Did you know Mama?" I asked, wiping a tear from my cheek.

"I didn't, but don't for a second think us meeting and going on this adventure wasn't fate because it was."

"Why did they send you money?" I asked.

"To help me out. So I could buy you food and help pay for rent. I'm not making big bucks at the bakery. It helped pay for the extra pie supplies."

I took another gulp of cold water.

"Did they know about me seeing my father?" I asked.

Mom crossed her legs the other way and rolled the water bottle across her forehead.

"Yes, I needed your social security number, help with the forms, and for them to call the prison to allow you to visit. Since I'm not legally your mom, I wouldn't have been able to get you in to see him."

That's why she'd whispered to the prison clerk.

"I don't want you to think that I don't want to be your mom. I did this because everyone deserves to know what having a mom is all about, even if only for a short time. I should've told you I'd talked to them. I should've told you the truth," Mom said.

Don't say it, I thought. Don't say it.

And Mom didn't. She didn't say that stupid word.

"That's why I never saw myself missing on the news," I said.

I could see Mom nodding her head yes out of the corner of my eye.

"I want to show you something," Mom said, standing up. "Something I've never shown anyone, not even my soon-to-be ex-husband. I think I'm ready to be courageous, just as you did with seeing your father. You, Miss Felicia-Sandy, gave me courage. Now let's go catch the bus."

"In wet clothes?" I asked, standing up too.

"It's a short trip, promise, and it's not like it's cold outside."

We laughed and then hugged before making our way through the rain.

Chapter 44 - Present Day - 2009

We walk up the steps to Elvis's front door with a group of strangers. I think of Mama and the joy she might've felt had she been able to see what I'm seeing. The desire to take it all in for her engulfs me as the emotion hits. Being an emotional wreck about to walk through a dead singer's house seems like a horrible idea, but it's too late to turn back now.

Robert taps me on the arm, and I turn in his direction. Standing next to him is a lady wearing an Elvis shirt, with an Elvis fanny-pack, Elvis cap, and Elvis's face plastered on the socks she has pulled up, nearly to her knees. The lady holds her hands together and continues to bring them to her mouth as though to cover her excited grin.

"First time here?" I ask the lady when she catches me staring.

"Yes, a lifelong dream of mine." She folds her fingers over one another. "I hate flying, and I live in London, so it took a while to gather up the courage, not to mention money to come over the pond."

"Congratulations on making it." Robert half-smiles at her.

"Thank you." The lady turns back to the front door as an employee appears. The tour guide goes over the rules and then opens the door.

Walking in through the hunter-green wrought iron encased front door of Elvis's house is the most surreal thing I've ever experienced, fan or not. A feeling of intruding sweeps over me as I stand between the front room and dining room. I take in everything in the rooms, from the peacock-stained glass windows to the glossy white piano. Everywhere my eyes look, they find mirrors, golden yellows, and royal blues.

The dining room is decorated in blacks, muted gold, and more blues. The voice of the tour guide goes in one ear and out the other. For me, I'm not the fan Mama was or the London lady. Yet, walking through a famous stranger's home causes me awe and uncomfortable steps. I don't think I'd want a million germs tramping through my home, even if I was dead and gone.

As the tour guide moves us from room to room, my eyes fixate on the continuous explosions of color, from shiny wood paneling to olive-green carpet on the walls that encase a set of stairs, to room after room of yellows and blues and a slew of leather sofas. I can't un-see the game room with multi-colored curtains running the length of the walls and ceiling.

I pause to take in every angle and ponder what Mama would be feeling. When I glance back at my father, I spot his eyes glassy as tears well up at the edges. Seeing this causes a lump to form in my throat as we step to the edge of the following room. I pull myself out of my uncomfortable notion of being a stranger and observe each room with respect for Mama. Elvis's music must've meant a great deal to Mama if my father is tearing up.

Robert and I don't speak as we move from the interior of the home to the outside and glance around Elvis's dad, Vernon's office. We exit and pause at the view of the horses and the rolling land around them before moving past the roses, graves, and fountains.

For some reason, which I can't explain, as my father and I stand side by side in front of Elvis's grave, I reach my hand out, and instinctively, his hand finds mine. We say nothing, but in my mind, it's as though we are standing in front of Mama's grave.

After viewing the meditation garden, I finally speak. "I'm starving; let's go eat."

He nods in agreement, and we get back on the bus to take us off the Graceland property. We decide on Gladys' Diner and make the short walk to it after getting off the bus.

"If I never see blue again, I'll be more than alright with that," I say as all I can see around us are sky blue chairs and booths.

My father grins and turns his attention to the menu up on the television over the counter. I glance at it, decide what I want in seconds, and turn my attention out the windows surrounding the restaurant.

Robert steps forward and orders. "I'll have the chili cheese fries and ..." he pauses and stares at the menu.

"Hmmm," he hums. "A chicken patty melt. Can I have an iced tea?"

He steps aside, and I order. "Grilled peanut butter and banana sandwich. Iced tea, oh, raspberry iced tea, please." After paying for our lunch, I cross my arms. "Go grab us a seat. Once the food's out, I'll bring it over."

Robert does as he's told. I watch him amongst the nightmare of the blue suede. Shortly, they call our number, and I carry the tray of food to the booth my father picked.

The scent of the chili cheese fries, although I'm hungry, doesn't appeal to me. When I slide the tray on the table, my face finally relaxes. I remove my hand sanitizer and coat my hands before offering the bottle to my father, who does the same.

As I stare, he shoves a cheese-covered chili fry into his mouth, and I sigh. "I didn't realize walking through a dead celebrity's home would be this ... emotional."

He finishes chewing, glances at me, out the window, and back at me. "You're a caring the weight of your Mama not being here to see this, it makes sense." His voice is shaky. "Thank you for ... " Robert brings his hand to his upper lip and closes his eyes for a second, "... for this short journey with you here to Memphis and Briscoe, and for allowing me to help you with your house." He takes a sip of tea.

Waves of happiness and exhaustion ebb and flow through my body.

"You've had such a horrible childhood without your mama and me. You deserved better than you were dealt." Tears flood at the corners of his eyes and mine follow. "My pride for all you've become is unmistakable. I know your mama is beyond proud of you from wherever she's looking down on you right now."

I reach my hand out, and my father slides his into it. Our hands clasp together. His palm and fingers are rough.

"I'm so very sorry for your childhood. But being able to share this time with you means more than you'll ever know."

Usually—*always*—the word "sorry" is never right, never okay to use. It means nothing, until now. "I'm sorry too."

I'll never forget the look on his face when those words hit his ears—a look of pride, honor, and love. Squeezing his hand, I pull back and use it to lift my glass of iced tea, taking a long gulp.

He shakes his head no. "You have nothing to be sorry for." Robert picks up his sandwich with both hands. "Everything you believed in your childhood was justified, Sandy. Everything."

"Doesn't feel that way now." I take a bite of the famous Elvis sandwich.

My father raises his glass of iced tea. "The good news is we have plenty of time to change it from here."

I raise my glass to his.

"Your mama would've loved this trip." My father glances up at the ceiling.

Following his gaze up, I add, "Yeah, she would."

Chapter 45 – Bayou La Batre

In front of us stood a periwinkle-colored house on concrete stilts. The grass needed mowing, and the trees were overgrown. I couldn't imagine a better sign than Mama and Mom being born in nearly the same place. The bus ride had only been as long as an episode of *Home Improvement*.

"Is this your house?" I asked. "I mean, where did you grew up?"

"It's the house I was born in, but I didn't grow up here," Belinda said, wrapping her arms around herself in a hug.

"I don't understand," I said.

"Hank, my dad, he isn't my birth father. I was adopted at the age of three. My first memory of life was here."

"What about your mom?" I asked.

"Leila, Hank's wife, is my adopted mom. My birth parents lived here in this house."

"Why?" I asked, looking around at the leftover puddles of rain that created small ponds. "Why did you need to be adopted? Are your parents still here?"

When I turned to face Mom, she had tears streaming down her cheeks. She stared at the house like it was much worse off than it looked. Like it had just been hit by a tornado and was nothing but a pile of boards and broken glass.

"My biological parents were not the best of people," Mom said, her voice weak. "They did some ... not so nice things, and when a social worker found out, they decided to take me away from them."

"How did you know about this house? Do you remember being here?" I asked, reaching for her hand. "Mom?"

"I have one memory, but it's too hard to talk about. And yes, I remember being here."

"Why are we here now? If it makes you cry?"

Mom wiped her tears with her free hand. "I came to forgive them."

"But you said they aren't here now?" I asked, pulling backward on Mom's hand as though I wanted nothing to do with this house.

"No, they're long gone," Mom said. "I wanted to show you that, even as an adult, it can take a long time to forgive. Sometimes you can't, and sometimes you can. It's a decision only you can make. There is no right or wrong decision for forgiving. And just like you, I needed to come here, in person, just like you did with your father in prison."

I thought about my father and not being able to forgive him.

"I wanted to come here so that I could move on. This forgiveness has been holding me back."

"Couldn't you have done that without coming here? It's making you cry."

"No, I needed to come here, to see it one last time."

The screech of a screen door opened. A lady in a cream dress with butterflies on it came walking up to the edge of the railing.

"Y'all lost?" she called out.

"No, ma'am, sorry, just—" Mom said before her voice stopped.

I squeezed Mom's hand.

"Just passing through is all," Mom added.

"Alright then, sugar, sure ya don't need anythin'—like some tea?" the lady called.

Mom turned and started to walk away, holding my hand tight. She lifted her free hand at the lady to wave.

"We'll just be getting on, thank you, though," Mom said.

As we made our way back to the bus station, Mom rubbed my hand with her thumb. "I'm going to tell you something else that you don't want to hear," Mom said, her voice calm. "You need to tell Jessica the truth."

"The truth?" I asked.

"Your real name and who I really am."

"Can't I wait? She is not going to want to stay my best friend."

"You have one week," Mom said.

"One week?" I asked, turning to her. "What happens in one week?"

"Your grandparents arrive."

Chapter 46 –
Present Day –
2009

"What do you mean, she signed the papers?" My voice cracks like a worn sidewalk. "What papers?"

I press my head into my hands as I pace near my Toyota in the parking lot of Krystal. The scent of breaded chicken and fries filters from the fast-food joint.

Robert has Chester in tow, who is searching for the perfect place to potty on the grass. Justin holds Dixie Lynn in his arms, a sun cap covering her head from the sweltering mid-day summer sunshine. I squint even with my sunglasses on.

"The adoption papers, turning Dixie Lynn over to you, legally." Justin rocks the baby; although she doesn't need the comfort, I do.

"She just ... signed them? Like that?" I throw my hands up.

"I don't know what happened to Molly, but seeing her today, she was not the same." Justin scratches his right ear. "Once we go through the process of the paperwork with the court, you'll officially be Dixie Lynn's mama."

I suck in my breath and bend down. My hands wrap around the tops of my thighs. "I don't know how I should be feeling."

"How ever you want to," my father's voice chimes in.

"I want to be able to breathe without hyperventilating!" I shout.

When I stand straight up, Robert, Chester, and Justin are frozen, their eyes wide open in shock.

"I didn't mean to holler." I glance around to make sure no Krystal customers are staring.

"Sometimes, we can't explain a person's actions." Justin adjusts Dixie Lynn's cap, followed by his own. "But I can't think of a better mother than you, Sandy."

My father steps toward me. "I would agree with him, and I think you already know it too."

"Know that I'd be a good mom? Or a better mom than what Molly has turned out to be?" I cross my arms and lean on the tailgate of my truck. Sweat forms at my hairline as I focus on my breathing. "I don't want to talk bad about her, but I don't know how else to handle this situation."

"She made you a mom." My father reaches his hand out. "The pavement is far too hot for Chester's paws. Do you mind if we start up your truck and put on the air conditioning?"

"Of course not." I run my fingers through my hair and then remove the keys from my pocket. "Do you think this has to do with postpartum? I mean, she could change her mind once she ... overcomes it." *If* she overcomes it, I tell myself.

My father takes the keys, starts my truck, and has Chester jump in.

"Why can't life be like the movies?" I go to Justin, and in one seamless motion, he places Dixie Lynn into my arms. She smiles and reaches out for my nose. "Why can't everything happen at all the right times, with all the right people, and none of the worry or stress?"

Justin's hand is on my back, firm and reassuring.

"Because life is not the movies, it's life, and it's beautiful in its own way. Like you and Dixie Lynn." Justin's lips caress the side of my forehead and had his hand not remained on my back, I might've wobbled backward with delighted weakness.

As I lean into Justin, I close my eyes, and for a few seconds, I forget about everything around us.

"Probably should get on the road." Justin's voice breaks through my moment of Zen.

I nod with a sigh.

After loading Dixie Lynn into her car seat, I climb in and put on my seatbelt. The window is rolled down, and Justin wraps his hands on the frame.

"Supper tonight?" Justin asks.

"I think tonight we all need to sleep." I squint at the sun, bold and bright over his head.

"Right, and I know I drive far too fast to follow you back." He winks. "I'll have all the paperwork filed and ready by tomorrow."

"Thank you." I glance at the clock on the dashboard.

Justin pats the door frame and steps back. "Drive safe."

"You too." I put the truck into drive and roll the window back up.

"Everything will be alright," my father mentions once we were on the highway. "I'm here to help you with anything you need."

I wince a smile in his direction. "Let's avoid the reality of life until we get home." My hand reaches for the radio button.

Hitting scan, the radio searches for a station, and once one is found, Elvis's "That's All Right Mama" filters through the speakers. I bob my head and mouth the words, unsure about signing my heart out in front of my father.

When the next line of the song comes on, my father's voice crackles ridiculously off-key as he sings the lyrics. I giggle at his horrible out-of-tune singing, but he keeps on going. So, I join him.

Together, we belt out every retro song we know all the way home.

Chapter 47 – You can throw a pie in my face

I held the strawberry rhubarb pie I made for Jessica in my trembling hands and I reviewed what I practiced.

- Smile and hand Jessica her favorite pie.

- Tell the truth about your name and your mom.

- Let Jessica throw the pie in your face if she is mad.

I'd been practicing for days on how to tell Jessica I'd lied to her. Now, there were only two days left before Nana and Gramps would be here. Every time I thought I knew just what to say to get Jessica to hate me the least, my mind switched to wondering why Nana and Gramps were coming.

"They only said they would come down," Mom had said. "They didn't say anything about you staying or going."

But Nana and Gramps always had a plan. Nana made lists for the grocery store, lists for recipes, and lists for my chores. She even made the weekly supper menu, which she stuck under a magnet on the refrigerator.

Gramps always had lists too. He had one for his chores that Nana wrote him. And he had one for the feed store fifty miles outside of Diamond City. Nana and Gramps must have a list for visiting Mobile. I bet it read: Bring Sandy back to Diamond City.

For some reason saying Sandy in my head no longer made my face wrinkle up as though I smelled a broccoli and cauliflower salad.

"Do you want me to come with you?" Mom asked.

I glanced up from the pie. Mom had dressed for work. She sipped on her coffee from the travel mug. "I mean, after work, I can go over with you."

I shook my head no. She walked over and kissed the top of my head like moms do, even if you'll be leaving them soon.

***

"Hi, Miles," I said.

He rode, or at least tried, to ride his bike without training wheels while Paul held on from behind. He was focused and didn't say hi back.

"Morning, Felicia." Paul waved.

My fake name sounded rough and ragged. It didn't feel like it used to. I knocked on the apartment door, and within seconds, Jessica swung it open.

"You made me pie?" she asked. "Is it strawberry rhubarb? Oh, I bet it is!"

I smiled and handed her the pie. She swiped two forks from the dish rack on the kitchen counter, and we headed down the hall into her bedroom.

Jessica sat crossed-legged on her bed with the pie in front of her. She patted the bed for me to join her. I sat, crossing my legs too.

"Guess what I got in the mail?" Jessica said, scooping a fork full of pie into her mouth.

"Tickets to an Aerosmith concert," I guessed.

I held my fork in my sleeve-covered hand but didn't use it to gather any pie. I squeezed the heck out of it until my knuckles turned white.

"I wish!" Jessica beamed. "No, a letter from Theresa."

"Did she say how she's doing?"

Jessica shoved another jumbo bite of pie into her mouth.

199

"She didn't mention her mama at all. She just said she felt bad for not writing me or calling me after she left. And she was forever grateful we brought her the photo album. She wanted me to say hi to you too."

I switched the fork from my right hand, then back to my left and back again.

"Jessica," I said, feeling as green as a lima bean. "I have something I need to tell you."

"Did you get Led Zeppelin tickets?" Jessica laughed. "Wait, do they even still play? Aren't they dead or something?"

No, but I'm gonna be dead as soon as I tell her the truth. I put the fork down on the bed. I had to stand. I couldn't sit for this.

"Belinda isn't my mom," I softly said. "And my name isn't Felicia."

Jessica lowered her fork of pie down into the pie dish. Her mouth hung open. Her eyes questioned me.

"I ran away from home in Oklahoma. Diamond City, it's a small town. Anyway, I met Belinda at the bus station and I kind of adopted her to be my mom. Not right then, aloud, I kept it a secret. She was my first-grade teacher, and my Gramps is her dad's best friend. But I guess it's not really her dad. She calls him dad. It's a long story."

Jessica's face remained frozen, but I continued. I needed to get my whole story out.

"My father, the one in prison, of course, you know that, you were there. See, he killed my mama, and so my Nana and Gramps have been raising me ever since. I wanted to know what it was like to have a mom. My heart hurt as though someone was sitting on it. I couldn't take it anymore, so I ran. And my name ... I never liked my name, it's Sandy, but I've always hated it, but Mama loved the beach, and there is sand at the beach. So now I'm not sure if Felicia even feels right. I'm more confused than ever."

The only movement Jessica made was the blinking of her eyes.

"I know lying is bad, I mean, adults say that all the time. I didn't know I was going to hurt anyone with these lies. But, then, I met you and Miles and your dad ... and Theresa."

I needed to sit down but knew that I might need to leave if she decided to throw the pie in my face.

"Jessica?" I asked.

She blinked and crossed her arms. "So you aren't Felicia, you're Sandy, and you're from Ruby City ..."

"Diamond City," I corrected, which I probably didn't need to do.

"Ruby, marble, gem, whatever," Jessica said. "Your mom isn't your mom, and you did all this, running away and lying because you wanted to know what it was like to have a mom?"

I nodded. "You can throw the pie in my face if that would make you feel better."

Jessica sat there. I stood there. I heard Miles and Paul come in from outside, and the sound of the television made its way under Jessica's bedroom door.

"I wanted to tell you, I really, really did, but I was worried you would stop being my best friend. I guess I hoped that I could stay Felicia and keep having Belinda as my mom.

"You got on a bus with a stranger and came to Mobile?" Jessica asked.

"Technically, my first-grade teacher. My Nana and Gramps are coming in two days, and they'll probably make me go back home. It's probably on their to-do list."

Jessica stared towards the picture of her Mom on the dresser for what seemed like minutes upon minutes.

"That's the bravest thing I have ever known anyone to do," she said.

Did I hear that correctly? "The bravest?"

Jessica stood up from the bed and pulled me into a hug. My arms hung by my side as she squeezed me and twisted me side to side like aunts and uncles do when they meet you for the first time and call you cute.

"You aren't mad I lied?" I asked.

Jessica stopped hugging me and picked up the frame from her dresser.

"I never would have been brave enough to run away, let alone get on a bus. All you wanted to know was what it is like having a mom—wanting to have a normal life. I would love to have my mom here. It's scary being a girl without a mom. You wanted something, and you did it! You adopted a mom ... at a bus station!"

I smiled, Jessica smiled, and then we laughed. She must've been laughing because of how funny it sounded that I adopted a mom at a bus station. I laughed because I'd been so scared she was going to hate me, and now she didn't hate me at all.

"No more lies, promise?" Jessica asked, holding up her right pinkie.

"No more lies." I took my pinkie and wrapped it around hers in a pinkie swear.

"It's okay," Jessica said, "you can go wash your hands."

"Actually, no, it's okay." I smiled. "When you told me you were jealous of my mom and me, I wanted to tell you then, but I was afraid. I wanted you to know that I understood."

"How did you get up the courage to see your dad? I mean, I thought you were brave already."

"I don't know. The room spun, and I don't think I've been more scared in my life. Even when I ran away!"

"I don't think I could do it. I would've screamed curse words," Jessica said.

I laughed. I wish I'd done that too.

"Can I ask why he did it?" Jessica sat on her bed. "Why did he kill your mom?"

"I already knew the story of why he did it. I found the police report in a big yellow envelope two years ago, snooping around for my Christmas presents in Nana and Gramps's closet. It had "confidential" in red stamped on it and read: To the Guardians of Sandy Evans. I undid the metal clasp on the back and slid out papers."

Jessica leaned forward as if I was about to tell her the best story of her life. It was not the best story of anything.

"I sat down on the closet floor and read all four pages of what was titled: R. Evans Written Confession. R is for Robert, my father." I attempted to swallow the lump in my throat, but it didn't go away. "I wish I'd been younger and not able to read, but I could, I could read every word. My father's words, telling the police what happened the night he took Mama's life."

Jessica moved next to me and put her arm around my shoulder.

"He said how he loved her, but that he had anger issues, but that he wouldn't hit her. He said Mama was not doing well, and it was an accident. He pushed her on accident. I don't understand how it was an accident. That night, that stupid, stupid night."

Tears welled up in my eyes and slid down my cheeks. I trembled. My mind sent me back to the closet floor—the memory of shaking from the shock of what I'd read. My tears had made bold splashes on the pages below, magnifying the letters "father." I carefully blotted them from the paper with my sleeve, trying not to streak the ink, and slid them back into the envelope.

Jessica once again pulled me into a hug as I continued to cry. I thought about Mama. I thought about my father. I thought about Mom. I thought about Gramps and Nana.

"I definitely would have cursed at him," Jessica whispered. "I know it sucks."

Chapter 48 -
Present Day -
2009

I stand in the doorway of my old room. The room where I grew up once Gramps and Nana took me in. As I lean against the doorframe, my eyes scan the room. The tan wallpaper with tiny pink flower petals is peeling at some of the edges. I donated my canopy bed a few years ago, along with the nightstand and dresser, both covered in stickers. There's no real reason why I'd kept them for so long. But after returning from college, Gramps and Nana were getting older and less able to care for the home. They needed more help than home décor fixes.

Now, this room is going to be Dixie Lynn's, I remind myself. Because somehow, I continue to forget this vital fact as I push reality into the front of my mind. I'm not sure if I can be a mom. The word causes my breathing to sharpen. And while I'm not sure of my future role abilities, at least I know I'll never do what Molly has done. This thought makes me question if I'm really a mom, but I can't think of anything else in the moment of trying to understand it all. But I do know that if Molly ever changes her mind ... I stop myself because one part of me hopes she does. The other part of me knows how horribly confusing that might be to Dixie Lynn. But if Molly does, the door is always open.

I enter the room and stand in the middle of it. Making a note in my head as I look around. Strip the wallpaper, a fresh coat of paint, a rocking chair, a small bookcase, and a crib. Maybe a nice soft rug.

The sounds of my father laughing travel up the stairs. I tip-toe out of the room, knowing where all the squeaks on the floor are, and head quietly down the steps.

About halfway down is a view of the living room where I can see who is in the room, but they can't see me. I lower myself and sit on the step, wrapping a hand around the staircase spindle.

Robert is on his stomach on the living room rug with Dixie Lynn on her back. Together from my spot, they form the letter T. Chester is asleep on the couch nearby. A box fan is humming, and evening sunlight causes shadows to cast around the room.

My father takes his hand in a claw-like form and places it over the top of Dixie Lynn's tummy. When his hand moves in a tickle motion, the baby cracks up, followed by my father. She kicks her legs, and her arms jet out. Hearing and seeing my father playing with Dixie Lynn takes my breath from me and leaves a lump in my throat.

I think about the photo album, which now sits on my nightstand. I've flipped through it at least a dozen times in the twenty-four hours we've been home. Everything around me seems out of place, as though the realization of the truth makes everything a question. I desperately want to visit Gramps and Nana's gravesite, yell at them for raising me with a lie, but for the first time in my life, I want nothing to do with the cemetery. Mama is there, and I'm not ready to face her. To face her memory. The true memory.

Instead, I focus on my father, yet it's all too much, too much change. I stand and tip-toe back up the stairs. Closing my bedroom door, I pick up my cell.

"Hi," I say as soon as Mom answers.

"Hi, sweetheart," her voice oozes through the line like honey.

"Are you busy?" I ask because she is still on vacation, and I hate bugging her.

"Never too busy for you. Is everything alright?"

I curl up into a ball on my bed. "No." My eyes are fixed on the curtains dancing in the wind of the box fan.

"Is it your father?"

"It's the truth." My voice startles me because it's shaky, and I don't expect it to be. "Everything I knew about Mama." I close my eyes. "I had it all wrong. All these years, I had it wrong."

Tears soak through my pillowcase. I take the edge of my thin blue blanket and wipe the corners of my eyes, but it doesn't matter, the tears aren't stopping. My emotions move to my mouth, and I'm ugly crying. There's a pain in my chest, and it hurts as I suck in my breaths.

"Sandy, it's alright. It'll be alright. Is Justin there? Call him," Mom suggests.

The tears and sobs continue as Mom tries to console me. "Sandy, you're dealing with a lot right now, and it's alright to feel overwhelmed." The line goes silent, and I know it's because Mom has nothing left to say.

I don't blame her; I don't know what to say either. Instead, I keep crying, and she stays on the line offering me calming words every minute.

"I should let you go. Thank you, Mom."

Before she can say otherwise, I hang up and drag myself to sit up. My feet dangle over the edge of the bed, and I slump forward to stare at them. I reach for the photo album and pull it onto my lap, knowing I shouldn't. Only this time, as I take in each photo, I notice something I missed all these times looking through it. I take the focus off Mama and move it to my father.

As I flip through the photos, I see him smiling when he looks at me. He's looking at my eyes for my reaction, searching for the joy he hopes I'll find with a new toy or board book. He beams at me as I'm laughing in one photo while Mama stares blankly without any expression.

Taken aback, I rush to flip the pages, searching for my father's reactions in each one. And in each one, he has joy, happiness all the way through the album. I flip back to the front and then to the middle, where the switch is noticeable in Mama's eyes, but his never wavered. I toss the photo album on the bed and hurry to the bedroom door.

I enter the living room. My father looks up at me with the same smile as in those photos.

"Is everything okay?" He eases off his stomach and stands. "Sandy?"

I stand there staring at him before I take a few steps and wrap my arms around him. He leans back as though startled, and then he slowly places his arms around me. I go to say something, but I can't find any words I need. Instead, we keep hugging, and at that moment, it's all I want.

Chapter 49 – The arrival

I flipped through the channels with the clicker, waiting for *the* knock at the door. Today, Nana and Gramps were arriving. According to Mom, they were driving down, so they didn't have a planned arrival time.

I spent the last two days watching movies and playing in the pool with Jessica. I brought the scrapbook over again to show Jessica the ghost's shadow. She convinced her dad to take her to the Oakleigh Complex next week. Jessica even helped me tell Paul the truth. Although he didn't seem surprised, I think Mom might've already told him. I wasn't upset if she had. I knew Paul and Mom liked each other, and Mom keeping that lie for me might've caused a problem between them.

A pair of footsteps traveled up the stairs outside, and I pushed the mute button. A knock at the door came. I sucked in a huge breath and let it out gradually as I opened the door.

"Hi, Nana and Gramps," I said, stepping out of the way so they could come in.

They entered the apartment, peering around. Gramps hugged me, but Nana didn't.

"She isn't here," I said, meaning Mom wasn't home. "She's at work."

"Let's sit down and chat." Gramps took off his cap and placed it on the kitchen table.

I pulled out a chair and sat across from Nana and Gramps. The television was still on mute, so when I swallowed, it appeared to echo through the entire apartment.

"We missed you, Sandy," Gramps said, breaking the silence.

Should I say I missed them too? Did I miss them?

"What is this nonsense about being called Felicia?" Nana asked, crossing her arms over her chest. "On top of that, running away, worrying us like that."

"Now, Marie, stay calm. We talked about you staying calm," Gramps warned her.

"I'm calm, but I want answers."

"Nana," I said, "I've told you I don't like my name."

"That's true, Marie. She has told us that before," Gramps reminded her.

"I know, I know, I'm not senile, George," Nana said.

"We can change your name if you want," Gramps said. "We can go to the courthouse out in Salliville and get a name change with the judge."

Diamond City had a post office, which was about all it had as far as anything official. Salliville had the courthouse.

"George, we're not letting her change her name. That's ridiculous," Nana stated.

"Marie, we talked about this. There's no harm in letting her change her name," Gramps added.

"Fine," Nana said with a huff. "Just let it be known that the only reason we didn't come and get you right away was because Belinda had convinced us you were safe."

"And having fun," Gramps added with a smile. "And she *is* Hank's daughter, remember Marie, not to mention she was her first-grade teacher."

Gramps elbowed Nana.

"And ... Belinda felt it would be important for you to deal with your Mama's death because we don't think we helped you deal with it well. Or with what your father did," Nana said. "We wanted you to stop looking backward. You're constantly thinking about your mama. At times, maybe too much. Belinda felt maybe you could work out some of your feelings."

"Not that thinking about your mama is wrong. It's just too much thinking," Gramps said. "Marie and I've decided that ..."

"Now, George, I didn't decide this," Nana said, shaking her head.

Nana looked at Gramps, then back at me.

"Yes, now, school starts next week, and we can't have you missing school," Gramps said.

"Why can't I go to school here?" I asked. "Stay with Mom, I mean Belinda?"

Gramps reached his large and wrinkled hand out and patted the top of my hand. "We're your legal guardians, and we promised the judge that we would raise you until you turned eighteen."

"We know you miss your mama," Nana said, uncrossing her arms and placing her elbows on the kitchen table. "But being motherless doesn't mean you can up and run away. You can't go adopting moms at bus stations."

"I ran because I didn't know what else to do. You don't understand me. You don't know what it's like."

"We don't know," Gramps said. "And that is why you're here with Belinda."

"And not at home grounded for pulling this stunt," Nana added. "However, it's time to stop feeling sorry for yourself and be what your mama would want you to be. You."

I nodded my head yes so that Nana knew I understood.

"Now, Marie and I are going to settle into our motel," Gramps said, squeezing my hand. "When Belinda is off work, we'll talk over supper and discuss the arrangements."

"Arrangements?" I asked, confused.

"Marie and I ... agreed that it was important for you to keep Belinda in your life. We're going to work out the details for upcoming visits. Belinda mentioned that she wanted you to be able to call her, write to her, and visit her whenever you wanted."

"Really? I can come back and visit?" I asked.

"We've always wanted you to be happy." Gramps smiled.

Chapter 50 – Present Day – 2009

Dixie Lynn is back home with my father and Chester as I focus on my flip-flops. My sweaty feet collect the dust along the road. I've walked this path enough times that they should rename the street after me.

I'm not carrying any of Mama's favorite flowers with me. Sharp pain in my heart reminds me as though my hands don't notice they're empty. As I reach Mama's grave marker, I don't sit. Instead, I pace back and forth with my arms crossed over my body. This is my first time being upset with Mama. I pause and stretch my neck as the tension travels up from my shoulders.

The wind picks up and blows my hair in front of my face. I brush it out of the way by tucking it behind my ear and kneel. My hand moves to my mouth, and I cover it as I sigh.

"Mama," I finally say. "I feel sick with the way I treated Robert and even Justin because of the story I believed. The only story I knew for ... all my life."

I wipe my hands on my knees and slide them into the grass in front of me. Then, with my fists, I yank out the grass in clumps. My nails line with soil.

"I don't want to hate you, Mama, or be upset with you. I should be mad at Gramps and Nana." The breeze smacks the side of me.

Gramps and Nana are buried next to Mama, and I eye their gravesite but don't move. I sit on my bottom and kick my feet out in front of me. The grass itches my bare legs.

"I'm upset with all of you!" I holler and throw my head back. "You lied ... or fibbed ... or twisted the truth. Whatever you call it, I deserved to know exactly what happened with Mama. Even if you thought I couldn't handle it."

Tears are streaming down my cheeks, and my nose is running. The wind continues to whip around. "Maybe if Mama had had help, she could've been saved."

Molly's image pops into my mind, and I lay down on my back. I drape my forearm over my eyes to block the intense sunshine. Tomorrow I'll be in court with Dixie Lynn and Justin at my side.

"Mama, my life is not what I thought it would be. Everything seems like it's wrapped up in a tornado. I held all this anger for my father that was unnecessary and unsupported. I pushed a man I love away and never gave him a chance because of his family's history."

I sit up and pick up a chunk of grass and dirt. I chuck it at Nana's grave marker. I'm upset with myself for living my life as I have. I close my eyes and shake my head. But when Molly and Dixie Lynn return to my thoughts, I run my hand over my forehead. It's then I realize I can't blame anyone, even if I want to. Molly, my father, Mama, Gramps, or Nana. And most importantly, I can't blame myself. I only knew what was told to me.

Tomorrow I'll officially be a mom. A time to start fresh, to live my life in a way that's best for me and those around me. I have to drop everything from my past to live the best way possible now, for Dixie Lynn and for me.

"Mama, I'm sorry for what you dealt with and what you went through after having me." I reach out and run my fingers over the engraving of her name. "I love you, and I know the only way to make you proud is to be me without the history I've carried all these years."

I kiss my fingers and press them to the grave before moving to Gramps's grave.

"I'm sorry you had to hide the truth from me," I tell him.

I continue onto Nana's grave, my hand running across the stone. "I'm sorry you had to give up your already planned out life to raise me."

I take the deepest breath I've ever taken in my life. My lungs fill up and release. As I head toward the exit of the cemetery, a butterfly flutters past me, pauses, and then dips up and away toward the baby blue sky.

Chapter 51 – The slumber party

"Why do my best friends always leave?" Jessica asked.

She sat on my bed as I packed my clothes from the dresser into a suitcase Nana and Gramps brought. They were picking me tomorrow morning at seven a.m. sharp.

"I don't want to leave." I scooped up my shorts and dumped them into the suitcase. "Your school starts soon, too, right?"

"In two weeks. Dad's taking Miles and me shopping for new school clothes next weekend. Are you sure you can't stay at least one more week?"

"My school starts next week, and with Gramps driving, it'll take a week to get back. Corn on the farm grows faster than he drives."

"Belinda doesn't want you to stay?" Jessica asked.

"I figured if she wanted me to stay, she wouldn't have called Nana and Gramps in the first place."

"I think she does," Jessica said.

I let Jessica's words warm my heart.

After I packed, Mom and I pulled blankets from our bed and the couch cushions to make one big bed on the floor for our girls' slumber party.

Mom rented *Weekend at Bernie's*, it was a PG-13 movie, but Paul said Jessica could watch it even though she wasn't thirteen yet.

When Mom popped the videotape into the VCR, she turned to us with a serious face and said, "Don't try this at home."

Jessica and I laughed, even though we didn't know what she meant until after watching the movie.

"Let's go swimming," Mom announced once the movie ended and the ice cream was gone.

"The pool closes at ten," I reminded her.

"How about we do it anyway? I bet the gate is unlocked," Mom said.

Mom and I dressed in our suits. Jessica still had hers on from earlier, under her clothes. Mom put her finger to her lips, indicating us to hush. We tip-toed across the grass to the pool gate. She turned the squeaky pool gate's doorknob, trying to be as quiet as a caterpillar. The gate swung open. We silently cheered.

We set our towels on the lawn chairs and sank into the cool water at the stairs. With the pool light on our skin looked like blubber below the surface of the water. We whispered and giggled to each other, trying to be as quiet as possible.

"What's going on over there!" a man's voice erupted around us.

Paul and Miles stood at the pool gate. Miles had his hand over his mouth.

"I did it," Miles blurted. "I was sneaky, Daddy!"

"We were going to go and scare you during your slumber party but saw you were breaking the rules by swimming after ten," Paul said.

Mom giggled. "Come on, Paul, don't be a party pooper."

Paul stood there, holding Miles's hand, his other hand on his hip like a pondering parent. Then he slipped off his flip-flops, and Miles did the same with his.

"Ready?" Paul turned to Miles.

"Ready, Daddy!" Miles cheered.

And then, just like that, they jumped into the pool, clothes on. Water sprayed up in the air.

When the water calmed, I observed Mom and Jessica, then Paul and Miles. I wished it would never change. This moment right now, with everyone happy, everyone feeling like a family without any missing pieces. An ending where everyone had a mom, a dad, a best friend, and an annoying little brother.

Chapter 52 –
Present Day –
2009

When I arrive home from court with Dixie Lynn, I locate my father upstairs in my old room. I've only been gone three hours, but the room has been painted a fresh pale yellow that gives all the other yellows in the world a run for their money.

"How'd it go?" He asks as he sets the roller into the paint tray.

I'm wearing a skirt, which makes me feel completely out of place, even in my own home. Not to mention, I'm sweating in the summer heat in my button-up sapphire blouse. I hold Dixie Lynn, who's wearing a petal pink onesie, as she shoves her fist into her mouth.

"The judge signed off on everything." I want to smile, but it doesn't feel like a victory. "I lost one part of my heart and gained another part. But it's an open adoption, in case Molly changes her mind."

My father softly nods his head, and I understand he doesn't know what to say. I don't blame him.

Over the last few days, he's been sleeping on the downstairs couch instead of on the porch.

I turn into the hall. The upstairs has three bedrooms. Mine, Dixie Lynn's, and a guest room, which Nana and Gramps never used for anything other than collecting dust and storing jackets.

"Do you think you'll be staying in town for a while longer?" I ask as I turn back to him.

"Once I finish up all the little stuff around this house, I figured I'd get out of your hair." My father rests his hand on his hip.

"What do you plan to do, or where do you plan to go?" I rock Dixie Lynn, even though she's not fussy.

I'm grateful to have her as my daughter, but the fact that it's now real is beyond comprehension.

"Not sure. Maybe to Briscoe and stay with Tony and Jewel, see if I can get a job of some kind." He paces the room as though he's lost in a box and can't get out.

"What about if you stay ... here?" I mumble.

My father pauses and turns to me. "Here?"

I eye the guest bedroom. "Yes, you could have the empty room. You're great with Dixie Lynn."

"And you want my help with her?"

"I do, and it would be nice to have her cared for in her own home instead of in childcare. When summer is over, I'll be back at work, and some days, I end up in class for several hours after school is out." I swallow so loudly it sounds like I'm swallowing my pride. "And I'd like to have you here."

My father cracks a smile. "I'd like that more than you'll ever know."

I step forward and wrap my free arm around him in a hug. He's warm and smells of paint and citrus.

"Me too, Dad." The words slide from my mouth, and I mean them, but I don't expect them.

As I let him go, we pause, awkward, straight in our posture. The doorbell echoes through the house.

I hurry out of the room and down the steps. Dixie Lynn kicks her feet as I swing open the front door and find Justin on the other side.

My eyes widen. "Is everything alright?" I was just with Justin in court. "Did I not say thank you for being with me in front of the judge?" My brow creases as I search for what he might need.

Justin steps forward into the open doorframe, takes his hand, and places it on my cheek. His thumb caresses my earlobe, and my legs go weak. He leans in and presses his lips against mine. The taste of cinnamon and the warmth of his lips mix with mine. I have to focus on Dixie Lynn being in my arms, so I don't drop her with all this euphoria.

He continues to press his lips against my lips, and when we part, I'm trying to find my breath. Justin's eyes glitter with happiness, and I blush. His hand passes over Dixie Lynn's hair. "I know you have a lot going on, being a new mom and all, but I'd like to see if you'd entertain the thought of having me for supper."

"A date?" I whisper because his face is still close to mine, and anything louder would be too loud.

"Yes." He presses his chin to his neck as though he's embarrassed.

"Absolutely." I pet Chester, who is now standing at my side.

Justin's hand wraps around my waist. "What made you have a change of heart?"

"Sometimes people make mistakes, misjudgments. Or judge someone by their past." I take a deep breath. "And I'm sorry for pushing you away all these years and using your father against you. I was so very wrong."

He pulls me into the best embrace he can do with a dog and baby glued to me. "All is forgiven if you give me another kiss."

"That seems like—"

I don't have time to finish as Justin presses his mouth on mine, this time with less urgency and more passion. I start to melt into him. He holds me up with his strong hand around my waist as our lips part.

"It seems like we have a lot of catching up to do." He runs his hands through his hair.

I bite my lip as he follows me inside and takes off his shoes.

"Are you hungry?" I ask, shifting Dixie Lynn to my other hip.

"You have no idea."

My dad clears his throat as he comes down the stairs. "Don't mind me." And I know right then and there that everything will be more than alright.

Chapter 53 – Back home

The first morning, after arriving home from Mobile, I walked past the refrigerator and noticed a list stuck to the refrigerator door. It read: Sandy's name change at the courthouse.

I took a pen from the junk drawer and crossed it out. Sandy was not so bad a name after all. It reminded me of the beach in Mobile and my adventures with Mom.

The sound of a truck barreling up the driveway caught my attention as I pulled out my box of Powdered Sugar Squares from the pantry. I opened the door to find Molly jumping from the truck.

Molly was what Nana called a talker, but she never said it in front of Molly. Nana said there is nothing wrong with a talker unless you have somewhere to go or you had gravy on the stove that needed tending to.

I bolted down the porch steps, nearly tripping.

"I heard you were back," Molly said, wrapping her arms around me.

"I missed you." I squeezed her tight.

"I came over earlier, and your Nana said you were gone. So I asked where? Some adventure in Alabama, she told me. Alabama! I've always wanted to go to Alabama, of course, I don't know why, but I do. I called every day, but your Nana said you weren't back yet, and she didn't know when you would be. And here I am, and here you are. Right plumb this morning!"

We hugged again.

"Well," I said, breaking away from Molly's hug, "I'm back."

"Yes, yes, you are, so grand, isn't it? You must tell me about everything. I mean *everything*. Oh, and I made you this mixed tape."

Molly handed me a cassette tape. The label read: While You Were Gone Songs.

"It has all the newest songs. Listen to it, so when I come back over you know the lyrics, and we can sing together. But I better go now. Mama is waiting in the truck."

I leaned around Molly and waved at Mrs. Dwyer.

"She's letting me drive," Molly said. "To the end of the stop sign on Fourth and Chilton Street. The shifter going from first to second is right tricky. But Mama says I'm doing great. She's taking me clothes shopping for school. You'll have to fill me in on Alabama when I get back!"

We hugged one more time, and then Molly dashed back and hopped into the driver's side of the faded tan pickup truck. The truck lurched forward as a grinding sound came from it. It squealed as it shot forward, kicking up a puff of dust behind it.

I finished my cereal, dressed, and walked down the long driveway, stopping to pet Hazel and Heidi before turning right at the T in the road. I could close my eyes and find my way without a problem. I'd walked this path at least once a week for as long as I could remember.

I picked some wild sunflowers at the edge of Mrs. and Mr. Thomas's property and carried them to the cemetery.

The dried-up flowers I left last time had blown around and were not in a neat little bunch anymore. I placed the fresh flowers next to her name and laid down, looking up at the cloud-covered sky.

"Missed you, Mama," I said aloud. "I saw my father. Don't worry. I didn't forgive him."

I didn't know if I should say the next part. So I laid there silent for a while, my eyes closed, feeling the breeze stir around me.

"I hope you aren't mad, but I adopted a new mom when I ran away. I wanted to have a mom. It sounds silly now when I say it aloud. Maybe some of us are just supposed to be a little un-normal. Nana says un-normal is not a word, but I believe it's just the right word to use. Belinda and I made a scrapbook.

She let me keep it when I left. We watched your favorite movie too. Belinda said it's okay if I kept calling her Mom, and I wanted to see if that would be okay, now that I'm here to ask you."

I lay there, waiting, hoping for a sign.

I waited some more.

A butterfly, gold and black, landed on the tip of my flip-flops. I pushed my back up off the ground. Perched delicately on the rubber, it fluttered its wings.

"Thank you, Mama."

The butterfly lifted off, flying into the distance.

※※※※ ※※※※

Three weeks later, the phone rang in the living room.

"I got it!" I hollered and picked up the receiver.

"Felicia, hi," Jessica said. "I mean, Sandy. I keep forgetting. So guess what?"

"What?" I asked.

I could hear Miles yelling, "Hiiiiii, Sandy!" in the background.

"Miles, Sandy doesn't want to say hi to you," Jessica told him. "No, you need to guess," she said to me.

"Your dad and my mom are dating."

"Yes, they are, but that might change because of the news my dad received."

The line went silent.

"Tell me!" I exclaimed.

"My dad got a job at the OU."

"That's great! What is the OU?"

"It's the University of Oklahoma, in Oklahoma!" Jessica hollered.

"I'm in Oklahoma!" I screamed.

"It's in someplace called Norman. Dad says it's only a few hours from you."

"Does that mean you're moving to Oklahoma, and we can have sleepovers and watch movies?"

"Yes!"

We both screamed into the phone.

"Belinda said she is going to call you," Jessica added. "She wanted to tell you something. It's good news, but she made me pinky swear not to say anything to you."

I said a quick goodbye to Jessica and dialed Mom's number. I couldn't wait for her to call me. She wasn't working today unless she had to switch schedules.

"Hello?" Mom said.

"Mom, it's me."

"Hi, sweetheart."

"Jessica called and told me that her, Miles, and Paul are moving to Oklahoma, but she said you had news too."

"Are you sitting down?" Mom asked.

"Yes." I picked at the pillow on the side of the couch.

The phone cord had wrapped around me several times from all the excitement of talking to Jessica.

"I applied for a teaching position. Specifically, a dance teacher at a university."

"That's great, Mom. I bet you got the job! Did you? Mom, is that the big news?"

"I did, but the job isn't in Mobile."

Silence fell over on the phone.

"Mom?"

I heard Mom giggle on the other end. "It's in Norman, Oklahoma."

"Mom, you're moving back to Oklahoma!" I screamed.

"I am! It was a hard decision to decide to return to the state I ran away from, but I realized you faced your fears, so I will too. Mobile isn't the same without you. I know it'll be a few hours away, but it's better than being all the way in Mobile. Plus, if you decide on a college, maybe you can go to the OU."

"You went after what you dreamed you always wanted to do," I said. "Wait, you said Norman, so you and Paul will be together?"

"Yes, we'll be together," Mom added.

Was it normal to feel proud of your mom? I wasn't sure. We said our goodbyes, and I ran up to my bedroom.

I flopped down on my bed with my scrapbook, flipping through the pages. The final page had a photo of Mom, Jessica, Paul, Miles, and me in the pool on our last night. A neighbor came out to remind us that the pool closed at ten and that it was ten-thirty. Paul convinced her to take a picture of us.

I stared at the photo for some time. The opposite page held an envelope glued to the back. Inside were all the refrigerator notes Mom had left me.

Mama's picture still sat on my desk, but my heart no longer felt suffocated. I wondered if Mom and Paul would get married. Jessica could have a mom again, too, just like me. I was more than happy to share my mom. After all, if I could adopt a mom at a bus station, I could share her with my best friend. Maybe even a future step-sister.

Epilogue

Dear Molly,

I hate that I'm writing this letter to leave at your gravesite. I guess I should be glad you're finally home. It's been a year since I last saw you at Mark's parent's house.

I can't believe you're gone, or maybe I can and want to ignore the notion. Gosh, you should see Dixie Lynn; I hope you can, somehow. She's beautiful and feisty. My dad made the cake for her 1st birthday, and she giggled with every taste of it.

Justin and I married in the fall. We had a raspberry cake with a raspberry glaze, and it was the best thing in the entire world. Oh, Dixie Lynn's going to be a big sister! We're expecting our first baby on Christmas Eve. I know I said I never wanted to be a mom, but after Dixie Lynn came along, it's all I thought about. But I constantly pray that nothing ever happens to me, and it still weighs heavily on my mind.

We're having a boy and decided on J.J. for Justin Junior. And both my dad and Justin are fussing over me like I'm an antique piece. I can't think of the last time I lifted a finger for anything outside of work.

Also, the town decided the bus station was finally of no use anymore and bulldozed it down. I cried when they did; I can't lie, but you won't believe what they built in its place ... a Target!!! Just like in those '90s movies we used to watch, where they built a Wal-Mart in a dusty town, and it was the best thing ever. Do you know how hard it is to try and convince

Justin that we already owned something I just bought from Target?

As far as my dad goes, he's doing great. Helping out others around town with house projects and some legal work with Justin at the office. I think the variety keeps him busy and happy. He even got his own apartment but watches Dixie Lynn three times a week, so she is only in daycare for two days during the school year. And get this; my dad is dating Ms. Gilmore. Mr. Gilmore passed away from a heart attack. My dad was helping Ms. Gilmore fix things around the house, and after a few months, they started having suppers together.

I want you to know that I'll continue to love and raise Dixie Lynn as though she's of my own blood. And I'll be sure to share all the wonderful stories of our childhood with her as she grows up. At this point, I don't know how to tell her why I'm her mom, and I hope I figure it out before she's too old. I promise I'll tell her the truth because we all deserve that.

I miss you, Molly. Say hi to my Mama, Gramps, and Nana for me.

Love always,
Sandy

I place the letter inside the envelope and lick it shut. Then I take a tiny hand shovel to the fresh earth below Molly's grave marker and dig a few scoops down. I fold the letter into a tri-fold and set it inside the hole. Taking the soil, I cover it up.

Dark clouds are shifting in the sky as I drag myself up to stand and rest my hand on my growing belly. As I flip-flop over to Mama's grave, I rearrange the dry hydrangeas so they look a bit better until I bring out fresh ones next time. I take a swig of water from my insulated pink bottle and adjust my Sooners cap on my head.

"Well, Mama, how do I look?" I lean over her grave, pushing my belly out. "I feel like one of Mr. Miller's pigs." A giggle comes out along with a burp.

"If I'm honest, I worry about postpartum depression, Mama. But Justin and I have discussed it in length, and he'll be watching out once little J.J. comes along." I kiss my fingers and touch them to the gravestone. "I hope you know I love you."

Leaving the cemetery with one hand on my belly, a group of butterflies move like birds in the sky to my right—a raindrop lands on my shoulder, followed by another and another. I stop walking and lean my head up to the gray sky. My arms go out like a scarecrow as the clouds turn it up a notch, and the raindrops dump out. I beam with delight and stick out my tongue, catching the water.

Playlist

Reba McEntire – *Fancy*
Lisa Loeb – *How*
Madonna – *Vogue*
Carrie Underwood – *Blown Away*
Led Zeppelin – *Ramble On*
Aerosmith – *Walk this Way*
Little Big Town – *Tornado*
Cyndi Lauper - *Girls Just Wanna Have Fun*
Reba McEntire – *Is There Life Out There*
Elvis – *That's Alright*
Tim McGraw and Faith Hill – *Meanwhile Back at Mama's*
Mark Knopfler – *Darling Pretty*

Link to the YouTube Playlist

Acknowledgments

First, thank you to my readers! Without your support from sharing my books with your friends, family, coming out to see me at book signings, and book club meetings—please continue to leave reviews so I can discover what you loved and even what you didn't like about the book.

Thank you to Starla and Rachael, who always allow me to vent, bounce ideas off of, beta read, critique, and ask questions about all things writerly and publishing, plus their continued support.

A warm and delicious thanks to Mariposa Coffee Company—you fuel me with the best coffee in the world.

To my dad, who took me on amazing loop-road trips. My favorites being Tennessee and Montana/Wyoming.

For D.S., who figures out what I'm trying to say when I can't find the correct words in the English language, but I can find them in my made-up world.

If I've forgotten anyone, it's because I had to stop writing this to get up and play the 87th game of fetch for the day with Ransom.

About the Author

Savannah Hendricks (born in California, raised in Washington, and resides in Arizona) is a full-time social worker during the week and a devoted weekend writer. She loves all things dog-related and has a passion for red wine. Savannah enjoys gardening, baking, and watching for storms. You'll often find her hollering at the TV during restoration shows when they paint over the bricks.

If you'd love a digital personalized autograph or bookplate, you can request one here

facebook.com/authorsavannahhendricks

instagram.com/savannahhendricks_author/

youtube.com/channel/UCefa7Xu3c3KPfJ_j2_TRsRQ

https://twitter.com/AuthorSavannah

bookbub.com/profile/savannah-hendricks

tiktok.com/@wordsmithsavannah

SAVANNAH HENDRICKS

goodreads.com/author/show/7210922.Savannah_Hendricks

pinterest.com/AuthorSavannah/

amazon.com/Savannah-Hendricks/e/B00BO0RQK2

Also By Savannah

THE ALBUM
A hidden album unlocks a mysterious mansion's past and present.
Coming 2/23/2023

Are you ready to get dusty?
A Hearts of Woolsey Novel (3 Book Series)

A Desert Restoration - Book One

A Desert Romance - Book Two

A Desert Rivalry - Book Three

THE CHRISTMAS RENTAL

Two strangers, two dreams. They'll need more than a Christmas miracle; they'll need each other.

GROUNDED IN JANUARY
Winner of the 2019 New Mexico/Arizona Book Awards
A story of resilience and rebirth to warm your heart.

GROUNDED IN JULY
This summer, love is in at the inn.

TO WORK OUT OR TO WED - a novella
A romantic comedy story about imperfection.

WINSTON VERSUS THE SNOW

1st Place (tie) for Picture Book 5 & Younger in the 2019 Royal Dragonfly Book Awards
Finalist in the Children's Picture Book: Softcover Fiction category of the 2019 Best Book Awards sponsored by American Book Fest

Winston doesn't like touching the snow. While his friends play in the snow, he's stuck inside. Until one day when a neighborhood dog, Mac, provides a possible solution.

THE BOOK WHO LOST ITS TITLE
Shortlisted for the 2020 Little Peeps Book Awards for Early Readers a division of the Chanticleer International Book Awards

A book without a title? Where could it have gone? Webster and his friends go on a search to find the missing title for his book. See if you can help Webster find the title to his book. Who knows, it could be just a step away.

NONNIE AND I
Available in English, Spanish, and Bilingual editions
When a little girl must start her first day of school she will
need to leave her best friend, Nonnie, a giraffe behind. Can
she make new friends, but keep the old?

CPSIA information can be obtained
at www.ICGtesting.com
Printed in the USA
LVHW100732301022
731911LV00016B/309